Gates of Evil

Carinthian Thriller

By Peter Bergmann

Imprint
Gates of Evil – Carinthian Thriller
Author: Peter Bergmann

© 2013 by Peter Bergmann. All rights reserved.

Translated from German by Jonee Tiedemann

ISBN: 978-3-9504215-0-7

www.peter-bergmann.at

Prologue

Walking slowly, the girl came down the alley. It would be dark in half an hour. The high hedges left and right seemed like massive walls. Involuntarily, she hesitated. Perhaps she should have taken the detour along the busy street. A cold shiver ran down her spine. "There´s nothing there", she said to herself and started to walk faster. Many of us sometimes have this feeling of freezing up briefly, or a sensation that makes us look back over our shoulder for no apparent reason and continue to walk a little faster. This happens on deserted streets and in basements as well, once the usual background noise is suddenly turned off and there is an unusual silence seeping out from all directions. The same thing happens when we walk through a quiet building and pass a dark room with its door ajar. To some people, this happens in broad daylight while being in a crowd. It is not unusual for this to occur when walking home through a deserted neighborhood. Never had this alley been so narrow and long and its hedges this high. Even the sound of her own steps and of her coat rubbing against the fabric was louder than usual.

"You are crazy! There´s nothing there!"

Just those wide stairs, each one taking several steps, and down there she could see the lantern-lit street. Just one more minute. If it hadn't been so ridiculous, she would have turned back. Now she was walking really fast.

Half an hour before, he had walked into the alley and hidden in a niche. He was the hunter. There was no particular game, only game. From afar he could hear her steps. He heard her hesitation and her resolve to continue. He heard her thoughts and her sex and her age. Long, blond hair. He didn´t move a single muscle and hardly breathed. He kept his eyes closed. She was fifty yards away, thirty, ten, five, three, one yard. He lounged forward and grabbed her and took her back into his hideaway, as fast as a sharp-toothed moray eel hiding inside a reef.

Her only thought was a silent scream. It disappeared in pain and darkness.

He burrowed inside of her like a crazed butcher inside a warm pig. His jacket was soaked in blood up to his elbows. That was okay. Breaking up the game was part of the hunt. He ripped up another life connection with red, hot blood spurting out.

He sat up with jerk.

He looked at the luminous digits of the old traveling alarm clock. Half past two. The upper part of the pajamas was clinging coldly to the skin, the bed sheet was wet. The hairlines of the neck and forehead were wet as well. His heart was racing in a light gallop. A few stars were twinkling between the curtains. A cool night, just above freezing. It was very quiet. The ticking of the alarm clock sounded twice as loud.

The man in the drenched pajamas moaned. Where did these images, where did these dreams come from? Why was he continuously committing murder in his dreams? There had to be an explanation.

He turned on the lights, poured water into a glass and washed down two pills. He switched off the lights and reclined. It was awful to lie in the cold sweat, but he was battered, exhausted, way too tired to change clothes.

This had been going on for two years now. The only time he had been spared was during his health spa session. One would think it might have to do with the location or the house. But he had lived here before, long before the dreams. The start of the dreams - his private turning point in time. Seen from today´s perspective, the days before seemed like a golden age. And he had led a normal, average life. That was it! A normal, average life! Normal, average people cannot imagine what it means to dive into a bloody abyss night after night. His dreams were so brutally realistic, so full of fear and pain that there was hardly any difference to the real experience. He had been to the doctor and complained about sleeplessness. His body was healthy. The doctor prescribed a sedative and he took it. He got himself stronger pills and soon he was taking far too many of them, but pure sugar would have had the same effect. It was like he was cursed. During the day he did his job, at night he descended into a world of insanity and mayhem, walking in blood and fire, seeing things and doing deeds from which he could not get away. More and more he became convinced that he had once actually experienced and committed all of this. Almost everyone has moments where he is absolutely certain that he has previously experienced the situation he finds himself in. Not a similar situation, but exactly this very same situation, down to the smallest details. It only lasts for a few moments and then everything resumes its regular course. But it leaves its mark. In his case it was about much longer periods of time where he *was* the slayer, the knife-murderer, the man with fangs and all these ludicrous names, which from one moment to the next turned into bloody reality.

It was a miracle how he could keep up the appearance of his former life going on as usual. He was like a bombed building with a standing facade, while the inside walls and ceilings had crashed down like a deck of cards.

He was regarded as being calm and courteous, reliable, a man who kept his word. He had an office just for himself. His name was on the door. Curiously, he could not recall his name right now. Senior municipality councilor! Was this his real name? Well, whatever. Tomorrow he would read the name and remember it. Office hours from nine to eleven. He savored this for a bit. *Office hours*. Traffic. Yes, he had something to do with traffic. Roads …, wide ones and narrow ones.

And then he was standing again in the dark alley, bent over the girl who winked at him surreptitiously. Her face seemed familiar. There were veins protruding from her ripped belly

like truncated hoses. She said something he couldn't
understand. How was she able to speak if there was not one
drop of blood left in her? Bad blood. He was covered with her
blood. It burned through his jacket like acid, burning his
forearms and hands. He held his arms up high and ran through
the streets. Muscles and tendons were lying bare and the skin
had fallen off. Then he was standing inside fire and billowing
smoke. He heard screams of horror. The horrific screams of
those trapped inside.

He desperately fought to get rid of the new nightmare, but the
pills kept him from doing so. The night was not over yet.
Morning arrived, brilliant and cold. There was a thin layer of
ice with a fine web-like structure on everything where water
had accumulated, in vats, buckets, a plastic bag left behind.
Men and women dressed in work clothes and rubber boots
wearing thick coats and hats or scarfs on their heads trudged
into the stables. White vapor was trailing from their mouths.
Their faces were reddened, or still pale from sleep. Fresh
smoke came out of the chimneys as the women had added
wood before leaving the house.

The hamlet at the edge of the hills and its small church and its
two taverns, hardly worth the dot on the map, had come to
life. Many of its inhabitants first looked at the sky with a
scrutinizing glance. But none of them saw the bodiless black
star whose rays had been pulsating hesitatingly for a few
years, as if it too had just emerged from deep sleep. Nobody
saw it. But it stood right in the zenith of the town, day after
day, night after night.

1___

Dr. Terrazzo opened his office at nine. He was the only medical doctor in this region. His area included half a dozen villages and the scattered farms between them, as well as a couple of mountain farmers whom he could only reach by snowmobile during winter. He knew that several traditionally oriented settlers did not like the snowmobile, and his predecessor had used a Haflinger mare. But most of them were happy that there was a successor at all. Young medical doctors don't usually dream about becoming country doctors. He himself could not have imagined to swap his career at the university for one in the countryside. Now he was sitting in the darkest boondocks imaginable. He drank his fourth or fifth cup of tea and shrugged. Why bother? It wasn't so bad, after all. "It's a blessing", he thought with a touch of self-irony, "when you are endowed with a good sense of stolidity." Actually, he wasn't that stolid, really. His thoughts went back in time. Two, three years. It would be three years in August. And then?

In the secretary's office his assistant was preparing things for the day, which included four consulting hours and an as yet undetermined number of home visits. Sometimes he returned around nine or ten at night, exhausted and weary due to the fact that he was not only performing his duty but there was much time spent behind the wheel. The distances in his district were rather long. On the other hand - self-irony was gaining the upper hand again - he would never starve being a country doctor. It had taken him several months to realize that his patients were seriously offended whenever he rejected their offerings. Since that time, he had been stocking up on eggs and bacon, ham, bread and schnapps, pastries and doughnuts and butter and milk. The people liked it because he was *their* doctor, and therefore it was their duty to take care of him. Slowly he began to feel being really *their* doctor. He was amused.

Maria entered the room silently. She was wearing shoes with wooden soles and yet she managed to walk without making any noise. She was young and rosy and a little too serious with her glasses, which sat like a protective mask on her nose. Silently she put the first patient´s filing card on his desk and silently she disappeared. A mute fairy, still with inhibitions. A countryside fairy.

He read the name on the card and sighed. Whatever it was with old Körner, he would have to drink a glass of schnapps with him. He wouldn´t consider the fact that a doctor´s practice was not the appropriate place. The time of day didn´t matter, either. Why did this guy always show up so early? Terrazzo went for the glasses without thinking. He had spent an entire afternoon trying to find the smallest ones in town. After all, there were a few basic premises in the countryside which could only be ignored by paying the price of everlasting foreignness. And what good was a doctor whose patients were foreign to him? He pressed the button and said: "Mr. Körner, please".

2___

Pastor Paul Weilrich sat in his study and looked across an open book into the distance. He was troubled by dark thoughts. He would celebrate his 25th anniversary in five weeks. Twenty-five years! He could still feel the hope and the joy when he had moved into *his* church. But he could only feel it as a memory. How much faith had been in him back then! How he had clung to this sweet drug, always ready to give everything, to comprehend everything, to forgive everything. Now the drug had lost its effect. Now he was a man past his fifties, with trite and common problems, which due to his profession, he was not able to cope with as well as other people did. Becoming a layperson. Was he serious about this or was he only playing around with the thought? He could deal with the problems of a man past his fifties. Other pastors had dealt with this, they had found niches and created facts which were officially frowned upon but usually ignored. The problems of men over fifty! As if there were any ages without problems! However, the weight increases with each passing year. At some point it gets out of control and the crisis begins. For some unjust moments the pastor was angry with all the men whose troubles were lesser than his own. Because he had an additional burden, an additional weight to carry, one which a layperson could hardly comprehend.

Were Christians really allowed to confess to *everything*? Isn´t there a limit as to what they can expect of other people? Isn´t it true that a pastor is only a human being? But this was not the problem. Yes, every deed can be confessed, each and every one of them, no matter how grave. But it was different with this case, which brought him to the edge of his comprehension (and his wits?). Weilrich surmised, no, he knew that this sinner was not confessing in order to gain God´s pardon. He was confessing in order to make his father confessor an unwilling accomplice. He wanted to further explore his sadistic feelings by telling his deeds to the only person who could not reveal this knowledge. This rotten scoundrel had sneered at God and the world with what he had done, and now he sneered at God and his servant by boasting about it. He actually was not repentant at all despite his lying, solemn assertions. He still felt excitement when he remembered the unthinkable deeds. Pastor Weilrich saw the little devious smile of the man when he came to greet him, accompanied by his family and friends to attend holy mass. People thought it was the smile of a clever old man, but it was the knowing smile of an accomplice. A smile he wanted to knock from his face with his bare fists.

His gaze stopped at the cross with the Christ figure. "I don´t have your strength", he said, bitterly. "And my own is decreasing all the time."

The wall clock announced the second part of the morning. Had he told Grete he would be having lunch elsewhere? Yes, yesterday evening. He closed the book and looked at his image in the mirror. He had become gaunt. He wore the grey suit almost like a coat. It was good that a coat was still needed. No hat. You cannot hide the face of a pastor, but with a hat, it turns into a traveling exhibition. Other professions carried their stigma across the landscape as well, but they could be erased with water and soap, like that of a chimney sweeper. The face of a pastor can´t be scrubbed away. He curled his lips. It´s the soul. Slightly dry at the edges. Weilrich put on the coat from the wardrobe, left the church and sat in the small Fiat which was parked in front of it. Obviously a black one. He pursed his lips again. A group of laughing children greeted him, but not before taking a wide turn around his path. The Reverend´s driving style made it clear to his community that their pastor was close to God. He turned to the main street, without any accident, and took the road to town. He had told his housekeeper that he would be meeting with a colleague from the seminary. "If Grete only knew …", he thought for the hundredth time. The state capital was about an hour´s drive away. Weilrich parked the car in the suburbs and took a bus. He didn't like the busy traffic. At the central station he got off. The small inn where he had met several times before was only a few minutes away. Although almost all of the tables were empty, Monica was sitting way in the back. She stood up when he entered the inn. He shook her hand. They never kissed in public. The devil never sleeps. For the first time that day he smiled. They would have something to eat and then have coffee over at her place. This was only possible in the city. Country pastors without nearby cities could only resort to their housekeepers. He thought about Grete and his smile took on a tortured look, but it faded away quickly. Monica had taken off one of her shoes and touched his trouser leg. With time, Weilrich hoped, his face would become lively again.

3

It was good to see the doctor on a regular basis. Not because of health issues. He would be healthy until his last breath. It was good to visit people on whom he had little influence on a regular basis. Matte applied his life experience to gain influence. In other words: it was his life´s purpose. You have to stay in touch. Cast out nets. Talk. Particularly with those people who are independent. You have to talk to them. Not just anywhere but on their own turf. In the case of a medical doctor, that was during his office hours. People behave differently in their own environment than they do on the street or at a restaurant. The doctor met old Matte on the street, having heard quite a bit about him, at least enough in order to be cautious not to be too outspoken, friendly but cautious. During his visiting hours he was examining a man in his eighties. Unusually fit, but still, an old body. Sagging shoulders and torso, not much muscle on arms and legs, not an impressive sight. He doesn´t see the old Matte anymore, only the old man. There is no need for being cautious.

Yes, casting out nets, talking about any subject. Talk in such a way as to get answers to questions that have not been asked. That is an art requiring much patience.

It is also a good idea to talk to him in private. It is on a different level and the change in the relational level causes many people to be apprehensive. Doctors with their emphasis on being responsible - and there is often not much substance to this - have a hard time bringing professional and private contacts onto a common ground. He had known a lot of them. Some of them tried to keep them completely separate. During visiting hours they want to be nothing but a doctor, and outside of that they are strictly private persons. But it doesn´t work. It is still the very same person.

Terrazzo wasn´t easy to figure out. Somehow he had learned to be very clever and evasive. If he could only figure out the reason that had led him to his village … that alone would be something. Back then, it wasn't an issue, but now these relationships didn't work anymore. The old folks had retired and the young ones preferred to mind their own business. And they are much more distrustful these days. Too many journalists poking their noses into all kinds of things. Back then, if someone became a nuisance, you just invited him to a party and something would come out of it. Money, or a cunt, or some dirt from the past would come out while being drunk. Usually a piece of bacon and one or the other beer and schnapps were enough to spill the beans. Nowadays they are all so much more diffident. They don't show up when they get an invitation. And if they show up they don't touch anything. Of course there are still the corrupt ones. But there is a clear-cut separation. Back then, they were all somewhat decent and somewhat corrupt. Today, the corrupt ones are without limits and the decent ones are as sharp as razor blades. They accuse you if you only offer them your handshake. They in particular are often the important ones. Of course you can win over anyone of them, but it is not easy. Besides - he wasn't fooling himself here - he didn't know the rules of the game as well as he used to. Whoever knows only half of the rules will always lose. He preferred to skip it.

Although Dr. Terrazzo had an aroma of the past, there was something challenging in taking the difficult road. He would continue to visit him at his practice and talk about his virility. This thing about virility was a clever move. The doctor was confused by the fact that a seventy-six year old man insisted on doing it three times a week. It sparked his interest. If someone like him starts to show interest, you've made the first important move. Perhaps it resulted in him becoming more accessible. He giggled quietly. "I am not in a hurry, doctor. I will find the soft spot. If it's not an old one it will soon be a new one."

He thought about Maria, the lassie in the outer office, nice and tight like all the genuine treats. Something stirred in his pants. He would have to tell the doctor, next time.

17

Everyone called him old Matte. It was a title of honor. For forty years he had commanded all of the political activities in town. Most other thoughts as well. Independent farmers had consulted with him whether their child should marry such and such's child or not. There was no business that he didn't hear about, and he was involved with most of them. He knew who was screwing around with whom and he didn't think much of taking advantage of the facts because these women were not really in a position to say no. They didn't have to enjoy it. They just had to do it and shut up.

He licked his lips. All this talk about virility and all these thoughts sticking like barnacles to a rope were stirring his blood.

Of course he had enemies. A whole lot of them. Way more enemies than friends. That was okay. It was easy to get a friend to do what you wanted him to do. To bring your enemies to do that was an entirely different matter. That counted. Those who understand know it.

He could have gotten way up the ladder, dozens of times. But it wouldn't have been prudent. Several of his comrades had advanced just a little too far and they had to pay for it. He preferred to pull the strings behind the scenes as this was what he was best at doing. Even today he was still pulling strings, but they were much shorter than ten or twenty years ago. At any rate, there was nobody in town who could beat him at that. He would be pulling strings in town until he was gone. Each morning he did his rounds, greeting this way and that, having a few words with an old friend or simply ignoring someone who happened to pay him his respects by tipping his hat; he left him standing there as if he didn't exist. You have to let them know continually, man, woman and child. It is just like training a dog, like a hard pull on the leash at the right time. It is routine to those who know and a complete mystery to those who don't.

He walked up the three steps to the Sheep's Inn and opened its heavy door. It used to have a different name, but after they had the old innkeeper on the ground after a serious altercation, they had placed a plate made from wrought iron on the front of the house, which vaguely resembled a shorn sheep. *Let them feel it.* The loser had to put up with both the plate and the name or they would have run him out of town. His daughter had been running the inn for a long time now, and she wasn´t in her prime, either. Old stories were history, the name had stuck. Old Matte got along just fine with the Sheep´s innkeeper. They had fiddled around and all the rest of it. She was of his kind, not at all squeamish at the receiving end and even better at dishing out.

It was before noon and the inn was empty. He went over to his place at the head of his table and pressed the bell which had been put there just for him. He had lost his former voice, and when the mood became lively in the evenings he would have been drowned out. This had to be avoided. You have to be careful with those details. An old man ordering his beer with nobody hearing him ends up being a weak old man. He had known the meaning of image long before the word had been created.

While waiting for his beer he saw the stranger, sitting by the small niche with its window facing the garden. The stranger, middle-aged and bearded, briefly looked up from his newspaper. They exchanged a cursory nod. "An early tourist", Matte thought, "Mediterranean". But his fleeting attention span was quickly absorbed by Rosi. What an earth mother! Twenty-six or twenty-seven. The best age. Strong limbs, powerful like a young horse and nimble as a whip! There was no ungraceful move and not one bad angle. Her hair tied up, a classic skull and teeth like polished ivory to split walnuts like other women used to squash overcooked beans. And her eyes! He had never noticed a single tepid expression. They sparkled and gleamed with every expression, be it joy, anger, sympathy or rejection. When she slept there must have been more expression in these eyes when compared to ten other women. For him there was nothing good to be found in them, though.

For twenty-two months she had been the waitress at the Sheep´s Inn and old Matte had not even caressed her derriere. Considering that the waitresses in town and the surrounding inns had always been his standard prey. Most of them were flattered, but that soon changed, and by then it was too late. Rosi had been opposed to him from the very first day. It would not have taken more than a nod to the innkeeper and she would be out in the street, but that wasn´t what he was after. She wasn´t prudish. She had gone out with two young guys, for a few months with each, before they had broken down. But for some reason he was like a red flag for Rosi.

"The usual?" she asked.

"Yes."

She left and came back with a pint of beer and a homemade schnapps.

"Where is Bernd?" he asked.

"Stacking wood at Silbernig´s. Why? Got a job for him?" Not many waitresses talked to him that way. Not even afterwards.

"Perhaps", he said.

She shrugged and disappeared into the kitchen. They all have a weak spot. Even a strong one such as Rosi. For some reason she liked this moron. Mother´s instinct, he presumed. There was not much gentleness about her. But when she spoke with Bernd she was as delicate as a hen with her chicks. He in turn was completely obedient and took on any hard work if she allowed him to do so. Matte had observed her for a long time and had not discovered any other weak spot. Now it was time to press on it. The Silbernig farm was at the right place. You couldn´t see far down the street. Bernd avoided him as much as he could. Up there he wouldn´t have an opportunity to escape. "And your mother hen herself is sending me your way", old Matte thought blithely to himself. He finished his glass, left some money and took off. He did not notice the stranger. He had not caught the glance that Rosi considered worthy of him.

4

Bernd saw old Matte walking towards him and did just like his friend, the hedgehog. He tried to protect his soft inner core as best as possible with the outward pointing spines.

Some townspeople were friendly, some were not, some were helpful and gave him a hand, others looked down at him and made fun, some cared for him in an exaggerated way while for others he was non-existent. He could deal with all of that. He knew them and was aware of why they behaved like this. They were diffident. He had been born here and lived among them, but he did not belong here. He *laughed* in a different way. Sometimes he considered things to be funny which they did not, and sometimes it was the other way around. At times he had tears in his eyes because he thought about something terribly sad, then a happy thought followed the sad one and he smiled with tears in his eyes, just as rain may fall while the sun is shining. When they saw this, their timidity increased and the eyes of some of them also filled with tears while others made rude jokes. But essentially, and Bernd was convinced of that, they thought the same thing. They only dealt with it in different ways because their hearts were different.

Old Matte was different. He was the only one Bernd was afraid of. He could read someone else's thoughts and he was evil. This was why he was particularly apt at reading the evil in other people. Nobody saw this as clearly as Bernd, who knew much more about people than most of the rest. He just wasn't able to appreciate this gift because he lacked more basic ones. He was only dimly aware of it. It was just like fog in the morning hiding something unknown.

He would have preferred to avoid the encounter, but he had been so busy piling up the wood that it was too late for that. So he erected his spines and curled up his soft inner core.

"You're working hard", the old man said instead of a greeting. He only exchanged formal greetings with people who were on a par with him. There weren´t many of them in town.

"Good day", he muttered and kept stacking wood. Doing that was a good spine. To keep piling up wood might perhaps upset Matte so he would grumble a few bad words and get lost. But he only giggled. "Good day, oh yes. You have to be on good terms with God. He sees everything."

Bernd didn´t say a word nor did he continue to pile up firewood. That spine was broken. The old farmer winked. He had very light, pale-blue eyes. Eyes who had lost their color with time, so one would think they had become windows to look into his inner soul. But that was not true.

"You like Rosi quite a bit", he said. With this simple phrase the few remaining spines Bernd still had left fell like hay under a scythe. To him, Rosi was someone special. Nobody had the right to know this. Nobody was allowed to speak about it. Nobody was … his thought became a mess. He wanted to ask and protest and at the same time defend himself, and this caused him to stutter so hard that no intelligible word came out of his mouth. The eyes of the old man sparkled with joy. He stepped closer and said something mean about Rosi´s skirt and her legs with a low and clear voice, something about him bringing something down to the cellar for her and then walking up the steps behind her. This had been one of those things hidden in the fog, but old Matte had noticed it and peeled it out from the fog and now Bernd could see it, and just as the hedgehog´s spines were no good when a car sped towards it, he couldn´t do anything other than run away. He sobbed, dropped the piece of wood still in his hand and ran away like a hare, ran out of town to the forest where he had a small dark hiding place and hid there, half crazy with fear and sorrow and hopeless love.

The woman for whom he had stacked up the wood looked out of the kitchen window and shouted: "What did you do to the poor fellow for him to run away like this?"

"What am I supposed to have done to him?" the old man replied crudely. "He´s simply out of his mind, that dork!"

He lifted his hand and did a gesture with his middle finger which she had seen only once in her life. Blood shot into her face. She was close to crying out loud just like wounded Bernd. She closed the window with a slap and started kneading the dough which had been lying there once more. Her husband was sitting at the kitchen table with some notes. They didn´t exchange a single word, but suddenly the pencil broke between his fingers.

When old Matte returned from his tour to the farm he was still giggling. It had been quite some time since he had spent such a nice morning.

5

Franz Riement looked out the window with half-closed eyes. Images and thoughts combined to form a dark cloud, a pressing accusation. The landscape slipped past the bus like a monstrous desecration. Modern agriculture! What a four-letter word that was. No boundary ridges and balks were allowed to exist, not a group of trees, no lines of bushes, no pools or lagoons. They did not even leave the brooks alone, that had been streaming along in their courses for centuries and millennia. Everything was being leveled, straightened, flattened, drained, put into pipes, made *apt for machines*. All in the name of progress and provision and the Mercedes in front of the barn. It has to be worth it, though. The entire valley had been turned into a flat farmland, one single piece of raped earth. Raped by those to whom it had been given to take care of. Each turn of the tractor steering wheel had been too much to ask for, they had to plow ahead like tanks that were waging war against the soil they were plowing. Modern agriculture *is* war. The pillaged and poisoned enemy is not limited to the fields. Just look at the forests! Do they merit the name forest? They are timber fields, fir deserts. They stand tightly next to each other, as tight as to allow for their rapid growth, acre after acre. The soil of these forests are like barren, grey-brown shrouds consisting of dead needles. Not a single herb grows here, no bush, no shrub, only rarely a mushroom. To call this a forest is a blatant derision for every genuine, healthy, life-giving mixed forest. Riement sat on his window seat feeling more sorrow than anger, his portfolio next to him. The bus was barely half full, and during the off hours it was common that the driver drove around by himself. You had to worry constantly that this bus service would be dropped, or limited. Everywhere there were those people with pen and paper and calculator in hand. The complete control of the economy was already a fact, how long would it take to turn it into a totalitarian system? Teachers were not supposed to voice their opinions, that was obvious to Riement. In the company of entrepreneurs, producers and owners, teachers were a barely tolerated luxury. These people think it is adequate to teach children how to read, write and do math. That was enough. And to work! That was particularly important, getting them used to do work early on. We don´t learn for life, we live for work. This has to be drilled into them so it will last for an entire, long and hard existence. It should not waver or loosen. It has to be absorbed, it has to replace real meaning. *And we are their branding irons!* It was the teacher´s fault. With officials who dumped their pedagogic smartness like watery feces; with their stubborn refusal to recognize the positive aspects of their profession; with their tendency to perform absurd experiments; with their inability to talk straight, often linked to their highly poisoned party politics. Teachers should be and must be politically active, but here politics had degenerated into constant compromise. They were not politically motivated but grouped like little monkeys, all of them eyeing the highest rung of the barn.

He would write a letter to the editor. This time he would write a letter. He didn´t care what the colleagues would think of him.

"They do that anyway."

Yes, they did it anyway. His situation anger, as he called this anger about the state of things, disappeared in an instant. And if he were to write thousands of letters about agriculture, teachers and politics, nobody would take note of them. Writers of letters to the editor are part of those useful idiots of the system. They express what everybody knows, only not well enough. Their best contribution is to vent steam and to cause amusement.

"Why are people so blind?"

The landscape disappeared behind the thick curtain of his thoughts. At times everything was clear and pure, free of the intelligence of man´s logic, pervaded by the natural intelligence of being itself. The wrong way. Why did we take the wrong way? Was it our fault? Was this the fall from grace? For those who see, the eternal cycles are like an open book. Death and rebirth are stations of an indescribable journey. Every human being has experiences which reveal something. Only a few understand them. However, it would be so important that many would understand. Turning back is possible only when there is an inner disposition to do so. But we are blocked to such an extent that even the most simple truths are hidden from us. Everyone could achieve everything if he is in harmony with his real self. But there are so many obstacles in the path, apparently insurmountable barriers. They are built from the time we are children and we are stupid enough to eagerly help with their construction. Remove obstacles, remove all obstacles. If we achieve this, we are also free from sickness and death, free from all fear. Fear that pulls the rug from under our feet and robs us of the air we breathe. So much fear wherever we care to look. Even the fields seemed to fear the approaching spring. Soil after soil after soil …

Someone plucked at his shoulder. A girl said: "We are getting there, Mr. Teacher."

He sat up and looked into Sonja´s friendly face.

"Fell asleep again", he said, confused. "Thanks, Sonja."

She flashed her teeth and stepped off the bus before he did. Somewhat dazed due to the short nap he grabbed his bag and followed her. She waited for him because they shared part of their way home. They rarely talked to each other on the bus. Usually she would chat with a friend who lived a few miles further away, and he would be immersed in his thoughts. But he had started to like the fact that he chatted with her while walking the last yards to her parent´s farm. She was a friendly, open-minded girl. Although Riement taught at the secondary school and Sonja went to grammar school, the coincidences of the schedules and the limited possibilities of the bus schedule brought them together four or five times a week. She was willing to talk about school, family, and her favorite pastime, sports, while he reported from the other side of the front, the job of a teacher and the windmills of bureaucracy. At times he put in some of his ideas about life and death - very carefully, very carefully, because in the countryside, the church is still a power to be reckoned with and whoever has grown up in a small town knows that. The conversations were never longer than ten minutes or so, then she took a sideway and he looked at her and thought "My God! How young and fresh and joyful!" and the thought did not cause him to be happy, rather, melancholic.

Franz Riement still lived in the small house at the outermost edge of town, he had been born and raised there. His father had bought it after marrying and settling down for good. Before that he had held the position at the elementary school for many years. At some point he realized that his path would not lead him uphill anymore but towards his destiny, with wide, sweeping meanderings. Then he had bought the house and left it to his son.

The old school had been locked for a long time. Like a magnet, the county seat attracted everyone who had lived in the villages. Only the pastor and the inns remained. It had been pure luck that a successor had been found for the doctor's medical practice. Riement had become friends with Dr. Terrazzo despite the fact that he was openly skeptic and full of irony towards his theories. But at least he could *talk* with him. His wife Martha was waiting for him with lunch. Years ago he had lost contact with her. They talked to each other like cursory acquaintances. She managed the household and earned money as a dressmaker for friends. Back then, he had wondered whether she wasn't much better at her job than he was at his. After all, she had been the country's youngest dressmaker champion. Perhaps she should have kept her job and he should have taken care of the household. But twenty years ago this had been even more unthinkable than it was today. More so in a small town as opposed to the city. Martha had always preferred the city. During their first years of marriage they had been ready to pack their bags and move quite often. They had looked at apartments, talked to mortgage bankers and put up an ad to sell their house. But then he hadn't been able to pull it off. They had never talked about it, but most likely she considered his attitude a continuous betrayal. At least a continuous weakness, for which he could not blame her. One day she had moved into the room downstairs, including her bed. No comment. Ever since that moment their marriage had been limited to sharing meals and discussing pending repairs. Whenever he came home she said "There you are" and when he left, she didn´t say anything.

If she were to leave him she would do so without saying a word, just as she had left their shared bedroom. There was not a single day when he could be certain that she would still be there when he came home from work. He admitted that it was all the same to him, and had been so for a long time.

But she did not leave him and he never asked her how they would keep going on. They lived in a permanently unsettled state and had become used to it. But was this not an *unhealthy* state? He was weak, yes, it was true. He was weak. If he had been strong …

"Hello", he said while stepping into the kitchen. "What´s for lunch?"

"Smoked meat and sauerkraut", she said and dried her hands with her always meticulously clean apron. "And roasted potatoes. Sit down."

Sonja´s lunch was waiting for her, too. Her father and two younger brothers had finished their lunch some time ago. Her mother, a petite little woman, always friendly and full of energy, ate with her daughter. She thought it was wrong that the girl was sitting alone at the table, and whenever she thought something was wrong, she changed it. Her father was working yet again. He was one of the few people who were made for work and even loved doing it. All kinds of work. He was large and heavy but quick with his mind, and he had hands which could scare you when they held the soft hands of his wife. But they were unusually nimble. If there was a need for it, he lathed bolts and screws, which almost disappeared between his fingers. For Adelheid, he threaded sewing silk through the finest needles because her eyesight wasn´t as good, and when he did so it was a mute demonstration of his love that she enjoyed every time. But his hands were made for the hard work in the forest and on the farm, where they could prove their worth.

Sonja ate quickly. She had a lot to do. There were some of the twins' toys on the table as well as a box of painkillers.

"Is dad having headaches again?" she asked.

"Yes", her mother replied. "But I won´t take him to the doctor. He is as stolid as a mule. And he wouldn´t even have to go to town."

Sonja´s father hated going to town although he vehemently denied it. That didn´t change the fact that his family made fun of it.

"Perhaps he is afraid that it might be something serious", Sonja said.

"Yes. Don´t spook the horses, though."

Sonja jumped up from the table, gave her a kiss and went to her room. The days were way too short. She couldn´t waste one minute.

He had arrived yesterday. A cool March evening. Humid, gusty wind ruffled the forsythias and pressed the flowers against the walls and windows where they stuck like yellow dots. Wherever they stuck in a particularly dense pattern they looked like an unfinished mosaic.

Dark clouds made the sky look heavy. A gloomy atmosphere floated over the barren fields. Further south, where the plains turned into mountains, lightning was flashing. The conversations at the inn where he had put up also revolved around the weather. The farmers were unhappy. The last summer had been too dry and winter had brought damage to the forests. Now there was plenty of rain, but it was still cold. Five of them were sitting at a table, hats on their heads, drinking fruit wine and schnapps. They didn´t have much time as they still had to get into their barns. The other tables were occupied by people who were eating and drinking and apparently had nothing to do with farming. He had noticed that one- and two-family homes had cropped up between the dispersed farm houses. They were houses owned by commuters who had been attracted by life in the countryside and by the low land prices. He sat down at a small table inside a niche, one of its walls forming a large window leading to the inn´s garden. It might have been a nice garden during summertime, when the colorful leaves of the wild creepers were overgrowing the wire trellis. Now there was only rusty wire mesh which didn´t look any better in the vanishing light of dusk.

Then Rosi was standing in front of him.

Rosi immediately thought about the museum where she had been years ago. About the busts of Greek or Roman kings; or emperors she couldn´t remember. This man had such a head. But it wasn´t dead, white marble. The skin was dark, beard and hair were densely curled and black.

"This is how they looked", she thought. He did not notice her right away as he was looking out the window. After a few seconds he noticed her presence and looked at her. His eyes were almost as black as his hair. At first she was disappointed. She had expected a lot more fierceness and fire. His gaze was lively and interested, but more than anything he transmitted a sense of endless calm. Rosi was an unusually frank person. Whatever she thought was written into her face. He was reading it and smiled. Wrinkles appeared around his eyes like unfolding fans. Now they were sparkling as well.

"I would like to have something to eat", he said. "Can I stay overnight?"

"Yes", she answered without hesitation. She blushed a little. "We have four rooms available. Would you like to have a look at them?" He picked one of the rooms and ate and dreamed about strange things, and later on Rosi came to his room and they made love like people in the Middle Ages might have made love during the plague, starvation and war; with death always around the corner, they were completely resigned to life. Love and passion which deserve the name are no place for reassurance.

The following day Rosi´s eyes were glowing more intensely as usual. The man who was responsible for it was strolling through town. There was only one sight worth seeing. The small church from the time of the Turkish War, surrounded by a tiny graveyard. He returned to the Sheep´s Inn, drank coffee and read the newspapers. He nodded to one of the old farmers who left soon afterwards and whom Rosi attended without much enthusiasm.

He had registered as Jason Padoponos. So he was indeed Greek, although he spoke German without a hint of an accent. After lunch he took a long walk across the fields, untouched by the humid wind and the many rain showers. The trails were straight as arrows. Lonesome trees or effigies stood at many of the crossings. Forested hills grew near and far from the valley floor, some of them mere islands, others like long barriers, which divided the flat landscape of the mountain valley.

The atmosphere of the fields transferred to him. The flapping of the ravens sounded like the heavy breath of a dying person, their dry and hollow calls like the complaints of the dead from the underworld. He was gripped by a sense of unease. Gloomily he observed the countless elevations and bumps. The landscape was steeped in very old secrets, with sunken places of worship and altars where the earth around them was still particularly black and fertile. The millennia had erased the knowledge from the people´s consciousness. Vague memories were preserved in ancient customs, often overlaid with pagan and Christian rites. There was nobody around who could still interpret them. Time was slipping through his hands like fine sand. It would not be enough, it never was. Suddenly, a heavy burden came down on his shoulders. Soaked and tired, he reached the town and went directly to his room.

He laid down on the bed and closed his eyes. Small twitches of his nervous system caused him to shiver with fever, his fingers flapping on the bed cover like the wings of a butterfly weary of winter. He knew the indicators and did not fight them. The restiveness eased off and he slipped into a state of semi-consciousness, dropping all fetters of space and time. Images, cold like injections of liquid nitrogen, seeped into his settled mind: wisps of fog on a steep precipice, gloomy firs, bouncy forest ground, very old and very young people hurrying up the mountain in an endless procession, and then the young ones became old and disappeared. They formed a circle around a large clearing, they themselves surrounded by thousand year-old oak trees. Numerous little fires turned the mountain at night into a gleaming tongue, licking the black skies. A sad melody, a recitative, spread from one mouth to the next and finally draped itself like a coat around the flanks of the mountain and reached the large clearing. Men in long garments reaching to the ground were already waiting for the victims whose blood would help them overcome the separation between the times and the three kinds of lives. The melody stopped with the last hit, the fires expired and those who had been waiting sank to the ground, the morning dawn to the east being its heavenly mirror. Deep calm lay over the land. Clouds of fog crept up from the valley, up the hills and behind them the mountain vanished as if the fog had devoured it.

Padoponos lay as if he were dead. The mountain still existed. He had seen it.

9

Sonja was wearing a patterned pink running suit, keeping her hair out of her face with a headband. She was wearing running shoes whose advertisement wanted to make you believe they were running almost by themselves. They might run on their own. But once you had them on, they wouldn´t do that anymore.

She took the first slopes with light, even steps. Skiing was her passion, her biggest goal was to get into the state team. Whenever the weather allowed it she did extensive forest runs. She loved the forest. She loved nature. There was a large number of logging roads, which had been created over decades to facilitate the extraction of trees, then they had laid abandoned for years until a section of forest was ready for harvesting, or its owner was in dire need of money, or heavy snow damage or bark beetles made it necessary to intervene. Many of these roads and trails had been cut into the hills without any regard for the damage they caused; they ruptured water levels and created soil erosion. The main issue was to save time, heavy machinery is expensive and the price of wood was way down.

There was a positive side to it, too. Badly traced trails quickly formed continuous chains of pools which filled with all kinds of life a few weeks after the machines and trucks had left the area. Sonja loved the sections of pools where toads placed their yards-long strings of spawn and where frogs produced thick, jelly-like clumps of eggs. Diving beetles and hawkers were hunting here. Reeds grew in thick clusters at the moist edges of the trails, the long and round leaves dark green, the hard spikes brown and black. Not very often she saw a grass snake. Snakes had become a rare sight.

She used those pools as obstacles while running, jumping as high and as far as possible, always careful not to crush any of the small animals, which were walking, crawling or jumping between the sand and gravel.

Her father detested badly constructed trails just as he detested anything that was poorly done, as a sign of thoughtlessness and ignorance. He thoroughly thought about any job beforehand. The things he took on were designed to last, not to make a quick profit. Sonja had learned a lot from him. Her ambition was not the common ambition of young girls, bursting into flames and quickly fading away like a match. She planned years ahead and never wavered in her determination at working on herself. She had goals and did what she could in order to reach them.

She had been running for half an hour, mostly uphill. Now she chose a more level circuit to recover before returning home.

10___

He did not take the road but went directly between the trees. From a pile of wood he chose a walnut club, strong and well-balanced. Then he trudged through the forest covered in fog, parallel to the trail. The ground was wet and slippery. He didn´t walk far. It was not necessary. He stopped behind a thick pine and waited. A thought welled up in him like a gas bubble made from morass.

"What am I doing here? What?"

The question dissolved without echo in a kind of gloomy certainty. His view narrowed looking at the trail while his sense of hearing increased to infinity. He heard ants walking up the coarse trunk, a mouse digging, an early, wobbly fly ten yards away. Ever-present background noises increased to resemble a hurricane which almost swept him away. He bit his tongue under the unbearable pressure. The taste of blood threatened to suffocate him. The weight of a ton on his breast squashed his lung. But he resisted. The pressure subsided and he waited. Young, light footsteps, that's what he wanted to hear. He held the club firmly in his hand.

That evening Sonja did not return from her run. Nor the next day or the day after that. For the sleepy town, her disappearance had the effect of a kick into a nest of wasps. The parents sounded the alarm. Dozens of officials and many times more volunteers formed search parties. The Lassnig farm became the center of comings and goings. Sonja's father spent sixty hours without interruption inside the forest, her mother took care of the group of rescuers. Two helicopters flew over the area. After five days the search was halted, an accident was discounted. They had searched an area of six miles in diameter, turned over every stone, brought in tracking dogs, searched each and every old and overgrown path far into the underbrush, had dug at several suspicious-looking spots, all in vain. They found Bernd's hideaway and had it checked by crime scene investigators, without any result. Riement the teacher, who also dealt with dowsing and pendulums, tried his craft but came up with nothing. The police questioned friends and classmates but didn't find any indication about a love affair or suicidal thoughts. Sonja remained missing. Josef Lassnig, the man with the strength of a bear, suffered a breakdown. As most of them did, he suspected that the girl had been the victim of a crime and that the perpetrator had hidden the body very well. If you are intent on doing so, you can hide almost anything inside a large and mountainous forested area. A well-camouflaged shallow grave is all you need. The dogs can't be everywhere and people just step over it without noticing anything. Only Sonja's mother thought that this was impossible. "She is not dead", she insisted on repeating over and over. "I would know if she were dead". People were hurt to hear her saying that while ignoring all the facts, but none of them was willing or capable of contradicting her. A file was opened, suspicious people were checked,

among them the Sheep´s Inn´s guest, then the official actions
ceased. Sonja´s track led into the forest and there it
disappeared, like a light being switched off.

Rosi and the Greek were lying on the wide bed of his room. The girl had been missing for three days. There were search parties still doing their work. Flashlights could be seen from town shining around the hills out there. Rosi had put her head on his breast, now and then her hand passed over his belly, and deeper. Not in a demanding kind of way, more like a calm patrol checking on his state of virility.

"What did they want?" she asked.

"Information. Where I'm from, what I do, how long I plan on staying."

"What did you tell them?"

"The truth."

"Then tell me the truth as well. How long are you staying?"

He laughed.

"As long as I can take it. I actually wanted to rest."

Padoponos was lying on his back and observed the forays of her hand. He had never met a woman like Rosi. She was - whenever she wanted to be - soft and warm and tender. At the same time she was pulsating with pure, unused energy. She was so filled with life and love, with absolute will and absolute dedication, that many men *had* to recoil because they did not have the strength to withstand her.

Rosi felt the tension of the past days waning. Foreign faces had descended like a swarm of starlings on the town and the inn. Many people in uniform, criminal investigators followed by a bunch of reporters, mostly women, and curious people from the city. People who wanted to be there, see the tragedy with their own eyes, speculate about it and talk with everybody. Experiencing the tragedy up close and sitting in the first row.

One woman reporter said: "A young and pretty thing stirs the imagination. Pretty girls as victims, the reader eats it up. Hopefully they will find her soon, otherwise the story will go cold."

Had it been an old farmer's wife who had disappeared, it would have barely made it into the local news.

Rosi had barely known Sonja, there simply had not been too many occasions. The Lassnig family rarely came over to the Sheep's Inn. Nevertheless, they greeted each other and exchanged sympathies from a distance. Cold shivers ran down her spine while thinking about what might have happened out there in the woods. Perhaps the reporter was right. Young girls stir the imagination. She thought the hubbub was as terrible as the cause for it.

He had fallen asleep, his breathing had changed. She took her head off his breast. Now they were lying next to each other on their backs, the covers up to their chins. She dreamed with open eyes, protected by the protective warmth of the down blanket. Calmness and satisfaction. A feeling of happiness she had never felt before, even though she had been happy before his arrival. At least she had thought at times that she was, which is about the same thing. So there are several floors of happiness. Happiness is a house with several floors. But when you enter a house you know how many floors there are. With happiness, it's a different story. One can only intuit if there is more to come. Something on top of that, Rosi thought. But if there is anything else, then it is a roof garden, a small paradise, perhaps *the* paradise …

She was that three year old girl again, snuggling between the warm bodies of her parents at night, covered up to the tip of her nose. The bedroom was cold, there was snow lying on the roof window, but under the sheets it was just wonderful. She listened to her father's long breathing and the faster one of her mother. Sleep breathing. She wanted it to be like this forever. The darkness, the sleeping parents, the sense of safeness. It is something extraordinary to remember an early emotion. The sense of limitless safety had been so strong that even today the thought of it almost took her breath away. The three year old fought against sleep, afraid of losing the sensation of security. Of course it was futile. And then, it did not take long for her

41

to lose everything. First, her father and shortly thereafter her mother. She moved in with an aunt, went to school, learned a craft … All these years had left little if any memories. Nothing worth keeping. If she wanted to remember, she could, but these memories were stale. Teachers, classmates, the aunt, always trying, always drab, friends, acquaintances, neighbors. Even though back then she had already lived and felt with more intensity than others, looking back, it all paled against the three year old girl fighting sleep so as to protect her safety. Now that feeling had returned. Not as intense, but with a new and a broader base. She liked the smell when she lifted the sheet briefly. The skin between her thighs was tight while the sticky juices dried. He was lying next to her and breathed calmly. Again, she had to fight against falling asleep. Her memories mixed with the coming dreams. Faces started to appear, changed and sank away again. The tender face of a boy turned into the coarse face of a man, but she knew that it still belonged to the boy. Other faces were scolding the boy. Evil, distorted, mean faces.

Suddenly Rosi was wide awake. Her temples pulsed with anger. For the first time in two days she had spoken with Bernd today. He was so intimidated that he was unable to utter a coherent sentence. At first she thought the police officers were to blame. She had questioned him. But soon she realized that there was more to it. He was terribly frightened of *her*. A name had shot through her like an electric jolt: old Matte! He had asked her about Bernd. He had been looking for him. She asked Bernd about it. His reaction confirmed that she was right. He crouched like a beaten animal. But she was unable to find out what had occurred between the old guy and him. Only that he had been hiding in the woods afterwards. This had happened on the day Sonja had disappeared. Rosi´s anger changed into a strong feeling of unease. Apparently, Bernd had been beside himself … why? She would have liked to know why.

Padaponos was not sleeping. He had put himself into a

meditative state where his thoughts were as clear and bright as the Greek light where he had been raised. He saw his town before him - a village, but in another world. Distance did not mean anything anymore, as it was measured in flight hours. But the different worlds only seemed to have gotten closer because of it. One finds resemblances and might think that one village is just like the next one. But it is not so. There may be types of people who may be at any place, but the atmosphere, the consistency of the air, the age-old aromas coming from the soil - this original character of the land changes from valley to valley, region to region. People come and go, unsteady and short-lived. They bring along language and they displace language, they bring culture and take it with them. Only the soil remains. Light, rocks and earth and its history form a fixed base designed for other time spans than those of our fleeting hustle and bustle.

Young Jason sat on the polished rock high above the sea and thought he could see the glimmer of the desert far to the south. But again and again, ships appeared and he climbed a little higher. He would have loved to get up and say proudly into the silence which ensued after the teacher entered: I have seen Africa!

In his village, poverty had been omnipresent. There were no large farms like here. If someone had twice as much cattle than the rest, he was considered to be rich. And twice as much was still paltry. Nobody was actually starving, however, one of those overweight tourists could have easily wolfed down five of their rations. But there were no tourists back then. Now and then an emigrant visiting his former home, telling about the wonders of America. For decades, emigration and wars had been the only reasons to catapult the village men into the world. Many of them stayed abroad. At first, long letters arrived, then postcards with hastily scribbled greetings, thereafter, only silence. His own last visit had been a long time ago. What a long and miserable trip it was from his village to this! And it was here where he had found the woman he had been looking for all his life. But before he could tell Rosi about his plans he had to complete the task. He had told the officials he was working as a developer for a German software company. If they checked him out it would be confirmed. He thought it was unlikely that they would request a personal description. His papers were okay. He had been in his room when the girl had disappeared, later, at the inn, then again in his room. The innkeeper, some of the guests and Rosi in particular could confirm this. However, if they were to find Sonja, most likely dead, he would have to answer more questions than he would have liked. But more than that, he was scared of the basic vibes of this place, the atmosphere. His vision was closely related to it and it was quite possible that the disappearance of the girl had something to do with it. Was his relationship with Rosi being influenced by it as well? He had learned to take everything occurring on the mental level as a potential unit.

His hand found Rosi´s and their fingers interlocked. The calls from the search parties were being swept away by the wind.

13

Lydia Kern, the Sheep´s innkeeper - a surname she hated - looked at Rosi in a scrutinizing way when she appeared shortly after seven in the kitchen. The young woman was full of energy, as always. Not a hint that she had worked until eleven at night and then disappeared into the guest´s room. Normally, the innkeeper would not have tolerated this behavior, but Rosi was not one to accept such chiding. Particularly not in matters such as this one. Lydia would have regretted if she were to leave, as she was willing to work long hours and knew how to get things done. That was important. When two people work for a day, one can accomplish much while the other doesn´t get much done. Employment contracts don't differentiate between the two. Lydia knew perfectly well that Rosi was doing the work of another employee.

The innkeeper cut two slices of bread, still warm, added butter, ham, hardboiled eggs and pickled cucumbers and put on some fresh radish. She made a pot of coffee and placed it on a tray, adding a cup and a large glass of milk.

"So he doesn´t like jam?" Lydia asked.

"He likes our bread and ham. Where he´s from, there´s only white bread and the smoked meat is pale as a cadaver if they don´t inject enough coloring."

She picked up the tray and brought it to the upper floor. When she returned she prepared a sandwich for herself.

"Any news?" The standard question these days. No conversation where it was not asked. The innkeeper shook her head.

"They keep searching."

She cut up cabbage. A large bowl was almost full. There was much food being ordered because of the officials and the curious people. Her cabbage salad had become popular rather quickly. She looked at Rosi.

"I told Matte that our guest thinks you are likeable. And that you like him."

"What did he say?"

"He just swallowed it. According to his face it was like bile."
The women laughed. Concerning Matte, they were both on the
same team. The old man who thought he knew everything
going on with other people was very wrong concerning one
thing: Lydia had not forgotten the story which had brought her
the "Sheep's Inn" moniker, not one bit. Of course she had
fiddled with Matte, perhaps a bit more than that. There was no
way around it if you wanted to get somewhere around here.
She was ambitious. She did not accept the weak position
which her father had left her. Now, as some said, she was the
second man in the village. But the old anger and the old hatred
had not disappeared, they were just tucked away in some part
of her head until the right moment came along.

They both couldn't stand the old man. Lydia had high regards
for Rosi because she had not spread her legs for him like all
the other waitresses and servants before her. She liked Rosi
because she didn't mind showing him her disregard. *Let them
feel it*. That was what Matte had told her during a private
encounter. He didn't have to tell Rosi, she had it in her blood.
Steps and voices could be heard outside.

"Unlock right away", Lydia said. "They are coming from the
forest and they're hungry."

Rosi put the remaining sandwich into her mouth and
disappeared into the dining hall. A moment later, steaming
coffee mugs stood on the tables. Tired men, either silent or
talking quietly, waiting for their meals. No news about Sonja.

14

He was squirming in his bed like a skewered grub. The bed sheet was ripped off the mattress, the blanket had slipped to the floor. He held onto the cushion like a drowning person to a much too small piece of wood. His face was white and wet. He groaned and gasped. He was actually sitting on top of a steel locker, looking at his naked body, which was lying on a sheet of shiny, stainless steel. A figure dressed in a grey rubber coat wearing transparent gloves leaned over him. He saw the scalpel and felt its sharp tip sink into his belly. He would have loved to jump up and run away, but he was sitting on top of the locker and his body was lying down there and could not move. A smooth cut split his abdominal wall into two sections. Two more cuts made a Y-shape. He felt an uncomfortable pull while the sections of flesh and fat were loosened and flipped to the side. There was hardly any blood. In any case, no more than if one were to cut up the shoulder of a cow, for example, in order to make a goulash. If you have a serious hangover, there is nothing like a spicy goulash with a fresh bun and cold beer. Absolutely nothing. That is, if one is not shaking so badly that the meat falls from the spoon. In that case you wouldn´t be able to get the glass to your lips. Not with one hand.

The figure in the rubber coat pointed to the gaping wound, grinned and waved at him. He saw the open cavity and was certain that he could do without looking at it. The hands rummaged in his intestines, uncovering organs and taking them out. Then they lay there in the cold light of the halogen spotlights. The large and dark one must be the liver, the bent pair, the kidneys. You can do whatever you want with kidneys. You never get entirely rid of the stench of urine. Not for his nose, anyway. They put them in water, in milk, whatever. There is always a lingering smell. Enough to make your stomach churn. Speaking about stomach. That one was likely lying there as well. But he wasn´t entirely sure of it.

Perhaps the spleen?

Suddenly the stench of kidneys reached him and he felt nauseous. He lost his balance and fell from the locker. His head hit the floor hard. He lay there, facing the bed, wondering where he was. After some time he knew where. He stood up, arranged the linen sheet, picked up the blanket and lay down again. He then took two pills. They weren´t having any effect, but he felt helpless. He *had* to take something. After the events of the other day he almost preferred the horror of his dreams to the waking state. *What had happened in the forest?*

He remembered deciding to go for a walk. He had stooped over to tie his shoelaces, that he could still see clearly. He had to try three times because his hands were shaking badly. Then, a cut. A black hole. Nothing. When his memory returned, he was sitting with his back against a trunk, not far from the village, and he was terribly cold. He returned to his home with the vanishing daylight and immediately took a hot bath. His tongue felt thick and throbbed. His forehead was hot and it hurt when he swallowed. He was certain he had gotten a cold. Why was there a memory gap of several hours? He couldn´t go from door to door asking if someone might have seen him. Had he just walked about or had he *done* something? Apart from the dark spots caused by the damp forest soil there were no traces on his hands or his clothing. He should do something, urgently. But how could you do anything in this condition?

And then "it" took control again and perforated his forehead and the back of his eyes with pointed, glowing spikes until he lay calmly on his back, paralyzed by the pain, dissolving in the pain like a piece of metal inside molten steel.

The next morning, when he found out about the commotion in the village and the disappearance of Sonja Lassnig, he had forgotten everything. Only the dream in which he witnessed his own autopsy was still clearly present.

It was Saturday, no work. Despite him not feeling too well he joined one of the search parties. This kind of situation required them all to stick together, nobody should stay on the sidelines.

15

One week had gone by. Rüdiger was lying on his bed feeling
terrible. No results so far. He still felt terrible. He would have
preferred that they be straightforward right from the start.
After all, they were old enough. Now, on top of the secrecy
there was the forbidden, as well as a much worse suspicion.
He saw her face in front of his inner eye, her hands, her hair.
Tears welled up in his eyes as he realized he was thinking in
the past tense. *She* had wanted the secrecy. She said her
parents would have never agreed. He thought he knew it was
an excuse. But it was impossible to get the truth out of Sonja
if she was using an excuse. So they met at secret spots in the
forest and made love. Then she jumped up and continued with
her run. Sport was not supposed to take second place to love.
Rüdiger was pretty much in the same situation as those wives
whose husbands dedicated five intimate minutes to them,
between bowling and the newscast. Sonja loved him, but it
was not supposed to take up too much time. That was during
summer and autumn. During winter it was too cold. On half a
dozen occasions they had met inside the barn. It was cold
there, too, but it was okay if you dug yourself deep enough
into the hay. Afterwards, the entire body was itching and you
had to brush your hair for several minutes. It was actually
quite funny. Funny and a bit ridiculous. But nice, too.
Now he was suffering several pains. He suffered the loss and
the fact that he could not confide in anyone. He was also
afraid of being discovered. It didn´t take much imagination to
suspect the secret lover. Suspect of what? What had
happened?
He *had* been in the forest. He *had* seen something. He was so
confused that he started to lose his mind.
Until he learned to love Sonja he had hated the village. He had
been thirteen years old when they had left the city to move
into their own home. His parents realized their dream, which
he could not take pleasure in. Building a house meant a lot of

work and little money around. They were saving on everything. Food, clothing, vacations. During construction, vacation was synonymous with building. Carrying buckets, handing tools, holding planks, painting, puttying, vomiting because of the stew´s fat meat. If you turned around every dime five times, much of what would end up in the trash ended up on the plate. And then, moving. Until the very last moment he hoped that something would happen to the house. It could burn down or collapse, a plane might crash into it or the hill might slide away. Unfortunately, catastrophes couldn´t be asked for, same as they couldn´t be prayed away. They moved into the house, his parents cried for joy while he wept from sadness. His friends stayed back in the city, his classmates and everything he was interested in. The folks in rural areas were different. He did not know what made them different, and why, but he felt it. So his new friends were not locals but comrades in destiny. Fortunately, his parents had not been the only ones pursuing their dream of their own home. Within five years a neighborhood of happy homeowners had been built whose offsprings would have preferred to return to the city as soon as possible. This formed a bond between them. Then he had known Sonja and the highs and lows of love. And now he felt the same as he did during his first day in the village. He had to talk to someone. If he couldn´t talk to somebody, soon he would go crazy. Ever since their craze about their own home he had discarded them as people he could talk to. They reminded him of those couples from the American movies who only talked about grill parties and cars and dreamed about their own swimming pool. The pool would continue to remain only a dream. There had not been enough money for that much land. At least they had a masonry grill, now with a roof, and a horrific sitting room suite made of thick planks, which they called rustic. He got anxious thinking about sausages, chops and hamburgers, eaten with thick mayonnaise salad from wooden or cardboard plates. Sometimes hot, sometimes cold, sometimes burnt.

Sometimes semi-raw, sometimes so tough that you could hardly bite into them, sometimes covered with a thick crust of grill spices. But always *so* good and *so* practical and *so* nice. There was not one summer day when you could not smell the turpentine which they used to light the charcoal. Now there was another summer coming up and Sonja had disappeared and he was all by himself and close to losing his mind due to what he had seen. Who could he talk to? Who?

16

The kitchen was the most important room of the house. It was used for sitting, eating, quarreling, children did their homework, there was ironing being done, TV being watched, there was drinking, and sometimes someone would sleep off his hangover. In addition, there was pretty much continuous cooking going on. A large farm had to feed so many stomachs, although not as many as in former times. So the stove and the table, which could seat fourteen people, were the most important items. The stove was about three feet wide and ten feet long. It was heated with wood. A large copper bowl provided piping hot water. It had compartments for heating plates, drying nuts, mushrooms or fruits, to keep meals warm and - of course - an oven.

The old man sat at the narrow end of the table with his back against the wall. This spot gave him a view of the entire kitchen. There were two of them in the kitchen. The elder daughter-in-law stood at the stove, her bottom filling the coat like a fat sausage its skin. Sometimes he tapped her derriere. Only because it was so tight, no other reason. Presumably he could have grabbed her between her legs like a cow and she would have continued to stir the pot. Perhaps her feet would have drifted apart a little as it would be more comfortable, but she would not have turned around. "It´s more fun with a cow than it is with you", he thought maliciously. His sons were such idiots!

"The old pig is staring again", she thought. "I can´t put on a tighter skirt or it will split apart." She moved her hips a little. "He´s only thinking about one thing. Come on, why don´t you dare, old fart. Get over here and give it to me, I don´t mind. I couldn´t care less about which one of you puts his thing into me. But if you were to do it I´d have you under my thumb. It would be over with playing the big kahuna and all, you couldn´t boss us around anymore."

"Where´s mother?" he asked.

"She´s lying down", she said with her thick dialect. "The feet."

"Tell her to get down here", he replied, imitating her tone.

"She´ll be able to get this far. With the feet."

"She´s hurting", she said and kept stirring.

The face of the old man turned sinister.

"Look here!" he barked.

She turned around, large and heavy and sweating from the heat of the stove. Her mouth with these soft lips, way too soft, was tight with resistance and fear.

"If you don´t like it", he whispered, "then take a hike! With your husband and your brood. Today!"

"Michael is your son", she replied. Her voice had become higher and thinner. Hatred and fear. Fear, always this fear. To be booted off the farm. To have no rights. None she could rely on as she was not up to the old man.

He didn´t say anything, observed the crumbling of her weak defense without any joy. She lowered her gaze, "Pardon, father. I´ll go get her."

He waited until he could hear the heavy steps of his daughter-in-law and the arduous steps of his wife, then he got up and left through the other door. He slammed it hard so they could hear it. *Let them feel it.*

Old Matte had two sons, who were living on the farm with their families. And three daughters, who were married and lived elsewhere. Both his sons had been disappointing. "Bumbling peasants", he thought, which was strange as he himself was *the* peasant. But there´s always those and those. They had absolutely no talent for the "game", for pulling strings, for letting them feel it. Their only worry was when the farm would be handed over. To whom. Just wait, he thought. Two of his grandsons, one of fourteen, the other eight years old, stood at the narrow end of the stable and were slaughtering chicken. The younger one brought them outside, one by one, the older boy chopped off their head. After a dozen birds had lost their lives, the younger one was free to go. He picked up the heads with the bleeding stumps and went behind the stable. Less than a minute later there was the regular sound of a dry knock against wood, five or six times, then a pause before the next series, and so it continued. This aroused the old man´s curiosity and he took a quick detour to reach another building from where he could observe his grandson. The fellow had built an improvised shooting range. An old door leaning against the wall with three nails bent upwards with one chicken head on each of them. At about ten steps´ distance he had drawn a line in the ground. From there he was throwing small darts against the dead targets. He threw well and with much concentration. Deliberately, evenly, calmly. Each throw a new throw, otherwise, an error would cause further errors. After each series he walked up to the door, checking his hits and pulling out the darts. He wiped off the bloody tips of the short darts and sniffed at them. Now and then a smile crept over his naturally peevish, small face. Then he pulled the used head from the nail and replaced it with a new one. It took old Matte a while until he understood the rules of the game. Both eyes had to be hit.

17

At lunchtime, twelve people assembled in the kitchen. The old man and his wife, both sons, the daughters-in-law, four grandsons, the maid and the servant. When he was young, the farm had fed more than twice as many eaters, the work had been harder and the treatment rougher. A large and tough farmer actually reigned over his folks. Perhaps not according to the law, but according to customs. And of these simple people, who could barely read and write, who would have dared to complain elsewhere? Of course it had happened. There are always courageous ones who insist on their rights - or what they consider to be their rights. This does not mean that they would get them. And in case they got them it did not mean it would do them any good. But most importantly: how many cowards were there for each courageous one? Ten, twenty, a hundred? More than enough, old Matte thought for himself. Back then as today. If you control the cowards you don´t have to fear those with courage. He looked at his family and felt contempt rising up, like bad heartburn. He emptied his jug and felt how they seemed to wince with each of his moves. They were not aware of it, like beaten dogs. Only the young one with the chicken heads seemed to be different. He gazed into the distance, three vertical wrinkles on his forehead. Matte looked at him sternly, so the daughter-in-law elbowed him so as to look up.

"What did you do behind the stable?" the old man asked.

"Throwing darts", his grandson answered morosely.

"At what?"

"At the door."

"That´s right", his mother said nervously. "I told him he could use the old door ..."

"Shut up", Matte said. It was even more humiliating as he didn´t mean it to sound offensive. It was as if he had turned off the radio. Nobody protested.

"Are you practicing for moving targets?"

Now the boy´s eyes were shining.

"Perhaps this one is of my kind", the old man thought.

Something in the boy´s eyes reminded him of his own youth.

"But not on my farm", he added, grumbling.

His grandson understood and nodded.

"Fill up!" Matte told his wife, who obeyed without saying a word.

Matte´s elder son thought: "Mother is in pain but not allowed to stay in bed."

Matte´s younger son thought: "Each time Traudl opens her mouth she gets on his nerves. Can´t she just shut up?"

Traudl didn´t think of anything.

Matte´s second daughter-in-law wished: "When is this old pig going to die!"

18

Grete Strutz had been taking care of the pastor's household for eighteen years. She was two years away from retirement. Before Reverend Weilrich's employment she had been a maid, a cook, anything she could get. She could not avoid the destiny of having a child out of wedlock. Only a few with a bad start in life can avoid such a fate. Who was going to marry someone who had absolutely nothing? One who carried all of her belongings in a suitcase from one job to the next? The only interesting thing she owned could be had, anyway. A few promises are easily made and easily broken. These young girls, it is their own fault to continue to fall into the same trap. They are hot. They don't have much fun. Today it is different, but not that much different. Back then, it was the barn or the stable or a summer pasture, today it's the car at the country roadside, or a dark parking spot. Today they could avoid the consequences more easily, but it still happens almost as often as back then. Dumb young things. Poor girls who can't control their longing and fall on their faces. The Reverend had taken care of her and given her a steady job. The demands of life had changed her back then already, her daughter had made her a grandmother when she was seventeen, but she didn't provide a son-in-law, either. They've got pepper in their backsides, these young girls, and they were in an area where nobody locked up his zipper. That's how they are. And her granddaughter was already of age, may God protect her. Her mother made her take the pill, and until now it had worked, but some of them got pregnant just by someone looking at them. Those guys, they certainly have to pay when there is proof of paternity. But often they don't have much, except for debts. You first had to buy that car for the country roadside and the dark parking spot. Grete knew about money, she had saved money all her life. She went from one bank to the next, from one branch to the other, negotiating every fraction of a percent. She read everything concerning savings in the newspapers. There were radio shows with tips about saving money. Finances. It is such a resounding word. When the reporter said the word finances it sounded like the church bells during the holiest of days. Whenever she found out about a good return on investment and she was getting less than that, she was on her way an hour later. She took the bus to town and complained at her bank, and if that wasn´t enough she went to each and every institution. Those employees with experience quickly disappeared, but she disregarded this and waited, stubborn as she was, until she could not be overlooked anymore and someone had to deal with her. Everything she owned she had saved, so she was entitled to get the best deal. She knew about commitment periods, bonus savings and capital savings, but she didn´t get into shares, way too risky, bonds earned good money, but she was not willing to park her capital for too long. She already owned a small lot, construction would start in summer. She would need her own home in two years. Reverend Weilrich would get a new housekeeper and she would have to leave, there was no question about it.

If the Reverend were to be in office by then, that is …

Grete knew the cause of his suffering. The Reverend didn´t know she knew, although he could have imagined as it should have been obvious to him that, after eighteen years, Grete knew everything. Some called her a taleteller, so what? If people weren´t so keen on telling stories, there wouldn´t be any taletellers. They gossip about everything, without exception, some more, some less. And she simply listened, so if someone asked her, she didn´t remain silent. Actually, it wasn´t really necessary to ask her not to remain silent. The Reverend had two hearts, she believed, a big one and a small one. The small one had been implanted by the church, the large one was his own. With some Reverends it was the other way around, they weren´t really good people. His small heart protested whenever she told him about this one and that, his big heart commanded him to listen because her gossip was not underhanded or cunning, and he saw that she had two hearts, a small one and a big one. The big one was implanted by God, he believed. If people only listened to their big hearts they would not need to feign so much. They wouldn´t have to lie as much and to think badly about others. It would be nice to be able to get rid of the small hearts. But, apparently, they were part of it all.

So now Rosi had an affair with this early tourist and suddenly she was interested in old Matte who had been after her ever since she had started out as a waitress. This early tourist was a strange fellow, anyway. He had a Greek name but German vehicle number plates, Rosi said. The police had been questioning him after the Lassnig girl had disappeared, but actually it was only because he was a foreigner and he was single. Certainly old Matte had been helping along. He was bothered by the fact that Rosi did not sleep in her own room ever since the foreigner had checked into the Sheep´s Inn.

Rosi wanted to know what the old man had been up to back then. Way back, before the war and during the war, when his father was still alive. The housekeeper was past sixty, so she knew stories which everybody else had forgotten by now. At the end of the war she had been fourteen years old. Back then, Matte had shown up early, much sooner than the rest, some of whom returned only years later. There was much to tell about him, but nothing about his time before and during the war; she did not know anything about that.

Strange thing that Rosi was interested. Perhaps it was not her who was interested, but her friend the tourist. So she told the Reverend while serving lunch. Grete Strutz smelled a romantic affair. For example, the result of a love affair during the war, searching for his father many years later. These things had happened again and again. Or, a first wife whom he had never divorced. That one she liked even better. She was one of those who really wished some kind of trouble for old Matte.

The Reverend had remarked she should read less romantic

fiction. He left half of his plate. That was not okay, either. Usually he was the one saying so, but what was she supposed to do? She gathered the scraps and put them with the rest of the trash. Every evening she took the small bucket over to Stanislaus, who was happy about the delicacies from the pastor's kitchen. He shrieked with joy every time he saw Grete Strutz. The other pigs grunted with envy, but that was all they could do. Stanislaus was a guest at her stable. Guest for life, not even a year. After that, he would fill the freezer and the smoking rack of the rectory while the next Stanislaus was already shrieking with joy watching the housekeeper coming his way.

19

"A person doesn´t disappear like a shirt button you lose while taking a walk. Perhaps in Paris, or New York, but not here. I had talked to her. She was happy and content and terribly *present*, you know? Such a girl just doesn´t dissolve into thin air a few hours later."

"You would think so", Terrazzo said. "But where the hell is she?"

"There must be a clue", Riement said, stumped. "Whatever may have happened to her, there must be a clue."

"There were up to two hundred men combing through the forest, for days on end. Hard to imagine they missed much of anything."

"I am not referring to a shoe or a bangle or deep footprints. The clue could be something very ordinary, something obvious. Something that anyone would recognize if he knew the context. Every event leaves a hint. It doesn´t have to be secretive or well-hidden. It just has to be recognized. A person is embedded in his environment, physically and psychologically. If he or she is ripped out from it, there are ripples left behind. Someone knows something. There are probably several people who know something. They could provide clues."

"If that´s the case", Terrazzo said skeptically, "they have to open their mouth first."

They were sitting in the doctor´s apartment, which was directly above his surgery. It was ten o´clock in the evening. A bottle of red wine stood between them, its level decreasing inexorably.

"I hardly knew her", Terrazzo continued after a long pause, "but it doesn´t look like she disappeared by her own volition. Not like this. Not with a tracksuit in that forest. Unless she is a different type of person than we suppose. Not impossible."

"Totally impossible", his friend objected. "Such an open person ..."

The doctor made a face.

"Particularly open-minded persons are sometimes very apt at only showing what they want to show. I can vouch for that, I am an open-minded person myself."

They laughed.

"No", said Riement. "Not Sonja."

"So, not voluntarily", Terrazzo conceded. "We can discard an accident. She would have been found after an accident. What other possibilities remain? Kidnapping? Murder?"

"That can't be. However ..."

The teacher fell silent. Both were following their own thoughts. Somewhat maliciously, Terrazzo broke the silence.

"A crime. Okay. No, not okay. If we are dealing with a crime, then there is a criminal living among us. Or can you imagine that a murderer from wherever would choose this godforsaken place to do his deed?"

"You have chosen this godforsaken place yourself."

"Yes. To myself and our murderer."

The doctor emptied his glass and refilled both glasses.

"Your sense of humor is macabre", said Riement.

"Doctor's humor. Perhaps you are right. Imagine what we have thought about is correct and he tries again."

"There aren't that many nice girls running around in the woods", Terrazzo remarked. "And the police is on alert."

"The police?"

This time Riement's question sounded spiteful.

"Well, they must be thinking something, too."

"They are treating Sonja as a case of a missing person", the teacher supposed, "and that's it for them. There are runaway teenagers all the time."

"Perhaps ... On the other hand, we're not that smart, either. They have a lot of experience. Perhaps they are right."

"Not in Sonja's case", Riement insisted. "Something bad happened, count on it. And I tell you this: if there is a criminal among us, a murderer, then *you* should be the one to provide the clue. These people are never normal. You should be able to notice something unusual."

The fervor of his friend erased the doctor´s derisive attitude. "You mean, a patient? Signs of madness?"

"Yes."

Terrazzo dismissed this.

"Sure, psychological problems. But a crazy murderer … I don´t think so. Such a person is most likely totally inconspicuous. Furthermore, I am convinced that any person can become a murderer under the right circumstances."

Riement shook his head.

"That´s not the issue here. That is way too vague. Too general. You have the training. You should be able to *smell* a madman."

"Rubbish", Terrazzo replied. "Presumptions, hunches … That´s not sufficient."

"But you do have them, do you?"

"Of course I have them! Do you think you have a monopoly on fantasies?"

"That", the teacher complained, "was yet another hit below the belt by a non-believer. What kind of suspicions do you have?"

"Professional secret", the doctor smiled.

"Even if this is about murder?"

"As long as it exists in our imagination …"

Shortly thereafter Riement went home, not swaying, rather, elated. Terrazzo sat at his desk and thought if there was anything to his friend´s opinions. Perhaps there were clues. Perhaps he knew them without being aware of it. Did he have to look at every patient as a potential murderer from now on? He shook his head. As if he didn´t have enough problems already! Again he unfolded the telegram which he had received the day before. It was written in that curt style he knew so well.

The last sentence said:

"You know what this means. I am sorry."

He knew what it meant. It just had not fully dawned on him yet. But now was the time. Now, the realization spread in him like an epidemic in a refugee camp. That was exactly how he felt. He put his face into his hands and sat there for a long time.

20

Hannes had taken a day off without really knowing why. Lately he was prone to take spontaneous decisions which he could not explain in hindsight. But that was alright, he didn´t have to explain them. Sometimes he had to, though. Sometimes "it" demanded something and he assented, asking himself later on what "it" wanted to accomplish. Some time ago he would certainly have wondered why he was fulfilling these commands without protest. But by now he simply agreed to them. "It" did not like any questions and "it" did not provide answers, either. "It" demanded and he obliged. Somehow "it" also had to do with the dreams. Strange. Now and again he did ask questions, whenever "it" was not around to punish him. And although he certainly did not tell anyone about these questions, "it" was always well-informed. And then it punished him, anyway. As soon as "it" appeared it took him to task, and denial was futile. "It" had to have informants, people who wanted to cause harm. If he could grab one of them he would … There were those pains again. It was obvious, "it" protected his informants. "It" would not allow him to question his informants. Hence the pain. He needed a new approach. Perhaps this was the reason why he had taken a day off. Yes, he had taken the day off to see the doctor about the new prescription. If the doctor was out of office, Maria would give it to him. The doctor allowed this, she said, in case he had previously prescribed the medicine and the dosage was low. Nevertheless, this only happened with people whom she could fully trust. It was not according to procedure. She didn´t want the doctor to get into trouble. The doctor was still at his surgery. At this time of day he was always there, he should have known that. The waiting room was packed, but he met Terrazzo at the anteroom and they chatted for a while. "Everything okay?" the doctor asked when they were parting.

He wanted to say no, but "it" said yes. He wanted to tell the doctor how he really felt, but "it" said, "Thanks, I'm fine." Did the doctor hesitate for a moment? No, he had imagined it. Terrazzo himself looked tired.

He got the prescription and stood in the street again. The day was only a few hours old. Should he drive to town to the drugstore? The pharmacist knew him. He always sold him the large package instead of the small one. He understood the fact that nobody wanted to run to the doctor all the time. No, he could see the pharmacist just as well tomorrow. He took a newspaper from the rack. It was cold and gloomy. Usually you could sit in the garden of the Sheep's Inn around this time of the year. But today they hadn't even taken out the tables. He entered the inn. Almost empty around this time of day. He wanted to order a beer and read the newspaper, but "it" ordered red wine. And he didn't tolerate red wine at all. Beer was okay, but red wine made him antsy. "It" had to know this. If "it" was ordering red wine rather than beer, it meant that "it" had less and less consideration for him. Why was he in this situation anyway? Why did he tolerate all this? Immediately, pain again. No questions! Drink the wine and quickly order another quarter. The letters of the article he was reading didn't hold still. They slipped up and down, left and right, not one sentence was legible. He got angry at having spent good money buying the newspaper. What were they thinking selling this crap? The anger slipped into his stomach and further down into his intestines and sat there, clutching with his familiar claws like a thousand-headed tick which was slowly digging into his skin. "It" ordered a third quarter. He washed down the pills he still had with him.

The pastor's housekeeper entered the inn. Her gossip club was already waiting. Today there were three women who had too little work to do. They met every morning to exchange the most important news. The fact that he had taken the day off and was drinking wine in the morning was certainly part of it. A terrible suspicion arose in him. These women, particularly the pastor's cook, that Strutz woman, knew everything about everybody around the village. They would certainly know if he posed these forbidden questions. So she was the informant who ratted him out so he could be punished. Or was it one of the other women? No, it must be Strutz. He observed the back of her head with the blond curls, which were lying flat across the collar of her vest. It was her fault, that old, skinny goat whose mouth wouldn't stop for a minute. The sharp claws were digging into his intestines. He was close to jumping up and grabbing her chattering throat to rip it out. Then the tourist entered the inn. Hannes' ire cooled down. After more than a week, everybody knew the guest at the Sheep's Inn. He spent hours taking walks across the fields and far into the hills and mountains. At the end of March. Strange man, strange vacation. The gossip girls were electrified when they saw him.

21

It hit Padoponos like a poisoned dart in the back of his neck. There it was. Very powerful, unbearably strong. Compared to this one, the vision of horror he had felt after his first walk around this area had been a mild graze. Right now, in this seemingly peaceful restaurant, the same horror had moved in. This time it was pure viciousness, concentrated evil. One of freely moving, age-old evils, a demon of prehistoric times, perhaps older than the world, perhaps the cause of the world. Padoponos had never met it with such intensity and at such close proximity. The collision paralyzed him and covered his skin with a coat of cold sweat. Fear, naked fear of the enemy who was superior. Demons need people to enter them, like parasites. One affected person was sitting in this inn. Only three of the tables were taken. Three women, including the innkeeper, sat at one of them and pretended not to notice him. But he sensed their curious looks as if they were touching him with their hands. Rosi observed him, too. She seemed surprised. The other two tables were occupied by one man each. A mechanic in dirty overalls was wolfing down a plate of sausages, an inconspicuous guy wearing a tie was browsing a newspaper, drinking wine. Seven people, one of them possessed. He could discard Rosi. That left six of them. He looked closer at the mechanic. The man was eating noticeably fast, unnaturally fast. He was swallowing the food almost without chewing it. The Greek put out his antennas with care, but at that moment the contact had disappeared, it was extinguished. Whatever he might have picked up, it had retreated. It had not taken more than a second, all the impressions and observations matched the short time span while Padoponos had hardly moved one single step. It had been a cold lightning. A lightning which did not come from the sky but from the deepest abyss of being. *The abysses of being.* They exist. Only that we have chosen to ignore them in order to not endanger our countless compromises with reality.

Or was he simply imagining all of this? His hands, usually as steady as if cast from bronze, were shaking a little. He smiled at Rosi but did not say anything, instead, he went up to his room.

Startled, Hannes looked at the empty glass of wine. Why on earth had he ordered wine? He didn´t tolerate wine. And why was he sitting in the Sheep´s Inn at this time of day? He heard the women´s whispering and felt that he was blushing at the roots of his hair. This was just what they had been waiting for. "The bill, please", he said.

When the waitress billed three quarters of wine he wanted to protest at first, but he didn´t. Rosi sensed his hesitation.

"Is something wrong?"

"No, no", he said. "Everything fine."

Most likely it was due to the horrible nights that he stumbled into such memory holes during the day. Lack of sleep. While he was leaving, he felt the prescription in his pocket and had a look at it. So he had been at the doctor as well. Should he return to the surgery and tell everything once again? How could he tell something like this? "I was at your place today, wasn´t I?" "Perhaps I will return tomorrow because I forgot I had been here today." "Are you going to commit me right away? Can I pick up some clothes?"

Rubbish. Anyone could have such a gap. He was just too tired, that was all there was to it. Since he had a day off, he could finally get going with the garden. It was about time.

22

Today there were only three of them. Grete Strutz, Martha
Riement and Lydia Kern, the innkeeper. It was the women´s
regular table. Half an hour, one hour tops before noon. The
men who got all worked up about this sat around until
midnight and thought their chatter was smarter than the
women´s gossip. Well, of course they chatted, they were
simply interested. Or curious? So what, they were curious!
Whoever lacks curiosity will not learn anything.

"What is Müller doing around here at this hour?" Grete asked
after saying hello.

"He´s working on his third quarter", the Sheep´s innkeeper
said, partly with maliciousness and partly content. After all, it
was her business. "Perhaps he isn´t feeling too well", the
teacher´s wife presumed. "I saw him walking into the doctor´s
surgery today."

They briefly discussed whether the consumption of wine
indicated being well or rather, being ill.

"He´ll likely have his troubles", the innkeeper said.

"In earlier times he was at least a bit more friendly."

"The guest", Martha whispered, facing the entrance. She
referred to Jason Padoponos who had just entered the room.

"I can understand that Rosi is crazy about him", the innkeeper
said.

"Yes", the teacher´s wife pondered. "I could start to like him,
too."

The pastor´s cook and the innkeeper exchanged a glance of
silent agreement. They knew that things weren´t that great at
the Riement household. For way too long already. Martha was
just about forty and a posh woman who dressed well.
According to her friend´s opinion, the teacher was quite a
screwball. A teacher, after all. In the long run this could not
end well. But if she had a boyfriend, as some presumed, she
was hiding him masterfully. However, she often went to town.
Because of her tailoring business, she said.

The "guest" didn't stay for long. The women's regular table ordered coffee and went on doing its business. Then Grete Strutz and Martha Riement left as well. They both had husbands to take care of. Grete had prepared a piece of boiled prime beef in the morning. The Reverend liked the meat so tender as to fall off his fork. She prepared some carrots and boiled Kohlrabi and potatoes with parsley. She ate in the kitchen and the Reverend ate in the dining room. Lately he didn't have much of an appetite. They hardly spoke with each other at noon because he was listening to the news. Then he went for his nap while she did the dishes. She thought about how many plates had gone through her hands over the past fifty years. She liked to calculate such things. She liked numbers even though she had done only four years at a primary school and even back then, she had to work more than she could study. She knew the balance of her savings accounts down to the cent. She even knew the number of each account by heart. It was safer in case one got lost, or stolen. After cleaning up the kitchen she went to her room. There was one folder with four estimates from contractors, which she had been reading over and over for days. She couldn't be careful enough, in a few days she would have to make a decision. Construction season was coming up, and the roof had to be done by fall. Everybody told her there was nothing to it, and at the same time, everyone warned her about unforeseen delays. If there's just one chain in the link failing, the entire job comes to a grinding halt, said the experts. They are all experts. But deep down inside, Grete was certain she would pull it off. She was now a client who was getting a house built for herself! She, Grete Strutz, the pastor's cook and child out of wedlock, mother of a child out of wedlock, was building her own home. All by herself, without a single cent of debt. She told herself every day. It was not unusual that a tear welled up from the corner of her eye and made its way down the creased cheek. Who could know what it meant to her? Today, where everybody was building his house. A faded black and white photo of her mother stood on her bedside table. She told her mother everything. She had never had a better friend.

Not a really good friend.

She took a sheet of paper and wrote a letter to the lowest bidder. He had to vouch for the estimate, in writing. The Reverend had suggested that. Without this warranty she wouldn't allow anyone to put a foot on her property. Be careful, always be careful. The contractor would do his job, right now they were keen on getting any job. Furthermore, she paid cash. The craftsmen liked this very much. Work done, money on the table. She left the letter at it. There was time to write it tomorrow. It was past two o'clock.

23

Maria stayed at the surgery until two thirty. The doctor was already on his way to do house calls. She cleaned up the small laboratory and put away the blood samples which were sent to the city by mail for analysis. Then she took off her white coat and looked at herself in the mirror hanging in the waiting room. She crinkled her nose. Her belly was bulging about as much as a wall carpet covering a hole in the wall. "Yogurt", she thought, with much determination. Otherwise she was happy with her physique. Maria had a sensual relationship with her own body. She liked her legs, which showed off rather nicely when she wore stockings, she liked her breasts bulging under her shirt.

"What a waste", she said to her mirror image.

"He wouldn´t notice me if I walked around completely naked."

That was an idea! Serve his tea in the morning, totally naked, say good morning as usual and leave the room without saying a word. Then, slip into the white gown in case he called her. But he would only call her to fire her.

She shrugged and put on her skirt. A touch of lipstick - were those glasses too stern? - her hair combed, putting on the coat, one last check to see if all the gear was switched off, locking up the surgery and goodbye, see you tomorrow.

Maria followed the path to the county road, crossed it, past the Sheep´s Inn and the fire station, into the small eastern neighborhood consisting of eight houses and as many gardens. It was yet again a gloomy day. Spring just didn´t want to show up. Thank God it wasn´t raining. She had forgotten the umbrella. But it could come any moment now. So she was rather startled to see Hannes at his house, raking. She waved at him and shouted "Looks like you´re waterproof!"

He waved back but did not say anything. Lately he barely opened his mouth. She had asked her mother whether he was sulking. Perhaps it had to do with his insomnia.

Maria was still living with her parents. One of her sisters was married, the other one lived in the city.

To find a job as a nurse, here, that was about as much luck as winning the lottery. In the city, she would have had to rent a room at the nurse´s home. She didn´t own a car, and with the shifts at the hospital, commuting was out of the question. At home she didn´t have to pay rent and it took her about five minutes to get to the doctor´s surgery. She also did not pay for her food because, as her parents said, she didn´t eat much anyway.

"Beauty has to suffer", mother said. "Stupidity too", the father said. Deep down inside they were both proud of her. Only she wasn´t much interested in men. It would have to be someone better.

But the better man did not notice her existence!

Every afternoon Maria studied Italian for one or two hours. She dreamed about living down south one day. In Tuscany, Siena or Florence. She looked out the window, at the gray sky, the fog, which the wind was driving through the treetops - and she stuck her nose into the book again.

At five o´clock she had had enough. Hannes was still working in his garden. She started ironing and frowned at every other piece of clothing. Why was she spending money on silk clothing? So she could admire herself in the mirror? Cotton undies, a dozen for a warm handshake, would have done the job. Or nothing at all, even cheaper. But that was too chilly. She shook her head. The approaching spring was driving her crazy. Vigorously, she put the small pile of ironed clothes into the shelf and placed the large remaining pile into the basket. She would visit Isabella. Perhaps they would go out to have a coffee at the café. It sounded ridiculous. A strange idea to call a coffee house a café. Actually, it wasn´t a coffee house, rather, two small rooms at Pernjak, the second and smaller inn of the village. When young Pernjak had taken over the business three years ago, he had simply put up a wall through the large room. One half remained the old Pernjak, the other half got another little room and was converted into the café. They played music and sold pastries. Not bad ones, not at all. The youngsters met at the café if they didn´t drive to a real disco. Word had it that the Sheep´s innkeeper was not too excited about Pernjak´s idea. Maria called Isabella and arranged to meet with her. She left the house at seven.

24

When Padoponos passed the cemetery wall, a man dressed in black came towards him at the gate, as if he had been expecting him. It was a gloomy appearance, partly because of his attire, partly because of his face and his demeanor, which expressed a profound seriousness. For a split second Padoponos held his breath. At some point it could be just such a man who would stand in front of him in order to kill. Sober and objectively, without any personal feelings. Would he be able to preempt him? Would he try?

But it was not the time, not yet.

The gloomy man said "I am pastor Weilrich. I saw you coming down the path and I was wondering whether I might accompany you along the way."

"I´d be happy", said the Greek. "I have heard about you. You are a respected man."

"You got some wrong information there", said Weilrich dryly. "Let´s walk for a little".

They took a rural trail which divided the field in a perfectly straight line before getting lost in the distant forest. When they were walking in the open countryside, blasted by the cold wind, far away from the nearest homestead, the pastor broke the silence. "I have to apologize in advance. Grete told me about you and Rosi. Of course you don´t even know Grete. She said that Rosi has been asking questions lately. This has piqued my curiosity. You might be surprised at this because Grete is a gossip monger, nice and caring, but an incorrigible gossip monger. However, this story is so important to me that I am grasping at every straw."

The pastor fell silent and smiled with sorrow.

"You may think I am confused. You would be right. Let me start again. I don´t know you. I am just speculating. Perhaps I am about to tell you a story which makes sense to you, perhaps you don´t understand a single word. In that case you can simply make fun of the crazy cleric who got you to take a walk in the fields to tell you utter nonsense."

He made a short pause, but as Padoponos didn´t say anything, he quickly continued.

"It´s a peaceful area with hard-working people. They are not better or worse than any other people all over the world. They work, they eat, they love, they cheat on each other, some of them are honorable, some of them aren´t, they do business, have children, build houses and have accidents. There are clever ones and dumb ones, healthy and sick ones, faithful and unfaithful ones. None who has never lied in his entire life, nobody who has never, at least in his mind, cheated on his partner, none who, at least in her mind, didn't allowed to be seduced. These are pardonable sins. I am not telling them this from the pulpit, but I cannot blame them for it. Who are we, anyway, thinking we can act as judges over customs and morals? Much of what we do is arrogation and self-righteousness. So many of us are more unstable and weaker deep down in our cores than the herd which we are supposed to be guarding." He listened to the sound of his own words and continued. "However, some members of this herd have done truly terrible deeds. They are violent, they steal, they enjoy evil thoughts and deeds. But even those we should not judge too harshly and much less should we look down on them because a small part of their guilt is always our own guilt."

The pastor took a deep breath.

"This sounds very much like a sermon, that was not my intention. It is so difficult. What I wanted to say is that all of those whom I have talked about are fellow humans, better ones and worse, which we should care for and whom we should comprehend. But there are those, a few, who fall into a different category. Perhaps I should use the expression 'they are under the devil´s spell.' I am convinced that there is something like pure evil. Some people have it in them or somehow they absorb it, I don´t know. When these people get into a situation where all their inhibitions are erased, they actually turn into monsters, human monsters. Human monsters are much worse than the most bloodthirsty of animals. They do things with careful thinking, and consciously, and with cold cunning. There is no animal capable of this kind of cruelty."

"You are right", Padoponos agreed. He was electrified by this conversation and his experience that same morning. He had *been* in the restaurant of pure evil, evil itself, he had met it and that was exactly what Weilrich was referring to. So he was not the only one to feel it.

"I can´t get much out of the notion of vengeance", the pastor said, suddenly very sober, "but I can´t bear thinking about the victims while the evildoer is boasting about his deed. I must have chosen the wrong profession." "It is not just about vengeance", said the Greek. "It is vengeance and punishment and compensation. Some things demand this compensation. When it happens, it is a good thing." Weilrich looked at him from the side with burning eyes. "I have not been wrong about you?"

Padoponos did not reply.

"I have to make a decision which is far beyond my capabilities", the cleric said anxiously. "I really did not want this to occur. You are much more convinced than I am."

The Greek stopped in his tracks and faced the pastor squarely. His relaxed manner seemed to increase Weilrich´s nervousness.

"For me, the only thing that matters at this point is absolute certainty. I believe you might deliver it, but I myself will definitely achieve it."

The pastor´s face turned white. Padoponos remembered the large black birds and their scary calls. Like the ravens with their wings, the pastor lifted his arms.

"I can´t", he gasped, turned around and hurried back to the village. But he briefly stopped after a few steps and called "Come with me!" and kept on walking without waiting for his companion. They did not speak a word until they had reached

79

the point where they had started out. The pastor indicated Padoponos to follow him to the cemetery. He stopped in front of a family vault with a fancy stone and a small candle burning inside a lantern. For a few long seconds he stared at the Greek, then he said "This is all I can do for you" and turned around abruptly. Padoponos did not move until the pastor had disappeared inside the small church. Calmly, he looked at the grave and read the name which was emblazoned in golden letters on the black stone. Calmly, he left the graveyard and continued his interrupted walk.

25

Hannes could feel the effect of the wine. It must have been three quarters after all. These memory lapses bore down on him more than he admitted. The heated food from the freezer was terrible. He wolfed it down nevertheless.

Then he looked through the mail. It was not much. Colorful brochures, flyers, a tool catalog, a postcard, two form letters. He kept the postcards and the catalog. The postcards came from Plattensee. His colleagues had taken a trip to the place. They had returned a while ago. He had to remember to thank them. In earlier times he would have joined them for such an outing, nowadays nobody asked him anymore. This happens rather quickly.

The garden. The fall leaves were still lying there. He hadn´t been able to muster the energy to rake them. But now it was about time. Three more days and the grass would start growing. He changed clothes. Work trousers and jacket. Would it rain? His father´s coat was still hanging in the closet. Thirty or forty years old. Waterproof like a new roof, but almost as heavy. It was gray, almost reaching to the floor. There wasn´t much else his father had left him. It was twenty years ago they had buried him. What are twenty years? Nothing, once they have passed. You worked and did this and that, nothing really exciting. But still, you are twenty years older. The temples turn gray, the face turns gray, the rings under the eyes become darker. Another twenty years, perhaps thirty, and you go the way of your father. Looking back, nothing much had happened, looking back, time had gone by quickly. Your grave is waiting for you. Your grave is very patient. At that moment when sperm and egg come together there is suddenly a new grave. Where there was nothing before, now there is your grave. Before you screamed for the first time it was already waiting for you. The living and the dead. So many dead, so many deaths. He was shivering. The coat was way too heavy for doing work. And it was not raining anymore. He left the house and went to get the rake from the shed. Leaving the leaves during winter! Now it was a tough, wet layer, almost like a thin sandwich board. He worked for an hour, then for another one. It had started to drizzle but he didn´t mind. After two hours he was done. There was a tall, almost black pile of leaves between the house and the shed. White grass roots and dark earth appeared where he had peeled off the layer of leaves. Thin, white roots, like thin, white worms which he had observed a few days ago while they entered and exited his arms and legs. He had taken a closer look and realized that his skin was like a noodle sieve at the affected areas. Each hole an entrance for a noodle. Noodle worms. When was the last time he had eaten vermicelli? It hadn´t been that long ago. During those five years he had been living by himself, he had had ready-made soups quite often. There were about two dozen varieties with one thing in common: the taste. For a while he played with the thought that Maria would take his wife´s place. What was the matter with Maria? The pain returned. Ah yes, she had waved at him and shouted something at him. He couldn´t remember what it was. Various sentences were buzzing around his head. He left the rake lying there and went into the house. Half past five. It had cleared up. A few sun rays found their way past the treetops to the ground. They appeared to be uncertain and shy, almost as if startled by what winter had left behind for them.

Why was she betraying him? Why did she do it? He had to defend himself. If he didn´t, she would do it again and again. Maria or the other one? The Strutz woman or the teacher´s wife? He would remember, eventually. By nightfall he would have to defend himself. He sat there in silence and listened to the voices, which were gathering like echoes inside a bottomless gorge.

Slowly the dusk started settling on the earth and suffocated the day. He got up, went to the locker and took out his father´s heavy coat. He put on the coat and the rubber boots and put on the hat, the bad one. He left the house without closing the door properly. There was a narrow passage between the house and the shed. He recoiled from the tall and dark pile of leaves as if it were a living thing. In the shadow of the fruit trees he climbed over the fence into the neighboring garden. He knew his way. He knew it as if he had done it hundreds of times. Two more fences. Somewhere a dog barked. Cars stopped, others started their engines. He could hear every whisper in the village. A gate and more fruit trees. Steps on the asphalt path. He stood there, mute, gray and black, the dark building behind his back.

26

After leaving the pastor´s cook, Martha Riement went on her way home. Despite of the distance, she still had the busy, tottering gait of a fashion designer who always wants to be where she is going to be anyway three steps later. She designed and made her own costumes. They were elegant, a bit austere, tight, but never too tight. Nobody had ever seen her dressed in traditional costumes. Nobody would ever see her wearing one. This was her personal protest against twenty years of living in the countryside. Nobody really knew *how* unsatisfied she was. No entitlements, no hope, no sex. Her marriage had not even produced a child. After that had become obvious, she had not wanted him in her bed anymore. She could not understand the change that Franz had gone through. At first he had been ambitious, eager to learn and to further his career. They had been making lots of plans. To move to the city, where his chances were much better and where she could exercise her profession. Then, build a home in a nice neighborhood, and then, have children. If he went for it, he could even become the headmaster. She would run her own shop, as far as the family would allow it …

Then, everything started to crumble. Month after month, year after year. No mention of further education anymore, and moving to the city was postponed so many times that they stopped talking about it. Their plans did not burst with a bang but they fell apart like an abandoned house. There, a stone fell off, over here, a brick was splitting and without anyone noticing, rainwater seeps in and the roof rafters start rotting …

Today, she knew she had not insisted enough back then. Not next year, not next month, not even next week, right now! She should have had insisted. But he had appeared so self-assured and confident. Her heels banged on the asphalt.

She entered the house and slammed the door. He got home early today. She would have to hurry. Putting the costume on the hanger, putting on a housecoat, changing shoes and off to the kitchen. She put on the rice and prepared the cutlets. All natural is how she preferred them, as long as the meat was sort of tender.

A hundred times she had wanted to leave him and return to her old profession. But she was not fooling herself. It is one thing to sew for two or three hours a day for fun, and another to throw yourself head first into the fashion business. It required constant contacts to acquire the sense for trends and customer's preferences, and to keep them. A surgeon who uses his knife for decades, only to eat his meals, can still perform operations, in theory. But who would like to lie down on his operating table?

It would take her many months to get into the groove. Who would offer such an opportunity to a forty year old? To do boring sewing work eight hours a day, forty hours a week, being a professional tailor, that was unthinkable. Not because of the work, but because of the descent it implied. If you sell yourself for low money, it is quite possible that you stay low. That would be even worse. So she did the housekeeping and gossiped at the Sheep's Inn. Not because it was fun but to talk to someone at all. The lesser evil doesn't have to be a small evil. At one o'clock she served him his cutlet. Then she retreated and made some adjustments to a garment. At least he was able to put the dishes into the dishwasher himself. You lower your expectations. She answered two letters. She liked to write and kept up with her friends. At half past five she prepared a modest plate of cold cuts. Some sausage, some cheese and bread. They had dinner together. They split a bottle of beer between them. He told her some trivia about a colleague she didn't know. He always felt obliged to say something. She said "uh-huh" and "I see" and regretted that he did not have a mute switch like the TV set. Or an off switch. At seven she changed again, picked up the dress and went on her way. She had promised her friend to drop it off tonight. It was cold. The clouds had disappeared and the pale moon was hanging in the sky. An unhealthy, unpleasant moon. A shiver went down her spine. The best thing about the village were the short distances. She didn´t like to drive at night. Every headlight blinded her. Her heels were banging on the asphalt.

27

Grete was scraping slops from pots and plates with a spoon
and threw them into Stanislaus´ bucket. It made for bad noises
but she couldn´t care less. She hoped they would bother the
holy man during his private prayer service. Usually she would
do almost anything for the Reverend, but sometimes she
wished the black plague on him. He could be such a stupid
and stubborn fellow! There he was sitting, torturing himself
because of his forbidden Monika, trying to keep her in the
dark, she who knew him better than his own mother. That was
sort of understandable for a pastor. In these matters they are
even more stupid than men in general. But to throw a hissy fit
just because she had started to talk about Rosi and the stranger
once again, that was over the top. Something had happened
that caused his mood to flip between lunch and dinner. She
had told him what she thought about people who simply eat
up everything and keep it to themselves, never sharing it with
anybody else, but on the other hand they had no problem with
venting their anger at anyone who crossed their path. That had
made him particularly nasty and he said that if he were to
keep a secret, he would rather put it into his Sunday sermon as
fewer people would hear it than if he told it to her in all
confidentiality. And when she chided him for eating so little,
he said that this was due to the fact that she thought more
about the pig than about him. She had taken away his plate
and all, even the dessert which he hadn´t even touched yet,
and had walked into the kitchen. She slammed the door so
hard that the weathercock on the roof was trembling. Now she
put all the food into the bucket, everything that was left over,
including food from the fridge, because if he got hungry later
on, he should help himself to a dry slice of bread. She locked
the pantry and took the key with her, and today she would not
hear him in case he called for her.
She put on the worn cardigan and rubber boots and put on a
red scarf, which somehow kept her curls in check. She put a

lid on Stanislaus' bucket. Today he would get more than ever. She left the rectory via the back door, which she locked with diligence. She then went on her short trek to the Huber stable where Stanislaus was being kept. The bucket in her right hand, the left arm slightly spread out so as to keep her balance, a gaunt figure with a large skirt with rubber boots sticking out like sticks. Half past seven in the evening. The sun had long disappeared but the vanishing dusk and the moon provided enough light. Only the main street had streetlights, presumably to alert drivers they were speeding through a village. It was less than a three-minute walk. Almost all of the houses had the lights on and the bluish glow indicated the running TV set. Grete Strutz didn't watch much TV but tonight she wanted to turn up the volume to annoy the Reverend. He shouldn't have said what he said about the food. Everything but that.

She took the shortcut past the orchard.

The small gate with its simple wooden bar was usually closed, today it stood half open. She closed it behind her. Here, between the trees, it was darker than on the open field, but she had good eyesight. Next to her a dry twig popped. She also thought she saw a shadowy movement. There was always some sound between the trees at night and a hundred shadows seemed to be hiding. When she had been a maid, she had had to walk up to a mountain alp two hours before sunrise. It had been a trail through the most gloomy and lonely forest. She had done the trail many times.

The back end of the stable had a small entrance, which made it unnecessary for her to walk around the building and across the farm. Inside, it was even darker. She could find the light switch a couple of steps away, even blindfolded. She turned on the light and heard and smelled the presence of four dozen pigs. Then she heard a noise behind her. Much closer now. She turned around. There was something. That was not a shadow. A figure wearing a long coat.

"Who's there?"

No answer. The figure came closer. A manly figure.
A man.

He wore a hat, which covered half of his face so she did not recognize him right away.

"Oh, it´s you", she said, somewhat annoyed, somewhat relieved. "What are you doing here? If you want to see the Huber farmer you have to go to his house. He´s always checking the stable when it´s late."

Now she also saw the pickaxe he was holding in his right hand. And the rubber gloves. The polished, sharp end of the tool was gliding over the floor of the stable. Something was wrong. The man still did not say a word. Fifty pigs were grunting and Stanislaus was shrieking particularly hard. After all, she was holding his bucket in her hand.

He had gotten even closer. The pickaxe was swinging harder, like a clock´s pendulum. Suddenly, fear poured over Grete Strutz like a cloudburst during a midsummer day. She had never been afraid in her life, no time for that. Now it was there.

"You stay right there", she said with a shrill voice. "What do you want?"

The pickaxe was swinging. There was a clock with a long bronze pendulum hanging in the rectory, with three bronze weights. The weights were small but heavy. At one time one of the weights had slipped from her hands and had left a deep dent in the floor. She was lucky it hadn´t fallen on her foot. The clock was not accurate, but the chiming was wonderful. Three times the Reverend had had the clock adjusted, but it failed to improve. Back then, five minutes more or five minutes less were not an issue. These days the Reverend was adjusting the clock every day after getting up. He adjusted it with the same seriousness as when handing the host to the believer. She trusted him very much, although, by God, he wasn´t a reasonable man. She hoped he wasn´t hungry. She shouldn´t have taken the key to the pantry with her.

"What in God´s name do you want?"

She stepped back even further. Fear is so terribly confusing. Her granddaughter wanted to visit her next week. They´ve got pepper up their backsides at that age. And later, too. She had become pregnant rather late. Would Birgit get knocked up, only eighteen years old?

The pickaxe swerved like an iron bird under the low roof of the stable with a buzzing sound, twice, three times, four times before it started its horrific nosedive.

"What´s the matter with those pigs today?" Cornelia Huber wondered.

Her husband did not take his gaze off the TV.

"The Strutz woman is over there."

"But they know her."

"Perhaps it´s the moon. Tomorrow is full moon."

The two young women were bathing naked in a small, crystal-clear pond. They were laughing and gasping for air as the water was pretty cold. Soon they climbed onto the shore and laid down on a large, even slate of rock to warm up in the sun. The dark rock was nice and warm, too. They could have been sisters. Both with long, blond hair, both of them slim, of medium height and well-proportioned. One of them had blue eyes, the other one´s were brown. The one with brown eyes was wearing thin golden bracelets around her ankles and wrists. Suddenly a painful expression appeared on her face, she put her hand on her forehead and moaned with a low voice.

"What´s the matter, Devva?" the other one asked, alarmed.

"It has happened", Devva said with a choking voice.

"The horrible thing has returned. We were not able to stop it." She sat up and wept silently. The younger one didn´t know what to do other than to hug her friend and tell her comforting words in a low voice. Devva cuddled up to her warm body but it took a long time until she calmed down.

The numerous red and blue robins, warblers, great tits, blue tits, marsh tits, wrens, thrushes and nuthatches seemed to twitter with a lower volume for a while, the light seemed to become dimmer and the sun less warm. The girls held each other tightly and sat very still.

"This is Cornelia Huber speaking", said the voice on the
telephone. "You have to come over here immediately, doctor.
Something terrible has happened."

"What´s the matter?" growled Terrazzo, who had dozed off
after a long day at his desk. "Where to?"

"To Huber, to our farm", the woman repeated, desperate.
"Right away! You´ve got to get over here!"

"On my way", he told her and hung up. He had recognized her
voice. And the panic. There were many Hubers in the area but
only one farm named Huber. His watch showed ten to nine.
Five minutes later he parked the car in front of the house and
wanted to go inside.

"Not the house!" someone shouted behind him. "Over here.
To the stable."

Terrazzo followed the voice and found Toni Huber standing
next to the stable door. In the light of the 100-Watt bulb his
face was as white as the whitewashed wall behind him. The
second thing the doctor noticed was the agitation among the
animals inside the enormous stable.

"What happened?"

"Go inside", the farmer said "and look for yourself."

The doctor bowed his head under the low door and took a few
steps into the dimly lit room before stopping and taking a deep
breath. He usually avoided taking a deep breath inside a pig
stable but he forgot the precaution at what he saw. He felt how
his stomach rose up, and it had nothing to do with the smell.
He fought against the increasing nausea and turned around.
The farmer had followed him but was looking sideways.

"You won´t recognize her. It´s Grete Strutz, the pastor´s
cook."

"Did you call the police?"

"I first wanted to wait for you to arrive."

"Then do it now. Did you disturb anything?"

"Pulled a little towards the front. The pigs were working on the calves. I …"

He turned around quickly and bent over. A sloshing sound followed.

"Leave", Terrazzo demanded, fighting nausea again. He heard the farmer's hasty footsteps and was now by himself. Before him was the most terribly battered cadaver he had ever seen, even though he had spent a few months at the emergency surgery. There was nothing left of the head and face but a crushed, bloody lump, the torso was partly ripped open, practically shredded, the feet and legs up to the knees apparently eaten by the pigs. The animals must have witnessed the violent crime. They still had not calmed down and were grunting, either disappointed or frightened or infuriated, he couldn't tell. His dismay had evaporated and the professional curiosity had gained the upper hand. He bent down and began a brief examination.

Temperature, flexibility of extremities, blood clotting, all this would be important later on. Then he looked around more carefully. The cement floor, the wall and even part of the roof were splattered with blood, the corpse - what remained of it - was lying in a large pool. Apart from these horrific details, the stable was clean and orderly, there was only an overturned bucket in front of a sty and a little further away in the dark background, a tool. The doctor walked around the dead body and knew he was looking at the murder weapon. It was a pickaxe, covered with blood, a kind of axe with a bent tip used for moving felled trees. The perpetrator must have swung it with enormous rage in order to tear apart the pastor's cook - if it was indeed her. Most likely the first blow had killed her right away, and that was a comforting thought under these circumstances. But what could an old, inoffensive woman have done to cause such an explosion of hatred and violence?

Nothing.

Except in case the offender was thinking in categories way beyond normal. He remembered his talk with Franz Riement.

A mad murderer from the immediate area, perhaps from the village. A few days ago this had been mere speculation. Perhaps the young Lassnig was indeed celebrating her secret wedding or was jobbing at a bar or was simply following the call of the wild, even if nobody could believe it. But now? The first officials arrived after fifteen minutes. They were just the advance guard, soon followed by the detectives, a duty judge followed by a stenographer, and a district attorney. Terrazzo noted how one after another turned pale. The pros weren´t doing any better than himself. The stenographer, a fragile blonde, was retching all the time even though she took down the judge´s indications with her back towards him. He handed her a sedative. The pigs were totally freaked out and caused a horrific noise, but it was impossible to put them anywhere else. The scene turned surreal in front of this grunting, shrieking, jostling orchestra. Spotlights, a corpse, plenty of blood, busy and nervous people and behind all of that, as the main actors, the mass of barrel-shaped bodies, a dirty pink, bristly and unruly, with anxious snouts and curly tails. For a long time the doctor stood apart, feeling like he was in a grotesque theater. A detective, a tall and gaunt man with gray hair, introduced himself.

"I know who you are, doctor. Thank you for your patience. The farmer said you arrived at nine o´clock after his wife called you. Is that correct?"

"One, two minutes to nine, yes."

"You don´t have to tell me about the cause of death", said the detective. "How long do you think had she been dead when you got here?"

"An hour, perhaps an hour and a half, not longer than that."

"Less?"

"Ten, fifteen minutes at the most."

He quickly did some calculations.

"So, between seven thirty and a eight fifteen?"

"Yes", Terrazzo confirmed.

"How confident do you feel about that?"

"I am not a forensic professional, but … very confident."

"Okay."

The detective noted the time in a notebook and put it away.

"Is there anything you can contribute to identify the corpse?"

"The Huber farmer thinks it is the pastor´s cook. Quite probable. But as you can see for yourself …"

"If it is her, we will soon know for sure. We have initiated a search. The perpetrator must be covered in blood from top to bottom after this massacre. Do you have a hunch as to who it could be?"

Terrazzo said no and then laid out the theory of a madman. He also noted the possible connection to Sonja Lassnig. The detective nodded.

"Now it looks really bad concerning the girl. Thank you, anyway. If you would like to wait until tomorrow as to the report …"

You could tell that he would have liked to get it done sooner.

"I prefer right away", the doctor accommodated. "I am quite busy during the day."

And, just like Riement, the policeman closed by asking "A madman from the area … you are a doctor and know the folks. Do you have anyone particular in mind?"

"No", said Terrazzo. What was he supposed to say? It was all too vague. He had to think about all of this. The teacher had put an idea into his head with these clues, which only had to be recognized. Only!

When he reached his home there was just enough time for a short nap, which he needed rather badly.

30____

The following morning a neighbor discovered the blood-stained, gray coat lying in the garden of Hannes Müller, spread out like a prehistoric ray. The news had spread like wildfire in the village. The neighbor called the police right away, which cordoned off the area and began a thorough search. Apparently, the culprit just wanted to get rid of the coat. While fleeing past the gardens, he seemed to have taken it off and thrown it over the nearest fence. A few steps further away was the road. The trail ended there. The coat was an important clue, but for now it turned out to be unrewarding. It had the victim´s blood on it, but no useful hints as to where the murderer was to be found. It was an old coat, just like those which had been used by the police while on duty. But that was three decades ago. After renewing their uniforms the old garments were taken out of service, they were presumably auctioned off or given away or they remained with the officers. Perhaps all three versions had happened, it was impossible to say. And there were no indications against the fact that this model had been available commercially. If the perpetrator was from the area, it seemed probable that he wore it before committing the murder. The officers went around questioning the villagers. But to their surprise and disappointment, the result came to nothing.

31

Many strange things were happening lately. There was the issue with the dried blood in the sink. He had discovered it when he wanted to brush his teeth in the morning. Had he hurt himself while working in the garden and forgotten about it? But there was no injury to his hands to be found. Most likely, he thought, he had awoken at night with a nosebleed. This had happened, only that he usually remembered it.

Then the story with the coat which someone had thrown over his fence. When the police had questioned him, he had willingly wanted to say "yes, one just like this is hanging in my locker". But "it" took over control in no time and, inexplicably, denied to ever have seen such a coat. Because of the officer's demeanor he surmised their suspicion was general in nature, without any direction. They hardly considered him. Which murderer is dumb enough to spread such incriminating evidence on his own lawn?

He was sorry to not be able to contribute anything to solve the matter. Last night he had slept like a stone. Not even a dream had remained in his memory.

The rubber gloves were lying over the lip of the sink to dry. They were still moist. What had he used them for? His memory lapses were growing at a surprising rate. By now he was not really worried about them anymore. Memories were not that important. They were quite overrated.

Actually, there isn't much of a difference whether you had jam buns or fried eggs for yesterday's breakfast. People stored all kinds of daily trash in their memory and got terribly upset when they forgot some minor detail. That's almost pathological. He did much better. It wasn't his problem whether he remembered the nosebleed or not. It's not that pleasant, anyway. Same for the gloves. He had needed them for something, so what? While using them, he was certain what they were for. That mattered, not the complete protocol regarding each and every small matter. When the police left -

they had had coffee together - he saw the old hat on top of the wardrobe. It was covered with dark spots. Fortunately, the officers had not seen it. That would have been embarrassing. What would they have thought of him? You wouldn't wear such a hat, not even for doing garden work. He soaked it. The water turned brownish. The stains faded but they were clearly visible. The shape of the hat faded as well. Angrily, he threw it into the trash.

He sat in the rocking chair and for a long time he looked at the wall where a picture of his father had been hanging once upon a time. He had given it away. He liked it much better now, the wall. You wouldn't believe the kinds of things you could discover while looking at a wall long enough. Entire landscapes, foreign landscapes which don't exist like this, anywhere. And faces!

Every shadow, every dent in the plaster, every stroke of the paintbrush resulted in a multitude of faces which move and change. You only had to take your time. They don't take impatience very well. He was convinced they were talking about him. Too bad that he couldn't understand them too well. There was only a murmur in his head. A slight rustle, just like inside large auditoriums before a show. It was wonderful to dream while sitting in the rocking chair and observe the changes in the wall with the passing day. Nice, pleasant dreams, not those horrible ones at night.

Did he have to go to work tomorrow morning? Ever since he had stood in front of the closed office one Sunday he had started to mark the weekdays on a calendar. There was nothing to it when you didn't know what day it was. You only had to know how to deal with it. There was the minor problem that he didn't remember when he had marked the calendar for the last time. But he was saved by the morning news on TV. They showed the date. They certainly didn't make mistakes. The newspapers were much less reliable. Lately, in particular. Several times he had been reading one which said Wednesday or Thursday while in fact it was Saturday or Monday. That was bothersome. If *they* couldn't handle it, he thought, they should simply watch the morning news on TV and copy the date. He decided he would help them out. It was just too ridiculous. He, a simple civil servant, had this idea while there were really smart people working at the newspapers, who could not come up with such an obvious solution. He took pen and paper and started to write.

32

Pastor Weilrich sat in his study, heavy shadows below his eyes, hands lying on the table like cramped eagle claws, incapable of putting them together for prayer. Dawn was chasing the night from its positions, but he still did not dare to lift his head and look into the face of his God. "Why does he punish me by punishing Grete?"

Around midnight they had knocked at the door of the rectory. Very polite, having a look at her room after some back and forth. He didn´t know she was not in the house. After their argument he had done some work and gone to bed, still angry about her and himself. By the way, he did not mention the dispute. There was no occasion for it. They took fingerprints from the photo on her bedside table, from the glass in the bathroom, from the soap dish, from the glass paperweight he had once given to her. Under it was a letter addressed to a construction company. A murder had occurred. There was the suspicion that Miss Strutz ... "Why a suspicion?" he asked with dismay. Everyone in the village knew Grete. Everyone could say whether it was her or not.

Not at all, unfortunately the corpse was terribly disfigured. At the Huber stable. If he would perhaps himself ... Not a pretty sight, however.

He slipped into his shoes and put the coat over his pajamas. They brought him over to her mortal remains. He got sick. He looked at her in detail. Her hand had remained unharmed. Her hand, there was no doubt. For eighteen years he had seen it several times a day. Up close while she served him his meals and when she took away the dishes. He got sick again.

"It´s her hand", he said. He didn´t know when she had left. However, she left every evening at about the same time, give or take ten minutes. They brought him back to the house.

He had sat down in his study and had not moved since then. God punishes quickly and without pity. It had happened exactly on the day that he, although he had remained silent, had broken the seal of confession. At least in an indirect way. This is silly, he thought. How many would have to drop dead on the day of their sins when they kept on living for decades? But his thoughts kept coming back to the stranger who looked like Zeus, to their conversation on the open field, to his mute clue.

And Monika? When had he visited her last? Not even a week ago. And then he had to part from her in anger. He would never again raise a Stanislaus to have him slaughtered and cut up just like Grete had been butchered. He would have switched places with the pig if he could lessen the burden of his mistakes, the burden of his share of the blame. There is a share of the blame beyond the legal, moral or religious concepts: the shared blame of the silent heart. He should have asked Grete for advice and he hadn´t done it. He would have loved to change places, particularly with Grete! But God, or destiny or whatever you name this undoing, would not take part in such a deal. When death interferes, there is no more chance to do the right thing. It never returns.

He thought about warning old Matte (of what?) to leave Monika alone, to quit his job. But the worst thing was that his hands would not find each other. Like irreconcilable enemies they lay on the table, signs of his own intense hatred. Easter was coming up. He shuddered at the thought. In these hours pastor Weilrich turned to ashes and, like Phoenix, a new Weilrich arose from the ashes. God had beaten him and he never wanted to be beaten again. His inner being turned to stone during the day as he did what had to be done. Then he called Monika and arranged for them to meet.

33

After the events of the past week the regular´s table at the
Sheep´s Inn had become larger than usual. There were several
groups who met here on a regular basis, but the regular´s table
was the oldest and most important one. In former days it had
almost exclusively been a meeting point of the rich farmers,
the pastor and the teacher, but this had changed over the past
years. Some of the newcomers from the city had connected
and some of the old-timers themselves were commuting now
and brought back fresh impressions. The content of their talks
had changed as well and it was not a political block anymore.
Old Matte knew better. The real core was still there. The
opposing voices always came from outsiders who wanted to
get attention. It was an opposition that said while winking: we
are actually of the same opinion, but you should know that I
am a real man, who can deal with others. And a brave fellow,
too, because I am not afraid to state my opinion openly, even
though it is not really mine. Because mine is actually yours,
you know that, don´t you?
The real core nodded a bit and smirked a bit and thought those
idiots would never get what politics was about. Politics in the
countryside had three goals: to achieve direct benefits on the
county level, to fight off disadvantages, and to unify in order
to exert pressure towards the top. For subsidies, against
obligations. That was it. There were idealists everywhere,
fools, you might say. Everywhere, except in the inner core of
the regular´s table. The Sheep Inn´s owner was the only
woman who was admitted. Not because she owned the inn,
but she knew exactly how things were going really. That
meant applying jaw-boned tactics, negotiation and barter. The
better one could see ahead, the better. Whoever plans well and
for the long run will get the most out of it. It is a fight of man
against man, woman against man, woman against woman.
Ideological garnishing is good for the appearance. Those
losers from the cities with their rental apartments, leased cars

and overdrawn accounts simply *could* not understand that. They think they are into politics when the read two newspapers, cast their vote and discuss about schools, human rights and the death penalty in America once a week. This was actually like jerking off. They prove to themselves that they have an opinion. At the same time, this is the only use of their opinion.

Matte drank his beer while following the theories about the pastor's cook's murder. He noticed that today all of the women were accompanied by men. He smelled the latent fear and thought about times long gone.

Nobody had any doubt that Sonja too had been a victim of the madman. The point of argument was, why he had simply butchered the Strutz woman and left her there, while the girl's body had been hidden so well. Perhaps she wasn't dead at all? Perhaps he kept her imprisoned somewhere? Nobody really wanted to believe this, considering the way he had disfigured the Strutz woman.

"It doesn't mean anything that Sonja's body has disappeared", one of the newcomers said. "We simply don't know what a madman comes up with. If we knew, we would be mad ourselves, or the madman would be normal."

"What is that supposed to mean?"

"It means that we don't know the thinking of a madman because we think differently than him."

"Why should we think differently? Everybody thinks the same way. Just that one is a nutcase and the other one is not."

"That's the difference, exactly!", the newcomer shouted, desperate. "A nutcase thinks in a different way. If everybody thought the same way, we would all be nutcases."

"You're one of them, anyway", one of them grunted. They laughed.

The murder of the Strutz woman didn't move old Matte. A week ago, one of the cows had died while giving birth. That had hurt him more. He was sorry about Sonja. Fresh meat … He didn't believe she was such an innocent angel like everyone else had declared. They move in a different way once they have done it. It had been sometime last summer. He had an eye for it. Too bad he didn't know her suitor. Nowadays they are often from out of town. However, there were a few folks in the new neighborhood who were the right age. He hardly had any contact with them. They were uprooted city folks who didn't understand the rules of the countryside. Perhaps the rules have changed, too. The tight structures were dissolving. There were less and less dependencies. The new settlers with their little houses on 6,000 square foot lots and their job in the city had no sense for the power of 1,500 acres. For them it was simply one big piece of agriculture. Much work, dreadful work, little spare time. With all his land he is actually worse off than I am. After all, he can't eat it.

For the first time it dawned on Matte that these newcomers had weakened his power base in the village considerably. There had been commuters before who were not dependent on the biggest farmer. But their parents had been. For these commuters he was a respectable person. He was quick to create new dependencies. A little favor over here, a good word over there and they were at his mercy. The new ones did not even address him. And if they did, it was on the basis of *equality*. They bought something from him like they bought something at a store. If he was cheaper, they took it for granted. You simply got it for less at the farmer's. That's only fair when you live in the countryside. At any rate, the political connections didn't work with them. Everybody voted differently. From house to house, even among the same family. Even from election to election! He grimaced. Undecided voters. People without roots. It was okay that the workers voted for the socialists. Who else could they vote for in their situation? And it was alright that the farmers voted conservative. It had much less to do with the Church than many assumed. The Church was part of the garnishing of the front. You got a few percent more with it and you lost a few percent because of it. The Church was depending on the conservatives more than the other way around. He had never thought much about the clerics or religion, but of course he played his role there as well. This was something the youngsters didn't have. They only wanted to play roles they believed in. They didn't want to realize that appearances don't have much to do with the game, just as the soccer player's outfit has little to do with his talent. They even wanted to believe in the advertising on their shirts.

"You're not saying anything today?" Lydia asked when she sat down next to him with a glass of red wine. "Nice bustle these past days. I had to take on temporary help. Rosi can't handle it by herself anymore."

"This one?"

Matte was pointing to a portly woman past her fifties, who was, as he knew, married to the janitor. The Sheep Inn's owner nodded. He smiled sourly.

"In earlier days your helpers were young and beautiful."

"And stupid."

"That's okay. Is this stranger still after Rosi?"

Lydia said in a low voice, "He is so much after her that I can't sleep half of the night."

There was a short pause.

"The village has changed", Matte said eventually.

"And it has taken you a long time to realize it", Lydia thought. But she said: "It's no wonder. First, the Lassnig girl, now Grete."

"I was not referring to that", he grunted.

"Then what?"

"Oh, nothing."

He was bothered a lot by Rosi's relationship with the stranger. So far he had never considered that he would *not* get her. But she was capable of disappearing with such a guy. From one day to the other. To never be seen again. The thought caused him physical discomfort, an almost unknown feeling. "I am not in love with this woman, am I?" He burst out laughing. He sensed the looks of surprise and realized he had to be careful. An old man can quickly turn into an odd and old man.

"I've just thought of a joke", he declared in his rough and slightly contemptuous tone. "But today is not a day to tell jokes. A murder like this is a bad thing, particularly in a small community. There's not one moment when you can't be sure that the murderer is not sitting at the same table that you are sitting at."

The newcomer laughed nervously and old Matte would have bet his hand before that he would do just that. He still knew his way around, even with the independent ones. His interjection had brought a new angle to the conversation. A village is small. Everybody knows everybody. So if the murderer was from the area, and much was indicating this, then everyone of them knew him. If there are so many individuals who each know a stranger, there is a natural effort to name him. A woman at a table next to them said: "I always get goose bumps when I run across Bernd. He is somehow scary."

Her husband asked: "What kind of skin are you supposed to have, anyway?"

Matte saw how Müller was giggling into his glass. This fellow was on a downward slide since his wife had buzzed off. Some of them start blooming, some fall apart. You never know beforehand. The old Müller had been a real guy, a comrade, a friend. The young one was worthless. Lately he showed up less and less and rarely said a word. Most likely he was drinking himself to death in secret. Matte had known two or three who had done just that. With determination and discretion. From one day to the next they had been toast. With these drinkers you could never tell how much they had had at any given moment. They never lost their composure. With ten half pints and a liter of schnapps they were able to walk home, straight as an arrow. Only when they are certain they are standing in front of their own bed do they lose consciousness and fall over.

Matte hardly took part in the rest of the conversation. He was waiting. He had made a decision which he wanted to translate into practice today. When he went home around eleven, he felt just as in those old times. Never let it slide. He spent about a quarter of an hour in the maid´s quarter. Fifteen minutes was enough. There was nothing to talk about.

34

The village was lying in the smooth bend between the plain and the hill ascending towards the forest. Where there had been the church and the adjacent farms and much free space, the small houses of the old settlement and, more recently, the larger ones of the new neighborhood had been built. The invasion of the new homebuilders had not exactly contributed to the village´s appearance, but the Sheep´s innkeeper had converted a dry pasture into 30 lots, which meant turning stones into gold. The Lassnig farm was the one closest to the forest. If you looked out the window of the first floor towards the church´s steeplechase it was exactly at the same height as the store. Towards the east, west and north the forest climbed up the hills, and further away these hills turned into mountains. Not very high mountains. Not one of them was higher than the timberline. Actually, the only difference to the hills was the roughness and the manners of speech of the area. Looking south there was the village and the valley floor leading to faraway forest islands and to "real" mountains, which fenced off the land like several rows of shark teeth. White, cold, with sharp edges. Many peoples had moved through this broad valley. Some of them known, many whose names are not known. Some of them peaceful, most of them belligerent. Some of them had settled and mixed their blood with that of the locals.

In the afternoon, dense clouds had come from the southwest. They brought rain and shortened the day. The winter grain stood about a foot high. The warmth was still missing. The atmosphere at the Lassnig farm was depressing. Sonja´s father had recovered from his collapse, but he found no joy in his work. His wife was still convinced that her daughter was alive, but she didn´t talk about it as it would have tortured him too much. The nine year old twins had become more serious. They tolerated the increasing number of hugs without blinking and they gave their parents a good-night kiss, something they would have previously considered to be unmanly.

The family went to bed early. At ten o´clock the farm was lying in total darkness. The weak light coming from the street lighting was barely strong enough to show the outline of the buildings against the black background. The village was quiet after midnight. The cloud cover opened up and the light of the stars filtered down to Earth.

A keen observer might have noticed the slim figure sneaking across the farm towards the working quarters. There it merged with the shadow of the roof and was invisible. Only the cat saw how the figure stopped briefly at the door. Then the door opened, creaking quietly, and closed again. The night visitor had disappeared inside the house.

Adelheid Lassnig was listening in the darkness. Now she often lay awake and listened to her husband´s heavy breathing. The nights in the old house had many noises, but there had been one which did not belong there. Quietly, she slipped out of her bed and walked barefoot from the bedroom to the short corridor leading to the staircase. She did not turn on the light. For a moment she stood in complete darkness, then she felt her way down, step by step. It was a masonry staircase which did not creak. Again a noise which did not belong to the night. It came from the kitchen. Only now she thought about the fate of the pastor´s cook and that the murderer had not yet been caught. She stood at the bottom of the staircase and felt how the cold of the floor crept up her legs. Suddenly something cold brushed across her face. Adelheid jumped back and hit herself at the railing. The iron knob hit her ribs so hard that she fell forward onto her knees. She wanted to scream from astonishment and pain when she heard the door creaking again. It was this noise which did not fit into the night and which had brought her down here. She sensed that she was alone. Carefully she stood up. She had lost orientation due to the fall and had to feel her way along the wall before she found the light switch. The door was closed. She thought briefly and locked it with the large bolt.

Then she went into the kitchen. At first sight there was nothing unusual. But there was a large jar of jam standing on the table which did not belong there. The table had been empty when she had gone to bed. She got closer and discovered something lying under the jar. A small piece of paper, no, a small piece of cloth. Adelheid took it and deciphered the message which someone had written with a piece of charcoal. It must have been hard to write on this cloth with charcoal. Her mouth started twitching, tears ran down her cheeks. She put the jam back into the cupboard. She placed the cloth between two sheets of paper and put it into her drawer. She laughed silently, put out the lights and scurried back to bed. She put her cold feet under her husband's blanket. Her feelings had never betrayed her. It is a talent closely related with trust. Trust is a gift which helps us to conserve the warmth of life. Few are able to do it.

35

Padoponos stuck to his extensive walks. Today he had gotten far into the valley and dusk was falling when he returned. He reached the edge of the village, the abandoned house with a derelict garden wall, a nostalgic ruin, which passed on its mute reproach to every passer-by. A tall nut tree with its bald crown reaching for the sky underlined the image. The Greek liked the place. It was a place of invocation. A place without words.

There was no warning. The blow to the back was so strong that he was thrown forward, landing on his hands and knees. Without thinking he threw himself to the side and avoided the next blow. The weight of the club dragged the man who was holding it forward. The pause in the attack was enough for the Greek to get on his feet. Now they faced each other. He had seen the attacker only once. At the counter of the Sheep´s Inn. A huge, bulky man with a coarse, distorted face which was now totally committed to the fight. A large, rough block. He had hands and feet which seemed to be too large, even for his frame, like paws and baseplates which provided him with enormous stability. He held a thick club of some five feet in length at an angle in front of his body, like a samurai his sword. Padoponos felt the pulsating pain in his back. He could still move. That was the most important thing. The blow could have broken his back. He was gripped by cold rage. The block feinted several times, then he made a quick step forward, aiming for Padoponos´ neck. The Greek evaded without effort. He was relieved. The attacker must have possessed enormous strength, but his club was too thick and too long. His enemy realized this fact at that same moment. He threw his club at him and charged after it. Padoponos was hit in the stomach and went down again due to the force of the blow. Now the giant was lying on top of him and hit him, blind and without thinking, with the force of a heavy hammer. Because of his position he was in his own way, he was impatient and his hits were inaccurate. His blows were painful nevertheless, but the force of their impact was only a fraction of what it could have been. He must have been a fearful opponent during bar brawls. Padoponos limited himself to hold him where he was, to prevent him from assuming a more advantageous position. At the same time he worked on getting his knee between the legs of his opponent. When he was ready he sprung it like a steel spring. The block sucked in a cubic yard of air and rolled sideways. Padoponos jumped up, still speechless with rage. He grabbed the right hand of the fellow and crashed it onto his knee with a rotating movement. Then he broke the left wrist in the same way. The giant moaned when the new pain surpassed the fading pain between his legs. He sat up with much difficulty and looked at his hand in disbelief, hanging there, large and broad, useless.

Padoponos stood before him, marked from the fight and the clay trail, but he was already calm and cool again. The crashing of the wrists had blown away his rage.

"Why?"

There was no answer. But the will of the man was broken. One step in his direction was enough for him to say with fury:

"Because of Rosi."

"Are you her boyfriend?"

The giant shook his head.

"Who sent you?"

He shook his head again. Padoponos kicked one of the dangling hands. Tears shot into the block's eyes. Coarse wedge on a coarse block. Wasn't there a saying? The Greek waited.

"It was the old man. I owed him."

Padoponos didn't ask any further. Rosi had told him a few things, the rest was easy to guess.

"Now he owes you", he said.

It was almost dark by now. He didn't want to walk through the inn like this. Without any further ado, he left the thug sitting there and found his way across the fields. He reached the back of the inn and went across the patio to the back door. He got into his room without anyone seeing him.

36

"What is the matter with you? Sneaking around like you are
wrapped in cotton."
It must be bad if his mother noticed. It was bad.
"Nothing", he murmured and tried to leave the kitchen. His
father sat at the table, the Saturday newspaper in front of him.
Every weekend he spent half of the morning reading it,
including the small print. He was particularly fond of the ads.
Not that he was looking for anything in particular (he would
never have done business because of an advertising), it was
the tone which attracted him, the sales pitch in five, six words.
From a chest of drawers to a whore, from a plot of land to a
spouse. Everything could be offered or desired with a handful
of letters. He cut out the most original quotes. Showed them
around when friends came to visit.
"Sit down over here", the father said.
Rüdiger moaned, inwardly of course. The last thing he needed
was a tell-me-what-is-on-your-mind-talk between parent and
child. He sat down, the mother sat down.
"Careful!" the father hissed. She had shoved the ads around
with her elbow.
"Nothing happened, anyway!" she hissed back. Two pots
boiling over at the slightest provocation.
"That´s not the point!" he shouted. "The point is you can´t
even sit down without causing some kind of mess."
The mother stood up so vehemently that her chair fell over,
said "ass" and left the room. "Stupid cow", the man
murmured while picking up the chair. Rüdiger was grinning.
If his father saw it, he would certainly throw him out. But he
didn´t want to see it. He got a bottle of beer and two glasses,
placed them carelessly on top of the ads and filled them.
"Thank God she´s gone", he said. "What I am going to talk
with you about is not for her ears anyway. You shut your
mouth, okay?"
Rüdiger nodded dutifully. A man-to-man and you-know-what-

I-mean talk was still better than a parent-and-child circus.
They toasted and drank.

"I think I know what´s bothering you", the father began, still
with foam on his upper lip. "Out here there´s not much
happening with girls and stuff. But at your age, girls are
important. They are always important."

He put on a conspiratorial face.

"It´s about time I introduce you to the matter. We could go
out, for example. We´ll just say we´re going to the movies."

"And in case mom wants to come with us?"

"Then we´ll pick a movie she won´t like. For a young fellow
the first contact, the first real ... you know what I mean ..."

Rüdiger made huge eyes.

"Of course you know what I mean", the father said, annoyed.
"If you don´t know it at your age all is lost!"

He finished his glass.

"There, the ads. Sex! The first time, you understand? The first
time is not so easy. You´re nervous, don´t know what to do.
Perhaps you´re so nervous that you can´t do anything. If you
are too nervous, you can´t get it up. If it´s the first time for the
girl as well, you´ve got the perfect storm. You don´t know
what to do, she doesn´t know what to do ... That´s why you
need an experienced woman to show you the way. One who
isn´t impatient. Who knows her way around. Are you getting
the point?"

Rüdiger shook his head.

"No, dad."

Dad immediately went bonkers. Easier than two plus two.

"Then we´ll just leave it at that", he shouted. "You just see for
yourself how you deal with it. You don´t have to ask me
anymore."

"I didn´t ask", Rüdiger said.

"I don´t care!" the father shouted while leaving. "I´ll just go
by myself. I am not your moron!"

"How can we tell?" the mother called from upstairs.

"You won´t be able to tell", he shouted back. "You need a few ounces of brain for that."

Rüdiger disregarded the fight. This afternoon dad would fire up the grill and, while having lunch with the neighbors, mom would praise his cooking skills for the hundredth time and he would believe it for the hundredth time and tell her that all this grill-thing would be for naught without her mayonnaise salad. Then they would talk about meat and charcoal and salads, one smarter than the other, all of it with almost the same words as on any given weekend. After the meal, they would play cards and drink wine. They would also praise the wine, no matter from which shelf at the supermarket it came from, and the game would get them to start a fight again. It is a major surprise for a teenager to find out that there are *indeed* stereotypes. For years you smile when you see them in movies and books and suddenly you realize that you are yourself in the middle of one of them. That not only are you living the cliché in your own home but you are actually playing along with it. Because for a long time, Rüdiger had been the sullen boy who was terribly irritated by pretty much everything - a perfect role.

Moods are strange. He wasn´t depressed in the morning, rather, amused. Besides, now he knew which ads his father was really interested in. For the first time Rüdiger felt a hint of this deep comedy which accompanies every single human, whether he likes it or not. Were they ridiculous or tragic? Was his fear ridiculous? A murder had occurred and everybody thought it was the second one. Again and again he had searched his memory for what he called the appearance. Often, on cold days there were clouds of fog drifting through the forest, bodies are distorted, silhouettes become unreal. He had a lively imagination. This came on top of everything else. He didn´t know anymore what he had really seen or what he thought he had seen after the fact. Figures in long, white coats lifting up something. Another figure, a girl. Fog. A gust of wind and everything had dissolved. Everything dissolves. Dad wanted to pay a prostitute for him. Mom was supposed to think they were going to see a movie. If it weren't for Sonja he would have accepted the offer, only to find out whether these things really happened. It *was* funny, after all.

37

The county town was only twenty-five minutes away from the village. By car. The bus took about forty minutes. During the past few decades a wide belt of business- and apartment buildings had grown around the city center - a castle from the Middle Ages, the city hall, a dozen town houses - interspersed with small businesses. The city fathers had allowed themselves the luxury of commissioning a development plan which then had been shelved immediately. The school complex stood next to a paint factory because the land was owned by the municipality, small and large apartment houses surrounded by a haulage firm with some forty heavy duty trucks. The haulage company had arrived there first. Everyone in the construction business knew that. Nobody had been bothered by this. Different times … But even today there was always a free lot to be found where a contractor, building permit in hand, would raise his four walls in order to complain later about the noise and the bad smell. The last population census had surpassed 10,000 inhabitants. Good for business. The city council thought it was worth having a celebration. The weather was now calmer, but there were no indications of it getting any warmer. With the continuous circulation of people in the municipal building nobody noticed the man wearing a trench coat and a Tyrolean hat. He was wearing dark glasses and continuously held a handkerchief in front of his face to blow his nose. A victim of the first spring pollen, one might think. But the man was not allergic. The coat wasn´t his, nor was the hat. He was walking quickly and with determination. When he entered the maze of side streets after leaving the main artery he seemed to relax. A couple of garages had been built along the narrow side of two apartment houses. The man opened one of the doors, took out a yellow Opel, closed the garage and drove off. He left the city and soon reached a dirt road which ended at a gravel pit a few yards later. It was a popular spot among young folks for trips at night in order to do what they wanted to do and could not do at home. During the day the place was lonely and deserted. A moonscape with traces of a clandestine dumping ground, with a few scrawny shrubs whose twigs had caught used condoms dangling from them. A cultured landscape, in the best sense of the word. The man did not get out of the car. He stuffed rubber pads into his cheeks and taped a bushy black hairpiece over his light eyebrows. Then he turned around and drove back to the road.

Once at the village, he turned to the right half a block after the bus stop, passed the road to the Lassnig farm and a few new buildings and stopped at the short cul-de-sac behind the last house. He stopped the engine and disappeared past the hedge which separated the Riement property from the rest.

38

Martha had gotten up at six. Franz had to leave early to catch
the 7 o´clock bus. She fixed him breakfast and checked his
clothing. Not because of her own personal interest, more as a
nod to her former profession. Her dialog was curt, arid. (Franz
taught geography and natural history.)
"Good morning."
"Morning."
"Anything new?" (This referred to the national news she was
always listening to).
"No."
"More coffee?"
"Please."
He glanced at the newspaper while eating his bun. After the
second cup he looked at the kitchen clock and got up.
"Gotta go."
She was putting the dishes into the machine.
"Yes."
He closed the door and locked it. Ever since the murder of
Grete, the village´s keys were turning a lot more often. She
could have watched his short walk to the street but she hadn´t
done this in a long time. Martha cleaned up things and took
the vacuum cleaner from its closet. Kitchen, vestibule, her
sleeping quarters, Franz´ room. Her critical look got caught at
his book shelf. She got a duster and started to take out the
books one by one to wipe them clean. Usually she didn´t care
about his reading material but now she could not resist. What
sort of titles! "Following the Tracks of the Angels", "Life in
the Divine Light", "Exercises for Direct God Experience",
"The Rediscovery of Transcendence", "Be Successful and
Wealthy - The Power of Cosmic Magnetism". She read:
"In order to achieve guidance by the astro-cosmic waves of
the universe you need to go into silence and ask specific
questions, just like you would do with any person on Earth."
There were examples:

"What kind of work am I best at? How can I make the money I need to pay my bills?

How can I become a songwriter?

Should I live in New York City, Florida or California?"

The man was serious. At first Martha was astounded, then a light, somewhat hysterical laughter started to come from her throat. Tears were streaming down her cheeks. The mere thought of going out into the garden at night to ask a higher cosmic conscience about an unpaid phone bill was simply too much.

"Dimensions of Esoteric Knowledge", "Invitation to Zen". She read: "Never clip your nails in the dark!"

There was much to be said for this. "Home in the Light - The Wisdom of Magus Strovolos". Paranormal abilities, guided by the Spirit of Yohannan ...

"Beyond Death - New Facts and Models of Reincarnation". She read:

"Death as the temporary resting place of thinking electrons". "The Spirit of the New Era - New Age Spirituality and Christianity", "The Human Aura", "The Practice of Meditation", "Peak Performance by Intuitive Management", "The Way of Silence", "Autobiography of a Yogi", "A Strange Profession" - The Life Story of a Medium.

Franz´ library ... there were still those science books he had saved his money for while being an assistant teacher. Martha did not understand this change. Contrary to him, she had never been religious. Suddenly she caught a glimpse of the *absolute* power behind the search and the need to know meaning. She put back the books, now almost hesitatingly. Was he very desperate? This thought immediately brought her to Grete. She had never thought about the pastor´s cook. Perhaps she had treated her a bit from the top down because she looked like a scarecrow, lacking the most essential sense for clothing and hair care. But now she was dead and as little endearing she herself and her whole life might have been, there was a gaping hole which could not be closed. Martha thought about that. When we think about the life of another person we most often think about ourselves. We recognize its uniqueness. It is not easy to come to terms with the fact that this uniqueness has to disappear from one moment to the other. Could it be that this was the power which had changed Franz?

Nine o´clock. She put the vacuum cleaner away and went upstairs into her study. Time to change. The neighbor had promised to get her a hemming tape. Then, shopping in the nearest town. There were no shops here. A quick detour to the Sheep´s Inn, later, cooking. Was her life any more attractive than Grete´s? She had been very close to the stable when it happened and at around the time it happened. Since then she had been feeling this slight coldness at the back of her neck. The horror had brushed her.

She took off the coat and smoothed her undergarment. Her body had not changed in twenty years. Martha held her back very straight, almost a bit stiff. Franz had once said mannequin prison. Back then, when they still had had a common language. The memory of those past times when they had lived as a regular couple, had invited friends, went out, had fights and laughed, today it was like a look into a gloomy world where wax figures were moving slowly while layer after layer of dust falls off and gently buries everything. It happens faster than you think. No melancholy. Foreignness appears like thin fog banks between people who had once been very close to each other. Imperceptible at first, and suddenly there was a white wall with a voice coming through it calling you by your name. Why does she know your name? You turn around and quickly walk away. She should have left earlier. She now saw her own situation clearly and at the same time distant like a starry sky in the mountains. Not only did she see Franz´ ridiculous chess moves, the endless moving of figures back and forth, she also recognized her own pathetic reply, her need for security, her cowardice, her lethargy and - this surprised her the most - her secret satisfaction.

The satisfaction of a worm inside rotten wood. A shiver went down her spine. It is still not too late. But this time she would not flee in silence. She would talk to him. It was better for him, too. She heard a door downstairs. Way too early for Franz. Of course sometimes classes were cancelled or changed, but it was only nine thirty.

"Franz?"

Everything was quiet now. Had she really heard the door or was it just a similar noise? She tried to remember whether all of the windows were closed. The window stops were not that tight. When the wind opened one of them it almost sounded the same.

"Franz?"

It must have been a window. She didn´t feel at ease. Grete´s murderer was still at large. She specifically had asked Franz to lock the small door to the basement. He had said he would do it. But he was often rather distracted. She pulled the gown over her head, a tight model. At the very moment she was helplessly stuck in the tube of fabric she heard quick steps from the staircase. Immediately Martha panicked, which was further exacerbated because she got stuck in her skirt. She tried to free herself with forceful movements but the fabric stayed put. She was stuck just like in a straightjacket. Finally, her head popped through the collar, almost blind with fear she looked to the staircase. There stood the tomcat.

"Ohhhh!" she moaned with indignation and relief and smiled about herself. He had entered the house through his cat door, had opened a door standing ajar and jumped up the stairs. When fat Fridolin used the staircase you could really hear it.

"You devil!" she said tenderly. "I almost ruined a couple of yards of silk because of you."

Fridolin meowed.

The skirt had not ripped. Good work. She fixed the deteriorated hairdo, brushed her eyebrows, put on her shoes, grabbed her handbag and went down the stairs with light feet. Now she was thinking about her decision again and she felt good and fresh, better than she had felt for a long time. Downstairs, she glanced at the kitchen - of course the windows were closed - and wanted to go towards the door. But there was someone standing there. A man wearing a long coat. Martha screamed.

The yellow Opel was rolling towards the main street. Old Matte was doing his rounds. Shoulders up and looking straight ahead. There was nobody else on the street. Again the man drove to the gravel pit. He put the cheek pads and the fake eyebrows into a small plastic travel bag which already contained a red-stained piece of plastic. A thin plastic raincoat. Then he got out of the car and filled the empty space of the bag with rocks. He went to one of the larger pools and threw it in a high arc. It sank immediately. Then he drove the car back to the garage. When he entered the public building a few minutes later, he was still fighting his pretended cold. A short while later both the coat and hat were hanging in that locker where a parting colleague had forgotten them months ago. Without a hitch, the man picked up his work where it had been interrupted by his excursion. His pencil went over some administrative forms with much routine. Suddenly, he jerked. The car keys. He strolled over to the wardrobe and pretended he was busy with his own coat. The keys slid into the other pocket from where he had taken them. For the second time he returned to his work.

The bookstore was so narrow that its only window resembled an embrasure with glass rather than a shop window. Its front was painted a pale pink. Between two wide, gray blocks, it had something of being desperately stuck. Sensitive people invariably took a deep breath before stepping inside. Inside, it became even more cramped as a freestanding shelf divided the room once more, lengthwise. There was not one spot of free wall from the floor to the twelve-foot ceiling. Back to back, dense like wallpapers or as the scales of a fish, they extended towards the gloomy depth of the shop. There was a cashier on a counter right next to the entrance. A slim salesperson could turn around, even after lunchtime, provided she was eating half rations. For fifteen years this had been Monika´s workplace. Ever since she had left school and taken the one-year course as a typist. She did not suffer from claustrophobia or being overweight and felt at ease in the quiet atmosphere which is created by a large number of books. She liked the smell of freshly printed copies which she lifted out of their boxes almost daily, and she liked that most of the customers lowered their voice involuntarily when they stepped from the bright street into the velvety silence of her small realm.

A nervous young man handed her a handwritten list with titles by Stendhal, Hamsun and Steinbeck. She had only two of them in stock.

"I can order the other ones", she said. "It takes a couple of days".

He couldn´t make up his mind. At first he said yes, then no, he wanted to try elsewhere. She placed the two paperback books into a paper bag and settled the bill.

A pensioner, a regular customer, almost blind from reading, nodded at her silently while burying himself in the books for hours before deciding, perhaps, to buy one. A girl asked for a calendar with drawings and jokes and got one. Her girlfriend stood silently next to her, stepping from one leg to the other and would have liked to giggle, but she did not dare to. They both departed with the calendar as if they had found a prized booty. Their purchase would certainly be the cause for a lengthy conversation without an actual beginning or end. Monika remembered briefly similar conversations with friends, they were always important and prolonged, although in hindsight, their cause was really not worth mentioning. But they had seen this in a completely different way. There are much deeper trenches between the age groups than we realize or want to see. Such thoughts were occupying her mind quite often. She was actually too serious. Serious people have a hard time. They waste their time with fruitless observations, which are bound to fill their lives with a little bit more sorrow. Monika had a small face, a little too pudgy for 34 years. There were no glasses which really fitted her. Wearing contact lenses, she looked like she would never stop wondering. That was even worse. She had thin, blond hair which was only suitable for short hairstyles. She was an open-hearted, affectionate woman willing to make sacrifices, but everything she was, it was overshadowed by the eternal insecurity which some people drag around their lives like an invisible anchor. She had had three relationships with men. The periods between each one had been rather long. Now she was the secret lover of a pastor twenty years older than her. It was Goethe´s fault. Paul had come into the store because he needed the trip to Italy. A present for a friend. They had hit it off right away. They were both serious, friendly, and lonely. He was hungry for love, so much so that the brief encounter had caused his feelings to overflow after denying them for decades. They made love, and despite her lack of experience she was vastly superior. She became his motherly lover, just like that. Understanding, patient, submissive. He was always the child in their relationship. He dealt with himself and his irreconcilable feelings like children did: with unrestrained egoism. It never occurred to him that she might also suffer due to the secrecy, the hiding game, her "impossible" status.

She was his temptation and his protection and his lust, his universal mother. Universal mothers are wonderful machines that give continuously and function without complaints, forever. You don´t ask machines how they feel. Not even wonderful machines.

Monika asked: "How long can this go on like this?"

Paul touched his forehead and replied: "Just leave it at that. I will handle it somehow."

She remained silent.

Three customers came into the store in quick succession. The first one asked for a magazine she did not carry, the second was looking for a rare non-fiction book and could not believe that it was not in stock. She patiently explained, not necessarily charming by nature but always friendly and trying hard. The customer left, complaining loudly. The third one smiled knowingly and asked about erotic works. Monika knew that he would press past her in the narrow room, closer and slower than necessary if she went ahead, so she let him go first. He was disappointed at the small selection and her unwillingness to recount the book´s content in detail. After five minutes he made a lewd remark and left the store.

She looked at her watch. Half past ten. Paul had called yesterday in the evening. A strange conversation with a strange voice. He talked about the murder of his housekeeper. He wanted to meet her at eleven. Not a single thought about the fact that she was working at that time of day. The manager acknowledged this. She was sitting in her tiny office at the back of the store. Feeding herself with books and numbers. If her only employee had to leave during business hours she closed the store. When she opened the door to her boss´ office at a quarter to eleven, ready to go out, she nodded and said, "He is quite inconsiderate, even for a man. Don´t you think?" Monika blushed and shook her head automatically without really wanting to contradict her.

She had read a newspaper article about the crime and thought about the shock that Paul must have suffered. But she was also irritated about the way he was in charge of her own time. It was not the first time.

They met at her apartment. Paul was late, over an hour. She was seriously annoyed because she had asked if it was okay during the lunch break. Then she saw him and forgot about the sermon she had prepared. That was not Paul Weilrich. Not her Paul Weilrich. Someone else entered the room. Both the hint of irony in his eyes and the glow of kindness which had illuminated his face from within had been extinguished. Before her stood a cold man with cold eyes, who forced the corners of his mouth to go up after a short pause. If you see a shark smiling you don´t believe the smile.

Weilrich was staring at the woman who had stopped in her tracks, helpless, while coming towards him. That was good. He had actually been worried about her giving him a hug. Before his inner eye she took off her clothes, one by one, as she had done so often, and then she lay in front of him on the bed with her shameless nudity, took on an even more shameless pose and smiled. This whore. What had she made him do? The thought made him dizzy. The Lord had tempted him and he had not resisted the temptation. He had fallen onto the soft body of the whore and had melted with her disgusting flesh like dogs do. Even worse: like two slimy slugs, hermaphrodites, who embrace each other and put slimy horns into slimy orifices.

"Hello", he said with his new, strange voice.

It sounded like a curse.

"Hello there", she said weakly and offered her hand with hesitation. He took it, shook it briefly and let it go again. They sat at their little seating area, Swedish style, Monika on the sofa and him in an arm chair, yet another rejection.

"You don´t have to tell me", she said, trying to provide some kind of warmth. "I have read all about it. It must be terrible for you."

"It is", he said. "A terrible sign."

A terrible sign. What did he mean by that? She was trying to find words, couldn't find any and left it at that, abandoned herself to his gaze, the restrained blaze of his eyes, his hatred. That was it. *Hatred*! She felt how he hated her. Not only her, but everything she signified. Her sex, her sexuality as such, even the consciousness of owing his life to a sex act.

Weilrich was shocked. She was reading him like a book. He turned into a business owner who jumps from one display to the other while being threatened, ready to pull down the blinds. He only left a small crack in order to peek out. Ready to close it as well.

He had to be careful. Now he had to be very careful. The Lord had shown him his errors and now it was up to him to make up for them. Until now nobody had become suspicious. Why cause a stir with hindsight? It was not in the Lord's interest for his servants to become exposed. He should not give in to his justified rage. He had to be clever about it.

"It was a sign", he repeated. Suddenly his old voice was talking to her. "I have thought about it for a long time. We have sinned. Both of us. But we can be forgiven."

He stood up and now he did sit down next to her and took her hand, which was lying lifelessly on her thigh.

"We have succumbed to a temptation we should not have succumbed to. We cannot extinguish our guilt. But we can go inwards and become better humans. Forgiving each other and being sorry, we are going to be forgiven."

Monika was almost paralyzed. She heard his litany without understanding the words. She remembered other words, long discussions about the pros and cons of celibacy, its despotism, injustice, against nature and hence against God. Could God have given the gift of love to humanity and approve of the fact that his priests were being deprived of an essential part of it? She remembered the long, agonizing talks and realized that they had had only one purpose. He wanted to sleep with her without the risk of feeling guilty. He was like an early capitalist exploiter who gave away part of the money to a charitable foundation. But, rather than the exploiters, he wanted to talk himself into having a clear conscience without wasting a single thought about his victim. She was his victim. At that moment of clarity she realized it, although she was unable to offer any resistance to him. Him, this hypocrite, liar and deceiver. Because not only did he deceive her. He also deceived his strange God, who had his innocent cook murdered just to make a point. And he deceived himself. But she let him talk, her eyes filled with tears and he attributed this to his power of persuasion.

"Promise me to reveal yourself only to God", he asked her. "We should not set an example with our sin. Talk to God, not to the people, who are themselves weak and who can be tempted, just like us."

"Yes", she whispered.

"I will always carry you in my heart, even if we will never see each other again. You know we should never see each other again, do you?"

"Yes", she whispered.

He stood up and made a move as if he were to bless her. But in front of him sat the whore, the temptation in a short skirt, the insidious seduction. He couldn´t bring himself to do it.

"Farewell."

"Farewell."

Monika was deeply divided. She was at the same time the observer, watching the scene with detachment, and the paralyzed woman who was told by this man that she was a sinner and, as she suspected, a whore. The observer was smiling while the woman fell apart piece by piece. But after he had left, she felt a new and unknown power rising up in her. The power of liberty, which defeated her insecurity, at least for a few hours. It had all been worth it just for this experience. This way the pastor broke up with his lover and got weaker, thinking he was getting stronger, and she was getting stronger although at first she thought she would have to dissolve. He would be hearing from her, eventually. But right now it was not important at all.

Old Matte liked the stranger less and less. First the story with Rosi, and now he had broken both of Kare´s hands. He had never dreamed that this could happen. Not that he had high esteem for Kare. He was an impetuous idiot. But usually his sheer strength was enough. The stranger looked as if nothing had happened. He had not made any noise at all, had not even mentioned the event. That was more unsettling than if he had caused a big scandal. Was it that he wanted nothing to do with the police? After Sonja´s disappearance and the murder of the Strutz woman, Matte had pushed the detectives' noses firmly towards this German Greek. But there was nothing. He had two watertight alibis, and back in Germany they had confirmed all of his data. Perhaps he didn´t say anything because of the broken hands. Should he perhaps entice Kare to turn the story around and to blame the stranger? Better not. Kare was scared shitless and did not want to have anything to do with him. Furthermore, he should not underestimate the enemy. He would probably pick apart Kare´s story in ten minutes and drag Matte into the affair. Well, if the tourist kept his mouth shut it was the best solution.

For the first time in forty years Matte felt that things were not going anymore as they were supposed to go. It was not something you could touch with your hands, more like a change in the general atmosphere. Perhaps he thought too much about the story with Rosi. Perhaps he also started to feel his age. Was he imagining it or were his friends not quite as attentive as they used to be when he said something? Sometimes he had this impression at the regular´s table. In earlier times they were quiet when he spoke. Nowadays, one or the other conversation continued in a low voice. Matte himself had founded the regular´s table, to bind them, to influence them. That had been a mistake. They had not allowed to be bound, on the contrary, they had loosened the firm structure. To put Kare against the stranger had been - in retrospect - yet another mistake. And when he looked at the pastor, he had to be afraid of having committed an even bigger mistake ...

Too many mistakes. Matte sat straight. As long as you recognize your mistakes, nothing is lost. Only when you don´t want to see them and try to interpret them you become a loser. A yellow Opel turned onto the main street and accelerated. There was not much to see of the driver´s face. He did not know the car. Perhaps a salesman, insurance or something. His thoughts returned to Padoponos. There was something wrong with this fellow. The papers were okay, the company he had indicated as his employer confirmed that he was on vacation right now. A software designer. He had checked what that meant. A guy sitting behind a computer all day. The same man broke both of powerful Kare´s hands and did not say a word about it to anyone. And *he himself* had been the victim of a perfidious attack. That didn´t jive. Much less the way he had broken his hands. Except if he had been to a special military unit. That´s where they learn things like that. They prefer to stay mum if they get into a fight later. That would be an explanation. Matte was not content with it. A small municipal truck passed him. The three men inside greeted him politely. He briefly lifted his hand. The municipality steered his thoughts over to Müller. Had old Müller been alive, the Greek would not be here anymore. He would have thrown him out of town in no time. He also would have caught the madman. Although it is not easy to catch a madman. Matte thought he could tell what most people were capable and incapable of. But that applied to normal people, not madmen. Crazy ones. They are totally normal for days and suddenly they go crazy for a few hours. He had his candidates whom he kept an eye on. He also had time. The more murders happened, the smaller the circle would become. One would remain. He was not scared at the thought of the victims. People die. That´s how it is. Whether someone dies of old age or is murdered or crushes himself with a car, it´s all the same.

During war they die like flies and it´s all the same. He hadn´t
been bothered by the war. It had been an interesting time with
many possibilities. You couldn´t be a coward nor stupid, then
you knew what you could risk. Of course they can get you.
Everybody dies sometime. Everyone knows it and yet there
are so many cowards and idiots. Neither should you have
compassion. Compassion is stupid. Suddenly, images of the
past came back and he giggled. Compassion! He had never
been stupid.

Rosi came towards him at the entrance to the Sheep´s Inn.
Matte felt that she had been waiting for him. She stood in
front of him with a malicious gleam in her eyes.

"What did you do to Bernd?"

Even his best friends did not speak to him like that. She
wasn´t a coward, but she was insolent.

"What do you care?"

She was about his height and now she came so close to him
that their faces almost touched.

"I care because I take care of him."

From the corner of his eye he saw that the stranger was
leaning at the open window, watching the dispute.

But he did not see the Sheep Inn´s owner, who was also
quietly witnessing the scene from inside the guest hall.

"I set his head straight", old Matte said derisively. Against his
better judgment he continued: "About his own thoughts. What
do you think he´s thinking while walking up the stairs behind
you? His eyes are popping out of his head."

To his surprise she laughed out loud.

"So what? Is that all? He is young and strong. Why should he
not think about it?"

Then she did something which surprised him even more. She
grabbed his hand and pressed it tightly between her firm
thighs. In broad daylight! It hurt. She was much stronger than
him. She laughed at him, ridiculed him.

"This is where *you* want to be, old fart! But you won´t get any
further than this", she screamed, loud enough so that half the

village could hear it.

He struggled to free himself, white with anger. But she let him flip around effortlessly for a few long seconds before she slackened the grip and he pulled back his hand. Without a word, he turned around and hurried away, so quickly that it looked like an escape. Rosi smiled towards the Greek and went back to work.

42

Bernd had also followed the event as it had been all about him. Why did Rosi do this? He was certain about one thing only: he did not want to run into old Matte right now. He quickly retreated further into the open barn. His head was like a washing machine drum. Nothing would stay where it was, everything got entangled. But this should not be. It was important that he put things in order. He crouched on his heels, closed his eyes and put a brake to the turning drum. Bernd was afraid. Ever since he had escaped from old Matte into the forest, fear had been following him. He had seen Sonja run past him, he had seen the hazelnut club being taken from the shed, he had seen the boy coming out of the forest. He had sensed his confusion. Sonja had not returned. Then, everything had become confused. They had asked about Sonja and found his hiding place. They had taken his clothes and shoes and brought them back later. He felt they didn´t trust him. They thought he had something to do with Sonja´s disappearance. But later they dismissed it as they thought he was incapable of hiding any clues. Clues! What did they know about clues and traces? Bernd had heard Sonja´s voice as well as other voices. He heard that she was doing fine. He had gone to Sonja´s mother and told her that Sonja was fine. She had grabbed him and asked many questions which he did not understand, but suddenly *she* understood and smiled. We both know it, she said, and I am very grateful.

Someone had done something bad to the pastor´s cook. He could not relate this to Sonja. What did the cook have to do with Sonja?

Again, Bernd remembered the boy who had come out of the forest and the club which had been taken from the barn. They did have something to do with Sonja, not Grete Strutz whom he had not seen anywhere. He would have liked to talk about this to Rosi, but after what old Matte had recognized in him and peeled from the fog, he could not look into her eyes anymore. Sonja´s mother was always very kind to him. She felt only a tiny bit shy. He too wanted to do something nice for her. For a long time Bernd thought about how he could do that. Then he knew. He had to find out something about Sonja. Bernd decided to ask the boy about her. And the man who had taken the club, of course.

After he had come to terms with this, his fear also decreased. He felt better. A man becomes strong when he has to make difficult decisions. Bernd was a bit proud of himself. He was a humble fellow. It was a nice feeling.

43

The bus was a few minutes late. A car had gotten off the road and had to be rescued by a tow truck. The traffic had been interrupted. Riement had plenty of space, as usual. If you take the bus on a daily basis, you quickly get to know every passenger and if you do this over several years, you can´t help but notice how they become fewer and fewer. What would he do if they decided to eliminate this bus line one day? He owned a car but he didn´t like to drive. Martha used it for shopping and for her trips to the city. Did she have a friend? An attractive forty-year old who hadn´t been sleeping with her husband for four years? It was likely, but he actually did not believe it. Martha was a cautious person. She certainly would have agreed to a divorce, but under no circumstance could she be the guilty one. Well, he was only forty-two. It is not an age where you deprive yourself easily. But he was cautious, too. He didn´t want to be the guilty one, either. No story travels faster than an infidelity. A colleague, married of course, had driven some fifty miles through the night in order to find a bit of change in the red light district. Just when the lady with the short skirt and the long boots had stepped into his car, with the interior lights on, a neighbor had passed and recognized him. Not just any neighbor, but the woman next door, same staircase, same floor, the door in front of his door. Nothing is unlikely enough as not to be possible to happen. Every single day. On the other hand, things happened right in front of the curious eyes of the teaching staff and yet they remain hidden. He had been very lucky. A year ago he had fallen in love with a new colleague, and she had fallen in love with him. Love makes you oblivious to danger. They had not really tried hard to hide it. In hindsight, a very risky game. But perhaps it was the effort to hide something which attracted the vultures. After three failures in bed they had split up. Nobody had noticed anything. It was like a miracle. Most likely it had been due to pure chance that they had not shown the traits which arise suspicion. Nevertheless, it was a miracle. If Martha had found out … she would have found out. A fist-sized hole in a water tank is tighter than the discretion of the teaching staff. Since then, he was careful of opportunities to have an opportunity. He looked at his hand. It would not betray him, but sometimes he was sick of it.

Without noticing and without really wanting to, he had always relied on Sonja to wake him up in time to get off. Now this unconscious security was gone and did not allow him to fall asleep on the bus. It was five minutes past three when he put his foot on the pavement of the bus stop. A cloudless sky, the first warm springtime day. You only had to give the spring sun a chance. Once the clouds were dispersed, it can show what it is capable of in only a few hours. Dandelions and daisies were blooming next to the path. The teacher waved at two women who were standing in front of a patch talking to each other. One of them shouted:

"Good afternoon!"

"Good afternoon!"

People liked him quite a bit. Of course they all knew about his marriage. A solid majority thought Martha was the one to blame. For once, she was the woman, and strangely enough, it was particularly the women who reproached her for this, on the other hand, she had never really adapted. She had a way of letting you know that she did not really fit in. Whereas he had been born in the village and had decided to stay. This was taken into consideration. He belonged here and she did not. So it was her fault. Small communities are not tolerant.

A warm day in spring is enough to unleash the most intense fragrances. They are much superior to any perfume because they are the fragrances of life. The scent of the earth, the growing grass, the trees, the blooming shrubs and flowers, even the stables and the drying wood. There is much natural wood around the village. Fence posts, rafters, even wooden benches and tables between fruit trees and in front of the old houses, the stable´s gables made from reddish larch. Even the smell of fresh paint is a springtime aroma.

A few steps before the entrance to his garden, the teacher was overtaken by the postman´s orange car. It was the new postman, just about twenty, still shy and very much paying attention to the rules. They greeted each other, he said:

"I have a registered letter for your wife."

"Can I take it for her?"

He hesitated.

"Your wife is not at home?"

Riement could have told him about his predecessor who sat for hours with his buddies at Pernjak´s place, buying pastries for the village children so they would deliver the mail for him. Whenever he needed a signature, old Pernjak took care of it. But times change. Why try to convince this serious young man that all the rules are meant to be broken? Was he himself convinced of that?

"I will send her out right away."

The door was locked. There was the fear of the madman making the rounds, of course. The police said they were following several leads. For the inhabitants this sounded like "The murderer is running loose. We won´t catch him anytime soon."

He unlocked the door and called: "Martha! The postman!" He left the door ajar and went into the hallway. The transition from the bright sunlight into the semi-darkness of the lobby left him almost blind.

The postman waited next to the front door and heard the scream. He didn´t dare to run into the house right away, he only opened the door a little more and asked: "Mr. Riement? Something happen to you?"

He saw the man kneeling on the floor in the background, bent over a body on the floor. His young eyes quickly got used to the dim light.

"Oh my God!", he said. "Oh my God! Oh my God!"

44

If the village´s inhabitants had been a single living organism, any doctor would have diagnosed a severe shock after the murder of Martha Riement. Sonja´s disappearance had caused much agitation and busy activity, whereas the murder of the pastor´s cook seemed to have the effect of a badly dosed anesthesia. People knew that something horrific had happened, in the immediate neighborhood, up close. Everybody had known Grete Strutz, her jittery demeanor and her propensity to gossip. This Grete was now not more than a piece of meat, shredded by the pickaxe and eaten by the pigs. The half anesthesia allowed for all of this to get into the village´s consciousness, but it was not really recorded and incorporated. It was as if one would meet the horror and thought it happened to someone else. As if watching while a knife was sinking deeply into the naked thigh and feeling nothing. But the second murder within only a few days made it clear: That´s me! This is happening here! This is happening to me!

Now they too felt the pain and the panic.

Martha Riement had been knocked down with a poker. Then the murderer had used a kitchen knife to stab her forty times. All of the stabs to the back. Two of them went through her heart and had caused her death, the rest of them were superficial, so Martha would have likely survived them.

The mystery about Sonja had hinted at it, the murder of the pastor´s cook had confirmed it, and now it was a certainty: the perpetrator knew his way around the village. He had entered the narrow back door from the garden into the basement and from there to the apartment. Martha Riement seemed to have surprised him in the hallway. When she had turned around to run away she had been hit with the poker. The murderer left the house the same way he had entered it. This time he did not leave a bloodstained coat. Although the tragedy had happened between nine and eleven o´clock, nobody had noticed anything. Two witnesses had seen a yellow car, a vehicle which did not belong to the village. They could not describe the driver and they had not paid attention to the number plates. This was contradicting the assumption that the culprit was from around here. Yet, the unknown car did not necessarily have a connection with the murder.

Again Dr. Terrazzo was one of the first at the scene of the crime. It was mere coincidence that he was in the village and not on some faraway farm. He was about to step into his car when the officers from the closest station, siren blaring and with flashing lights, stopped their patrol car next to him.

"Good you´re here", the co-driver said through the open window. "A murder attempt. Number 22, Riement."

The doctor arrived only seconds after the police at Franz´ house. Then they stood around the blood-soaked corpse.

"This is not a murder attempt", Terrazzo said in a low voice. "She is dead".

His friend sat in the kitchen, shoulders slumped forward, his chin on his chest. He was looking intently at the patterned linoleum floor. The doctor placed his hand on his back.

Riement did not look up. He said: "You know the worst part of it? I am paralyzed with horror but I don´t feel grief. I feel terribly guilty. I think if I had still loved her it would not have occurred."

"It would have happened", Terrazzo said. "Whoever did this is ruthless."

Suddenly the teacher covered his face with his hands. He was shaken by convulsions.

"My God!" he sobbed. "Yesterday she asked me to lock the basement door and I forgot about it. First Sonja, then Strutz, and I forgot nevertheless. She thought about it and I did not! You know what this means? I killed her! I sat at school without thinking about what could happen and at that same time I killed her with my absentmindedness. I will never ever get rid of this, not in my entire life!"

"We have advised all the villagers", said the younger officer.

He was about as shaken as Riement himself. "But who would think it can happen in broad daylight?" And then: "This time we will catch this pig."

Late at night the chief detective paid Terrazzo a visit. He looked more gaunt than the first time.

"We are doing what we can, doctor. And we will catch him. But if someone kills seemingly without a motive or because he enjoys it and there are no witnesses, this may take a long time. A lot can happen during that time.

Think hard! You are an expert and you know the people. A doctor gets to know about things that others don´t. Around here, everyone is your patient. Go through all of them, one by one."

Terrazzo was tired and exhausted.

"I will do that", he promised.

45

He awoke because of the burning pain in his chest. Why was that? He slowly turned his head and sat up, startled, when he saw the blood on the blanket and the bed sheet. The movement increased the pain.
At the same time he felt that there was something wrong with his right hand. Thumb and index finger were as if glued together. He held up his hand in front of his eyes and saw that his sensation had been correct. The two fingers were indeed sticking together. They held a razorblade, and the glue was blood. Was he dreaming? Not this time, for a change. It was his own room with that rip in the wallpaper where the fireplace meets the wall, with that view upon still-naked treetops and part of the neighboring barn roof. Morning dawn. He was not dreaming. While asleep he had cut three parallel gashes across his breast. He ripped the two fingers apart and in a sudden panic shook his hand until the blade fell off and hit the ground with a dampened "pling". Suddenly, his agitation decreased. Anyway, what had happened? These things happen. Other people are sleepwalking or they jump up in the middle of the night and empty the fridge. He went to the bathroom and used the nail scissors to cut up the pajama shirt until only the chest section remained. He filled the tub with warm water and lay down. Red swirls danced away from the fabric and wound in intertwined streams. Soon he lay there in red-stained wetness and slowly, not without some child-like pleasure, he loosened the sticky fabric. The cuts were not very deep, but they were gaping. He pulled individual cotton threads from his flesh. That swollen, red gaping brought him foggy memories. Too blurred to create clear images, but unsettling nevertheless. The more he looked at it, the more unsettling it became. Suddenly, he had the uncontrollable urge to do something about this gaping. He grabbed the shampoo and poured bluish gel into the open wounds. He poured until the wounds had been filled and erased. The pain sucked his

lips from his jaw and the skin from his face. The mask of pain imprinted itself on his face like a red-hot iron, but he did not move. He lay there, rigid as a piece of wood, the breast pushed out so that the water would not reach the gel. He lay there like this until his entire body started to shiver and shudder. Only now did he get up, stood on shaky legs and showered so hot that his skin turned red as a snapper. Then he put ointment on paper napkins and pressed them little by little onto the burning wounds and taped them with several strips of adhesive.

Cold anger swelled up in him. He had survived this attack. It was obvious they wanted to get rid of him, but this time they were wrong. He was not one of those who just take it. He would teach them, eventually. Something had happened in the village these days. Something unusual. There were never this many people around. Only during Church Day, but that was in autumn. He had talked about that with the detectives. Yes, now he remembered. Someone had stabbed the teacher's wife to death. She too had belonged to the traitors. But his burning wounds were proof that the other side had not surrendered at all. To the contrary: they attacked him in his own house, in his own bed, with his own hands. He stood for a moment, at a loss. *With his own hands* - what made him think like that? The blond girl, the old Strutz, the teacher's wife, there was a connection. Maria's face materialized in front of him. It was so much like real-life that he would have wanted to kiss it. But she didn't want to have anything to do with him. That was okay. That was entirely fine. That was good. "It" grabbed him and had him throw himself face down onto the bed and, despite the pain, break into a seemingly never-ending laugh. He was startled by the tone but at the same time he thought it was so funny that his laughter turned into a giggle, which he couldn't stop. So he lay there, fresh blood oozing through the bandage, tears streaming from his eyes and he giggled until he lost his breath. He quietly wept for a long time. Maria! Maria. He loved her. He could not forgive her his love and neither

her betrayal. If they were hurting him in his sleep, he had the right to defend himself. He would defend himself. Again and again. Nobody was allowed to hurt him.

He slept until the alarm clock went off. The ring was too weak to really wake him up. It sounded in his dreams as a door bell, a telephone, a tea pot. Then it stopped. Only around ten he managed to get up and called in sick. Total mystery why his breast was hurting. He swallowed a few pills, that wouldn´t be a bad idea. After all, it was best to simply leave things alone. Perhaps there was a change of weather. People become more sensitive to the weather with advancing age. That is totally normal. Nice, he had a free day ahead. For a long time he had wanted to clean up. Particularly the bedroom. You spend more time in your bedroom than any other room. Nevertheless it is regarded as much less important than the kitchen or the living room. People are stupid. He would tackle the bedroom first. For example, the fringes at the narrow sides of the rug. They were all over the place, and too long as well. It was about time to trim them. He took a pair of scissors and cut them off close to the edge of the rug. Good, he thought. The shorter the better. This would be good enough for a while.

46

"Hello", Rüdiger said. "May I come in?"

"Come on in", said Adelheid Lassnig. "You are the young Winkelhofer."

"Yes", Rüdiger said and stepped into the kitchen as carefully as if its floor were particularly thin ice. He had been going around the farm until he was certain that Sonja's mother was by herself. She stood there in front of him, dough scraper in hand, and looked at him with friendly interest.

"You are friends with Sonja", she said. "She told me about you. You would rather prefer to return to the city."

"That was back then", he said and felt the rising heat in his face.

Sonja's mother put the dough scraper onto a floury board. She did it in a way which made the small movement appear to be something very serious.

"You are very good friends."

It was more like stating a fact than a question, but Rüdiger answered it, red-headed and nodding sharply.

Adelheid suddenly looked at him with more intensity. Still friendly, but with the instinctive caution of a mother.

"Sonja does not tell me everything. I myself taught her that. She can tell me anything, but she doesn't have to."

"You talk about her as if she could come through the door any moment now."

"She will come", she said.

The sun will come up, the next winter will bring frost, May will follow April. Sonja will come. He had not been able to stand it any longer. Either he would talk to someone about the images in his head or he would hit this head against a wall. Sonja loved her mother. "She listens with ears and eyes. She smells what you mean." She had laughed while saying that.

"A few words are enough with her. Dad is nice, but you have to talk to him for hours. And when he says he got it, he still didn't get half of it all."

His parents didn't get it, really. Dad pushed a few coins into his hand and mom gave him a kiss on his forehead. They were balloons, nicely painted balloons. He didn't want to be close when they burst. At some time they would pop. He felt a dull sense of satisfaction.

"Are you in love with Sonja?"

It was her right to ask, but how could she?

"I love her." He heard his voice for the first time.

"I am sorry", she said. "That was stupid of me. You wouldn't have come here otherwise."

Adelheid was five feet and four inches tall and weighed just over a hundred pounds. She had delicate bones and the tough power and the will of ten field commanders. She had a sharp mind.

The young man was insecure and unhappy. He wanted to tell her something, otherwise he wouldn't be here. But it was something that was harder to tell than the fact that he had slept with her. He either was Adelheid's worst enemy or her best ally. She brought the piece of cloth from the drawer, where it was still lying between two sheets of paper.

"I received this. I didn't tell anyone about it."

She handed him the fabric and watched his face. He was an ally.

"I did see something", Rüdiger said with baited breath. "But it is impossible."

"What did you see?"

"You will not tell anyone?"

Adelheid took his hand and pulled him to the bench.

"Pardon me", Rüdiger said, relieved. "Stupid. Stupid of me." Suddenly, he felt much trust and much relief. They talked for a long time.

When he left, the afternoon sun was illuminating the house and the barn and the forest, fields, paths and colors. The village had changed. Rüdiger did not think of Sonja in the past tense anymore.

47

The gaunt detective visited Terrazzo again.

This time the doctor kept his position in mind. A colonel. He felt awkward to ask about it, but the colonel was not surprised. There really was not much that surprised him.

"Our experts agree with your theory. More or less. You know how experts are. They would rather bite off their own tongue before agreeing with someone completely. They prefer to state the exact same thing with different words."

He started to count off with his bony fingers.

"First: we are looking for a madman. Second: his madness is not obvious. He doesn´t stick out in everyday life. Third: he knows the village and the area very well. Therefore we assume that he is either from the village or from the area. Fourth: you are the doctor of these people."

Terrazzo was alone at home. Maria always left in the early afternoon. The woman taking care of the household was preparing dinner and returned to her own family at seven. He poured a cognac for the colonel.

"How do you proceed? You are certainly not relying only on me."

"We have several clues, but no specific trail. We´re left with the procedure of selection. Who can not have done it?"

"Alibis and so forth?"

"Alibis, among other things." The colonel grunted. "A whole lot of them. It will take days until they have all been verified. And there are still a lot of people left who don´t pretend to have one. It´s a village. But if you include the close surroundings, there are several hundred people who knew or could have known that the Riements have a direct access to the basement. And most likely there are a few people outside the village who know about it. As long as we do not have a specific clue, we are just running behind the madman. If he really is a madman. Well, he is certainly not normal. In the case of the cook, he was wearing boots size 10. Huber has the same size. His wife also makes use of them at times, like when she has to go to the stable quickly. Usually she wears size 8. It doesn´t matter much with rubber boots."

"At least we can discard all those with larger feet."

"A size 10 can squeeze into one, if necessary. And how many are there running around with size 11 or larger?"

"I heard something about a white Golf."

"When we heard it, it was still a yellow Opel", the colonel said dryly. "Apart from the fact that we don´t have the license number, there is nothing indicating it has anything to do with the murder. On the other hand, there´s nothing against this possibility. Of course we are working on it."

"Two women, three, if you include Sonja …"

"We are about to put together a new search party. This time with help from the federal corps and several dogs."

"Were there any indications with Martha that it was sexually motivated?"

"Nothing. The murderer entered, knocked her down and stabbed her. Then he seems to have used the bathroom. We found some blood stains on a towel. With the Strutz woman he wasn´t so meticulous. On the other hand, there´s no opportunity to wash up in the pig stable."

He emptied his glass, put it back and looked at the doctor with a somber expression.

"You are a smart man. I have high esteem for you, really. But it would be an overstatement to say that you have been terribly helpful. Nobody knows when this guy it going to strike again, and you are insisting on your professional principles."

"I am a doctor", Terrazzo said, annoyed. "I can´t send the police to my patients on the basis of speculations. On top of that, I surmise a mental illness for which they have never been tested."

"You just take your time", the colonel snarled. "No matter how many he kills until then, as long as your patients are left alone."

"If that's the way you want to see it", Terrazzo said coldly and stood up.

"I am sorry", the colonel conceded. "We are all rather nervous. I still think you can help us."

"You are right", the doctor said conciliatorily, but he did not sit down again. "I am nervous myself - and tired. I will do it as quickly as I can. But on my own terms, okay?"

"I have no choice", the officer replied and shook Terrazzo's hand. "Think about the fact that this madman doesn't need much of a motive to kill you as well. But if you give him a motive, it might be easier for him."

"I am a talented liar. He won't realize what I am after. If he is among my patients at all."

"Let's hope so", the colonel said when he left. It was not entirely clear what this hope referred to.

Terrazzo closed the door and went into the surgery. He looked at the computer with suspicion. He had never cared much about it. On the other hand … he sat on Maria's chair and turned on the computer. Now he needed to get to the patients' files. He found the program and clicked around for five minutes. Then he found it. Then the program crashed.

The doctor thought about this and took the telephone.

"I am sorry to bother you at this time", he said. "But I need to speak to your daughter."

Maria had apparently been waiting next to her mother. "Yes?"

"I need your help, Maria. Can I come and pick you up? Right now?"

"Just sound the horn."

No questions, no detailed explanations. He liked that.

Twenty minutes later she started the computer. To his astonishment the program had recorded the previous crash. He felt caught in the act. Maria continued without saying a word. She browsed the file, called up names, answered questions while he remembered each patient and searched for hints. Now and then, very rarely, he made a note. It took them four and a half hours. During a break Maria made coffee. He felt her presence to be pleasant. He was astonished. Until now he had seen her more as part of the equipment. Perhaps it was due to the starched white coat and the cap she wore at work. She wasn´t curious, but friendly and open. He had told her the basics of what this was about. She thought his approach was very reasonable.

"The famous list", he said laconically when they were done, pointing to a sparsely annotated piece of paper. "Six names. Before I pass it on I want to talk to the people. We´ll find some sort of excuse." He automatically said "we". "This is all way too thin. Less than a hint."

He didn´t show her the list and Maria did not try to catch a glimpse of it. Perhaps she should have acted with less reserve. He drove her back home and was pleasantly surprised when she briefly put her cheek next to his while parting. Quite spontaneously, he thought.

48

His fingers brushed over the book spines, row after row. He
didn´t want to read the titles anymore. There were too many
of them. He had absorbed every page like a drowning man but
his thirst had increased ever more. Now he could not make
use of the collected wisdom of dozens of cultures. Reality had
swept them away like wind dry leaves. All these artful thought
structures had collapsed, powerful, once solid voices had
turned into peeping little voices. This was due to a single
breakdown of reality, more terrible than anything he could
ever have thought of.
It had happened to both of them, but for Martha it would
remain her last experience. Her knifed body had not yet been
released. He imagined how she was lying in the refrigerator,
naked, covered with a sheet. There was probably a cardboard
sticker hanging from one of the rigid toes. Like a piece of
frozen meat at the supermarket. Name, date, no price though.
A dead person has no price anymore. Only the living can have
a price. And not only once. He thought about his own stations
where he could be bought. The motives were always low:
vanity, ambition, recognition. We don´t sell ourselves in one
piece. Slice after slice we sell our integrity until there is
nothing left other than an empty shell. He saw himself
standing in front of the class, hollow like a blown-out egg, but
outwardly with all the well-meaning, superior authority. It
hurt him even more to scan his pupils with this x-ray gaze.
Young people, already hurt by that ever-present corruption
which teaches us to give up all that is good in us in order to be
successful. At least there was still something good in them.
But how were things as far as he was concerned? Not worth
mentioning.
He took a bottle of brandy from the cupboard and skipped the
glass on purpose. To drink brandy from a bottle was another
humiliation he could inflict on himself. Deep inside he wished
his pupils could see him as he was sitting there, feet on the

table, head tilted backwards, the bottle pressed to his lips. What an image! A framed poster for every room, to be put up instead of the cross, or the photo of the president with his goofy smile. Look over here, dear teenagers! This is what will remain, if you dutifully observe whatever your teachers and parents are hammering into you. Particularly important, dear friends, is the tie in the photo. It shows you that you can be the worst pile of dirt as long as you are properly dressed. Also, good manners are essential for you to get ahead. You only drink brandy from a bottle in your own home. The same thing applies to hitting wife and children. But even if you should desist of such rough behavior, and even if you take care of your fingernails, you won´t get out of here much better. Even if handmade shoes and golfing were your worst habits, you wouldn´t look much better than this piece of crap in the photograph. You know why? Because you have sold yourself. Because you have discarded even your last little piece of soul at the bargain sale. And you can believe the following: there is nothing, absolutely nothing you can do to get back even the smallest morsel of this soul. The smartest and the holiest of books will not help you, the advice of the smartest and holiest of men will not help you, nothing will help you. Every help needs a small base from where it can develop, and you do not have it anymore. So, boys and girls, look at this piece of shit, do as he has done. I promise you, you are well prepared for it. You will make it! Say this to yourself, over and over again. You will make it. Me too! I am not that burnt out. I´m only tired. Moods, whims. One should not overestimate them. You should not give up on yourself, never. That´s a big sin. We have to believe. Why do we take ourselves so seriously, anyway? The big plan ... of course. We are specs of dust. But still, important. That´s the whole point of it. We are only too stupid to comprehend this. But there it is. This has been proven many times. It couldn´t be any other way. We are part of creation. So there is a creator. Why? It has to be that way. It is logical.

He would not give up. He would not go down. As horrible as all of this was, one had to see the positive side of it. Every end is a new beginning. He would start to live again, very slowly. He would forget. But humans need some sort of support. He put down the bottle, stood up and went to the shelf again without staggering. There it was, all of it, all the truths, thousands of truths before the one truth, the final one. His posture became firm and full of determination. He grabbed a book without looking and returned to his armchair. He didn´t notice the brandy anymore. He was fully absorbed reading aloud sentences with a soft voice. But soon his interest faded, he started flipping back and forth, went for a second and third book, read a sentence over here, a paragraph over there. In the end he put away the books, looked at the nightfall and felt for the bottle. He had lost more than he had thought.

49

The morning wind was wonderfully mild. Air, light and sun streamed through the open window. The concert of tits and finches in the trees turned the flowering fruit trees into fragrant banners of springtime. He jumped out of the bed and went to the bathroom, naked as he was, and was surprised that his feet didn´t touch the ground today. Nevertheless, in some inexplicable way everything seemed to be natural. He showered. He was floating under a waterfall in a shimmering white tub made from smooth marble and saw the deep-blue sky through the cascading curtain made from crystal. He returned to the room and dressed. A white linen shirt and a clear, light pair of pants. Linen shoes on his bare feet. He looked for a belt and found a beige leather belt with a red and blue zigzag pattern. He took it into his hands to thread it when the buckle of the belt turned into a gaping mouth with long, curving teeth. A forked tongue darted forward like a small harpoon. The body of the snake wound itself around his arm. With his scream, glass shattered and trickled to the floor as fine sand. While still in his scream he jumped back and tossed the animal away with all his force. It slapped against the wall in a long spiral, slid to the floor and disappeared into a hole which he had never noticed before.

His scream was the beginning of the snake invasion. They came from the walls and fell from the ceiling, grew out of the floor in all sizes and colors. Angry, highly aggressive snakes, which wriggled and jumped up like steel springs to grab him. He ran out of the room into an unknown stairwell. It wasn´t any better here. Snakes wherever he looked. Aggressive, attacking snakes. Screams of people who had also escaped from their rooms while being attacked by the animals, barely visible under the onslaught, staggering around like knots of worms. People turned to howling lumps which coiled and shimmered, thousands of lumps consisting of smooth bodies. He was the only one who could fight them off. The animals lounged towards him, but a mysterious command caused them to stop at the last moment and slide off his body. He jumped down the floors in panic without using the stairs. He knew he could not survive the fall, but he landed very gently. Ever more snakes. They grabbed his arms and legs, rained down on him. He ran out of the house. A stream of smooth bodies and flat, hissing heads followed him. He discovered a broad channel gleaming in the sunlight and jumped into it headfirst. The water would save him. But while jumping he realized his error. The channel was full with a flood of snakes as well. It wasn't water gleaming in the sun but the shiny scales of the enormous animals, some of them large enough to swallow a human. He dived right into them. Wildly moving patterns pushed into his clothing, his hair, his naked skin. Smooth, hard lips scanned him. He tried to reach the surface. Suddenly he fell into nothingness. A long, free fall through somber light. From up high he saw a bright room he was falling towards. Again he was aware of the fact that he would not survive the fall. Then he stood in the room and looked around. On a bed lay his wife. She wore black underwear. She was sleeping. Her mouth had opened. He remembered that she had a tendency to snore a little. On her lower lip sat a large yellow and black hornet. The insect was carefully cleaning its wings and tail where the tip of the sting was barely visible. Then it crawled over her small teeth onto the tongue and further into the open mouth. Carefully he bent over her and looked at the animal, which was building a nest inside the woman's throat. The hand of the sleeping woman lifted up and felt his sexual organ. He saw her arm. Inside sharply cut holes were fat maggots. At that moment he swung around and ran away. Without seeing it he knew that the hornet darted angrily out of her mouth and went after him. He ran along an upward sloping trail. His legs became heavy. The escape was getting terribly arduous. It took enormous effort just to lift the foot from the floor. His muscles were burning. Every step required as much effort as if he were walking through three feet of snow. For a while he crawled on his arms and legs, then he sank to the floor, completely exhausted.

In the next scene he found himself lying on his back, closely encased by millions of tons of rock. He didn't have one inch of wiggle room. The rock imprisoned him like a second skin. He would never leave this dark, heavy and imprisoning grave. Lie here forever, condemned to total paralysis, conscious of the tremendous weight on top of him. Immense fear gripped him. He could only roll his eyes from one side to the other, far past his temples. At this moment he feared for the first time to be mad. Then came the last of the snakes. A small white snake, more a worm than a snake. He felt it slide over his body, over his neck, chin and lips, he felt it enter the dark caverns of his head through the nose. It coiled up behind his eyeballs. It wanted to rest before it started its meal. He waited in the darkness and the pain and panic, unable to move a finger.

Maria could not stay quiet in her armchair. On her desk was
the Italian workbook, lesson 19, her old floral-patterned piggy
bank´s front legs keeping it from closing. Next to it was the
vocabulary book where she took down the endless rows of
foreign words using her meticulous small handwriting.
Whatever she wrote down herself stuck in her memory more
than anything she read. But today the trick was not working.
One minute she was writing, the next she was reading what
she had written and it was as if she was reading it for the first
time. She jumped up and walked the three steps to the mirror
to look at her face. A nice face. Evenly proportioned, smooth
skin. Nose and mouth neither too large nor too small. The
eyes behind the glasses were large, the gaze was still young
but already that of an adult. Could it be that the glasses were
too stern? When she took them off the clear lines blurred. She
felt that she changed, but she only saw it in fuzzy outlines.
She put on the glasses again.
He had noticed her! He had noticed her existence! It had been
on Friday. The list. Today was Sunday. She felt a gentle
glowing in her guts, which doubtlessly had to do with love.
She had never really known for sure how to recognize the big
love, the famous really big love. The gentle glow was *one*
clear indication at least. However, Maria´s busy mind still
didn´t grasp how one could discard - at least theoretically -
that there would follow an ever bigger love a few years after
the big love. But such details did not occupy her mind at this
time, only in passing. She walked up and down the room, sat
on the bed, sat at the table, parked in front of the mirror,
looked across green-black hills far away and wondered about
the question of all questions: how would it continue? And
when?
In such moments of faint-heartedness she asked: had there
been anything at all? Was there a spark? Am I just imagining
everything? But these were only a few moments. For now she

would have to wait, that was obvious. And this and that. She continued her stroll around the room, sparkling with plans, visions and bold designs.

In the house next door Hannes Müller was lying on the unmade bed, the sheet still stained with blood. He felt terrible. "It" was constantly giving him orders he didn´t understand. He felt like crying. He didn´t understand anything and nobody was explaining anything to him, but when he asked, or when he made a mistake, "it" punished him mercilessly. And he was not stubborn at all. On the contrary: he was willing and trying hard! But nobody was interested in that. A small misunderstanding, a slow movement and then … Desperate, he pressed his fists against his temples. Why did "it" do this? What had he done? It was somebody´s fault. Somebody who angered "it" so much that he had to suffer because of it. Maria. Why did he always think of Maria? He stared at the ceiling, at the many hidden faces, which were making grimaces at him and babbling along, and then he had a revelation. Suddenly he understood the connections! Suddenly he understood last night´s dream: Maria! It had been Maria! Maria was the tiny white snake eating behind his eyes! He went into the small workshop in his basement and took a hatchet from the shelf. The last time he had used it was to dig out the old rootstock. Tough and old elderberry roots. The blade was jagged by the stones. He put on protection glasses and waited until the corundum blade had reached its speed. Then he went to work, enveloped in a shower of sparks. Tools had to be serviced. A blunt axe is offensive. Tools need to be as sharp as razor blades. Again and again he checked the blade by pressing his thumb against it. He continued until small drops of blood oozed from the white line it left on his skin. Satisfied, he put the hatchet away and his thumb into his mouth.

Maria couldn´t stay put in her room any longer. There are moments in a woman´s life when she needs to talk to another woman or she will burst. There are women who need years to reach this point. Isabella, for example. Isabella had always confided in her. She went downstairs to call Isabella, the faithful one. Her parents sat in the kitchen and played cards. Every day they played a round of piquet. The loser had to do next day´s dishes. Because of this arrangement there had been a dishwasher for some time, but there were still pots and pans and silverware.

"Today she is completely crazy", the father said. "Running around like something stung her."

"Come on. She is in love."

"That´s what I meant. I´ll take all."

It was a tough game. Minutes later they heard their daughter coming down the stairs again. She stuck her head into the kitchen.

"I will be meeting with Isabella", she said. "Don´t wait for me for dinner."

"Be careful", the mother said. "This madman is still running around."

"It´s still daylight. And I won´t be by myself. Ciao!"

"Can´t leave her Italian alone", the father said.

"Game over."

The whirring grinding wheel, the taste of blood, the shiny blade had put him into an elated mood. He did not want to stop just yet. There was still a good selection of crowbars and woodcarving knives. He dealt with all of them, even the chisels. While working on the second chisel, the machine broke down.

NOT SUITABLE FOR CONTINUOUS OPERATION.

Red capital letters on a black sticker. Why hadn´t he noticed them sooner? He shrugged. It would recover, eventually, the machine. He only had to give it time and firmly believe it. Besides, he would not be needing it anymore for now. His thumb was cut up and bloodstained from testing so much. He went to get his first aid kit. While cutting off a broad Band-Aid "it" forced him to lift his gaze. From the shed´s window he saw the entrance of the neighboring house. The door opened and Maria stepped outside. He put the Band-Aid onto his thumb and gathered his fishing equipment from the locker. He put the hatchet into his belt. The long windbreaker covered the handle as well. You shouldn´t scare people. Particularly Maria, he should not scare her. At some point he would marry her anyway, but he had to defend himself against the snake behind his eyes. She would understand.

Maria was way too early. Isabella wouldn´t have time for her until six, now it was five o´clock. But she preferred to walk through the village in a zigzag. Anything but to stay locked up in her house. The winter-weary pastures had turned into green carpets within two or three days, some trees and almost all of the shrubs were putting out leaves and blossoms at a breathtaking pace. The intense yellow of the forsythias was glowing from the hedges like colored markings. Snowdrops, crocuses and spring snowflakes were crowding in the shadowy garden corners. Many neighbors were busy with their flowerbeds or were simply sitting outside, exchanging greetings, parts of conversations were flying around.

"Hello Maria!"

"How´s it going?"

"How is work?"

"Tell her I said hello."

"Good evening, Reverend."

"I really need that recipe. Tomorrow I will stop by for sure."

"Any news?"

"Yes, it´s terrible. You can´t sleep quietly anymore."

But despite the shock and agitation they had experienced they were already joking around, teasing each other and enjoying the sun. Springtime was stronger than fear.

Police was omnipresent in the village. Officers in uniforms and plainclothes were following clues and theories, one cruiser was patrolling slowly before stopping and waiting for half an hour. Showing presence, providing a sense of security. Some thought it was the sense of security of a child whistling in the dark forest. Discourage the perpetrator. Can you discourage a madman?

He put the fishing gear into the trunk and drove towards the access. He could not see Maria anymore but he would find her. He did not take the short route to the main street but took the long way around. Right, there she stood at the fence and chatted. He stopped next to her and lowered the window.

"Hi, Maria."

"Howdy."

She was almost singing it. She was so joyous today. "It" had taken total control and turned him into a totally normal man in his forties. Single, and therefore not really in great shape, thought the women, but still quite acceptable. Perhaps a bit bloated, rings under his eyes, a few spider veins - these guys drink too much. If none of them looked at them. It was about time he should get one again. Now was still time. But he couldn´t wait for too long. Strange that he still had not gotten one. After all, a reliable income, public official, pragmatic, a house. Of course they become somewhat particular after years of living by themselves. But the right one would change that in no time. All in all, not a bad match. Not good enough for Maria. Not yet. She´s looking for something better. She will see for herself how far she will get. She´s not that famous, either.

"I am going fishing", he said. "Want to come along?"

She had accompanied him several times, back then. She liked the river. She liked flowing water. Most people like it. Maria looked at her watch.

"I only have half an hour."

"That´s okay. It´s only three minutes. I´ll drive you back up."

"Okay."

She walked around the car and got inside. The neighbor at the fence waved.

Maria had an overflowing heart. So she chattered like a small child, cheerful and contented. He tried to smile and say a few words, but there was only one thought behind his forehead: there she sits, the small white snake, and this time I will defend myself!

They stood next to the street, a few yards from the entrance. About where Rosi had shown old Matte what she was made of. And it was about that episode. Lydia Kern, the Sheep Inn´s owner, listened while Matte kept on talking to her. He was irritated and annoyed. Behind his back they were making remarks and grinning. Matte the old fox was allowing a waitress to humiliate him in broad daylight.

"He was angry, he sure was. But he didn´t wash his hand, so at least he had something to sniff at …"

He had to react quickly. Lately too many things had gone wrong. He was lucky the madman was distracting people. But once they caught him, things would really start to get rolling. In the village they don´t forget things quickly. Particularly not if it is about getting even with one of the big ones. They are jealous and subservient, too. They do it but they don´t like it. When an opportunity arises …

Kern listened with one ear and faked interest. She was actually thinking about other things.

It was a large-scale conspiracy. He, who should be affected the most, did not even have the slightest suspicion. Lydia had learned a lot from him and proven to be extremely patient. She had been successful in that those who were willing to switch sides had come to her of their own free will, even though she was thought to be Matte´s ally. Nevertheless, not that much of an ally so as to make it appear futile to ask her …

It is a great art to achieve the same effect with many different interlocutors. The right mix between innuendo and winking and cleverness and honesty and promises of immediate and future advantages, without expressly creating a connection - her political masterpiece.

"You have to fire her", old Matte reached the obvious conclusion.

He still trusted her completely, at least as much as he trusted anyone else.

Most of her new followers would actually believe they had done things according to *his* wise suggestion. Matte might even agree to it to save face. Damage limitation. But *she* wouldn't make it easy for him. She wanted to deconstruct him piece by piece until he was at the point where he had put her father. Then he could rot while still alive, she didn't mind. She smiled at him and said: "Of course I'll fire Rosi, if that's what you want, but first I will need a new one. The place is too busy, I can't afford to not have a waitress for a single day."

Matte was content. Business before revenge. A few days didn't matter.

"Look around right away. Don't forget."

"I sure will."

He swung his walking stick for a greeting and wanted to leave. At that moment a car came rolling and stuttering, the engine sputtered a little more and then it died down completely. With a last tired swing it swerved into one of the parking spots in front of the Sheep's Inn and stood there.

"It's Müller", said Matte. "He won't get far with that bucket." Hannes and Maria got out. She was in a good mood, he was white with anger, or so it seemed to the Sheep's innkeeper.

"No fuel", he muttered. The old farmer giggled.

"If you want you can have a few liters from mine", the innkeeper offered. "It'll be enough to get to the gas station." Müller shook his head.

"I prefer to leave it here. It's a short distance to the water." His voice carried the tone of barely suppressed anger, which amused old Matte even more. If someone gets this upset about a mishap it's twice as funny. What a jackass!

"Never mind", he said with a snide voice. "This trash only contaminates the air anyway."

Müller gave him a mean look, quietly grabbed his equipment from the trunk, said "I'll get it tomorrow then" and trudged away. He only waved at Maria. She was in too good a mood to get angry about it.

"Come", the innkeeper said to her. "Let´s have a coffee."

They left Matte standing there.

He walked with great strides. The high boots made it difficult. Now "it" loosened the grip on him and left him to his disappointment, anger, and his hatred. So much hatred! Like a glowing mountain he was floating in the center of his ego, large and glowing dimly and menacingly, a destroying volcano, which did not blow at this very moment because of the whims of tectonic movements. Why not turn around and charge ahead? Clear things up?

He was now getting inside of himself and next to himself. At the same time. A completely startling sensation. An outgoing and incoming tide, inside and outside which was, again, only another inside. Borderland. I am borderland! "I am borderland!" he said aloud and laughed. Nobody heard him. There was the river up ahead. Somebody walked along the shore. He did not recognize him. There was still this hatred. Like a disintegrating army assembling again under the command of a great general he collected himself to form a unit. One hand went for the hatchet, which he was now holding hidden under his jacket. His gaze turned into colored glass with a violet shine around his eyes. The age-old shimmer of death. And somewhere deep down inside, the thin, lost voice asking for the exit and not getting an answer.

Robby was what is called a mongrel. Many races had left their paw´s imprint in his ancestral line. The result was a knee-high rover with long hair and incredibly smart eyes and an iron will to be his own master. For that reason he was either despised or respected, depending on the attitude. Speaking in general, there are three categories of dogs. One is that of faithful friends. They are bred and can be taught almost anything, except perhaps reading and writing. Humans praise their conformist behavior and good character, even though one excludes the other. A dog that is praised this way is lost for its own ancient tribe. Quite different are the independent, proud and cunning rovers. Humans have disparaging names for them and do not think highly of their character, a strong indication that they actually have one. These animals are extremely valuable for the conservation and development of the original dog existence. All the other dogs belong to the third category. They are tiny bags of hair pissing on the rug, sinking their sharp teeth into anyone´s ankle and are regarded to be the sweetest thing in the world by their female owners. Some of them are calf-sized, good-natured monsters whose stupidity is only surpassed by that of their keepers, who haul home half a pig on a daily basis in order to feed their sweethearts.
The dogs of this group are therefore quite uninteresting and useless and yet, they do not have a lesser right to life than any other being on Earth.
Robby kept an owner, pro forma. A kind of figurehead, who bought his brand, paid the vet and sighed at "his" dog´s occasional screw-ups. On the other hand, he had nothing to do with Robby´s education because Robby did not allow for him to be educated. He also took care of his food, basically. Just like old Matte (whom he couldn´t stand) Robby did his daily round. He knew exactly what kind of food was being served at which house, where it was worthwhile to stop by, who only gave away fat and tendons, and which nice lady sometimes

gave him an entire sausage, as long as *her* master wasn't
around. That evening Robby was trotting happily along the
river trail. There were trouts in the shallow waters, under the
stones at the shore. There were two or three cats with the
ability to catch one of them, now and then. Robby felt like
helping them out a little. See if the cats would appreciate it.
Robby lifted his lips as if he wanted to grin. Perhaps he did.
There was still no cat in sight. Other company was
approaching.
He knew the one who was approaching him well. A friendly
human. Always willing to share some of his food. Something
was different today with this human. It was him and it also
wasn't him. Robby couldn't make sense of it. Suddenly he
sensed the danger and his hair stood on end. But by then it
was too late.

Surfacing from a wild intoxication. Sudden fear. Looking around. Securing. Nobody had observed him. He ripped out tufts of grass and wiped the hatchet clean. He also cleaned the high boots with them. He could not get rid of the bloody stains on his jacket. It was a dark jacket, they weren´t too noticeable. And the light was fading, too. He would have gone home straight away, but "it" would not allow it. "It" forced him to follow the river in a long loop, with all of his gear. This way he returned to the village from an entirely different direction, tired and cut up by the alder branches through which he had pushed in order to stay invisible. He didn´t know what this was good for. Had not even known it while doing it.

He met an acquaintance (he could not remember his name). "Did you catch anything?" he asked. Not really with much interest. Just to say something. A chat while passing by.

"No", Hannes murmured. "Not one bite."

"Perhaps the weather."

"Perhaps."

He returned to his house, carelessly dropped the angling gear on the floor, took off his jacket and looked with surprise at the hatchet dangling from his belt. Since when did he take along a hatchet when going fishing?

Terrazzo got the call while he was forcing his car past narrow, badly-reinforced serpentines on his way to a remote mountain farmer. The road was poor, the driving was tough. He chose to stop.

"What are you saying?" he screamed into the radio. "Another victim? Not a human? Speak up, I can hardly hear you. How quickly I can get there? You are funny. I am a doctor, I have patients to attend to. What? Now you don't understand me. In the southern part, at the river road. Of course I know ... I'll do what I can."

If he postponed the house visit, he would save half an hour. At least. He looked up the steep road. Up there was a girl with a severe angina pectoris. People up here did not call the doctor for nothing. He accelerated and tried to take the incline with more speed.

When he stopped at the river it was dark. Several patrol cars and strong spotlights showed him the way. The colonel stood at the edge of an illuminated area. Officers with flashlights were searching the area.

"Took you a long time", the police officer said.

"I did hurry", Terrazzo replied curtly.

The other did not engage him.

"Have a look at this."

They took a few steps and stood in front of the mutilated body of a dog.

"That's Robby", Terrazzo said. "The most intelligent dog I've ever met."

The colonel didn't seem to be interested.

"Look over there", he said.

The perpetrator had chopped off the front and hind legs of the animal and put them on the ground so they formed a sign. An M or a W or an E, depending on how you looked at it.

Supposing it was indeed a letter and not a primitive sketch.

"What is your conclusion?" the doctor asked after a while.

"This is the first time this will be making the news. Nevertheless, we think it is the same perpetrator. Two homicidal madmen would be a bit much."

"Do you think this sign could be initials?"

"Quite possible. But it could also be some stylized lightning bolt or two mountain peaks. We will dig out a specialist who can tell us more about it. This doesn´t mean that this may be helpful."

"Doesn´t sound much like you appreciate specialists."

The colonel took on an owlish expression.

"We need them. Sometimes they are strenuous. Basically, these people tell you too much rather than too little. The more they know about their field, the more talkative they are. Only you yourself are an exception."

"I don´t understand much about mental disorders. But I think the perpetrator is becoming increasingly more dangerous. There are cases which stay on a level for a long time. Others develop with quick leaps. These explosions of violence are coming faster every time."

"Not very encouraging."

"Looks like it. At any rate, you can reduce the circle of suspects. Everybody who didn´t like Robby is excluded. The dog would not have let them get close enough."

"Perhaps he was lured", the colonel said with a skeptical look.

"Not Robby. He would have never fallen for something like this."

The colonel took down a note.

"You know quite a bit about dog psychology", he mumbled.

"We didn´t find a weapon. He must have used a hatchet or an axe. Every household in the countryside has at least two of those."

"Did nobody notice anything?"

"We are trying to find out. It all takes time. And it looks like time is running out."

He looked at Terrazzo with a quizzical expression. The doctor sighed and pulled a piece of paper from his breast pocket.

"I wanted to check it first. What I am doing is totally against the rules."

"This here too", the colonel said. "This here really is against them, too. Thank you."

Thursday was Rosi´s day off. They were cruising aimlessly, both happy to leave the village behind for a few hours. They had lunch at a well-known restaurant and then strolled along a mountain trail which offered always novel and breathtaking images at every turn, not made for humankind. Too beautiful, too deeply embedded in itself. Indifferent to the fleeting steps of its inhabitants. This most likely was true for all places, but to the Greek it was so obvious here that he wondered why nobody else noticed.

They talked about love. Then they laid down on a sunny clearing, holding hands and kept silent. Rosi was radiating with happiness. Not just a saying. In the past days she had acquired a beauty which had nothing to do with long legs, sensual lips, racy curves. It was the beauty of a strong, loving heart combined with a strong, contented character which enveloped her like an aura, more precious than the most exquisite jewelry. For Rosi these were perfect days.

Padoponos, however, was wavering between his happiness and his task, between knowing and sensing, joy and sorrow. He thought about the organization. He was lying there, her hand in his, and stared at the sky, saw past the friendly blue into distant black worlds.

Infinitely far, infinitely close. A difference?

The organization. They were murderers. At times he let the phrase drip over his lips so it burned like hot acid. "I am a murderer." It was so. They were an organization of murderers. They murdered while serving justice. Serving justice, not a national set of laws. They murdered those who had gotten away. Those whom Justitia, with balance and sword in hand, had skipped, blind as she is. Those who didn't have to worry about a trial. There are many executioners and torturers who are free and out there. Those old war criminals who have been living a bourgeois life for over half a century and who believe they are untouchable. There are the new war criminals and the new state terrorists. They are all over the world. Their numbers increase day by day and because of political and economic reasons many of them are never persecuted, some are honored and respected. Politics, particularly foreign policy, is among the dirtiest and most disgusting businesses of mankind. Because politicians find reasons for anything if there is a palpable interest backing it, they shake hands during state visits with people who are far from the integrity of a worm.

Padoponos let images of heads of state parade before his imagination, people whose hands were soaked with more blood than those of all the "civilian" murderers of their countries together. But those who still held power let them alone. Too involved, too many obstacles, too much publicity. There are plenty of others. Criminals, torturers and terrorists, retired. People who thought they could change their past like a dirty shirt. People who are upset when the past catches up with them. Now, after such a long time! But time does not heal wounds as long as the perpetrators are not brought to justice. They did not commit the mistake to let the small ones get away just because you could not get to the big ones. The small wheels inside the bloody machinery of terror are not one bit better than the big ones. There would be no big ones without the small ones. None of the torturers and murderers can get away by using duty and orders as excuses. There is only one duty of importance and that is not to torture or to kill. Nothing and nobody has the right to dismiss this duty, no state, no community, no religion, no idea. Only the idea of justice. So, was it an exception, after all?

They themselves were killers. They themselves committed injustices. They did so with full knowledge of the fact. They committed injustice to avenge much bigger injustice. Those who turn away from the much bigger injustice and keep quiet about it are not any better. To the contrary. They are cowards, too.

It was correct and yet there was something wrong. It remained being a contradiction. With each new day, with every new assignment, it became more intense. In some way they were acting against their own principles and justified it by referring to a higher goal. All ideologists have done this, from the witch burners to the genocidal maniacs. It is so convenient to blame the superior realm with zeal and scorn. In the end it is all about power. The power of the dictator, the power of the Church, the Army, the Party, the Company, the Small Elite Group. The Organization did not care about that. That was the difference. He was clinging to that difference.

Padoponos had killed several men. With his own hands and without regret.

They were chasing old and new criminals without caring about borders and jurisdictions. They had allies at the archives of which many justice departments have no knowledge. They had people inside these justice departments. There are people all over the world to whom justice means something, and it can't be chattered away. Presumably the Ancient Romans were the first to develop this powerful and pure sense of justice. The sense for justice itself, not only as a mechanism to unite opposing interests, damage limitation or psychology, but an original value. Something sufficient unto itself and which could do without the scientific justification of sociologists. That was, after all, correct!

They had supercomputers with access to the data of organizations and entities all over the world. Illegal, but highly efficient. Some of the chiefs of intelligence agencies would have given the right hand of their best buddy to join the network. And those of second-class people, of course. The sharp tongue of their wives, too, as an encore. But they did not let themselves be used, they used.

Padoponos and a handful of other people were the advance guard in their battle. He did not know any of the others. They always worked alone. They were given assignments which had been uncovered by experts in research and analysis. From that moment on they were free to do what they wanted. If there was anything else to check, they checked. If there was a doubt, as little as it might be, they desisted from the assignment. It would not be followed any further unless new information came up.

"I am a murderer." A killer. At the same time a highly sensitive medium. His strong sense for the charisma of landscapes, objects, animals and people provided him with the power he needed. A just murderer requires much more power than a scumbag who, out of pure sadism or stupid pigheadedness, cuts up women, children and men while alive. Stupidity is humanity's worst enemy. Even highly intelligent people can be profoundly stupid. Some of the most abhorrent beasts have been highly intelligent, educated and cultured. It doesn't keep them from being disgusting beasts. Masked beasts. Your best friend? You yourself? *Me myself?*

His thoughts drifted away. He should not allow this to happen. He had a task to fulfill and he had met Rosi. From one second to the next he had realized that she meant more to him than anything else. Perhaps even more than justice. This was a shock he had to deal with. And he was out hunting …

In this meaningless village, in this unimportant region, his destiny might come to him. He saw the forested mountain of his vision and remembered the forested mountain which ascended from forested hills behind the village. It was one and the same image. Things had happened here and things were happening which went much further than his specific assignment. The disappeared girl had to do with it. But he only sensed the connections, he did not recognize them. He only knew: it was about time. Soon, he would kill.

Padoponos was a master of his trade and he was in no hurry. He should never be in a hurry. There was too much at stake. Human lives. Any and all of the doubts had been dismissed. The right moment was the only thing that mattered. In this village, a circle would come around and close, after almost fifty years. Could it be that the timing of the murders of two women was coincidental? He knew that *his* killer was not the killer of the pastor´s cook. He knew because he had observed him. Furthermore, no reasonable person would connect crimes which had been committed hundreds of miles away and over fifty years ago with the deeds of recent days. There were no co-perpetrators. There could not be. And yet, there was a connection. It was this place from which Evil spread out, back then as today. It was in the air. He sensed it, like powerful, intertwined fields of energy. He sensed it on his treks, in his visions, he had met it at the inn on the day Grete Strutz had been killed. Back then, had he seen the murderer? Could he have avoided something from happening? The rules were ruthless. An assignment was an assignment. He did not concern himself with anything beyond that. A long and cruel story wanted to come to a close. He was chosen to put an end to it and he would do that.

The trail had gone cold for decades, then suddenly it had heated up and led to the target. The captain had almost succeeded in erasing his trail forever. Nothing is as final as your own death. But there was this note inside an old document.

"Presumably death by automobile accident."

For a bureaucrat this was not typical wording. The doubt about this note was partially due to the timing of the accident. The front had moved up close and the information was not coming through that much. There were other concerns than to check out some mysterious car crash. Nevertheless, the wording had had a crucial significance. It suggested that unusual circumstances had been present. The man who had written down the phrase must have had information which caused him to write "presumably". And the things they knew about the other man the note referred to - back then a mere phantom for all of them - caused them to react with much sensitivity to the slightest inconsistency.

The organization had access to databases and files which no German judge had ever seen, even half a century after the war. They managed to find the official who had written the note.

But they only found his grave.

They were not going to give up. If the wanted person had not been the victim of a car crash, where would he have gone? Again the experts behind the screens were at it. After several failures the news came: identification very likely to be positive. The wanted person lives in …

But this was getting ahead too much. The story of their hunt had begun earlier.

60

The camp named "Friendship" had floated for a long time through the data streams, like a bloodless ghost. One hint over here, a note over there, always in relation to the movement of captives. As far as they knew, none of those few whose names they knew had ever appeared again.

The ball got rolling only after a dying person made a statement. He had carried the burden of his conscience all his life, he did not want to take it with him into death without telling someone. When the end came near, he called a prosecutor to his bedside and told him everything he had seen, heard about and done during five years of "Friendship". The prosecutor was very pale when he left hours later. Three days later his witness was dead. There was a huge number of grisly details and a list of names, nothing else. Heilmann, the prosecutor's name, was not fooling himself concerning the value of his tape. He was convinced that the confession was genuine. But what kind of court would make a conviction based entirely on the statement of a dead person? However, he tried to locate at least one of the alleged perpetrators. In vain. Against the will of his superior, who wanted the case to be left alone, Heilmann sent his files to an organization for historical studies. It did not cause much of a stir over there. Too thin, unverifiable. One staffer, however, was alarmed. The next day, a copy of the tape was sent to the contact person at the organization. Secret files, independent of state control, got moving. Eight names. Eight men. Eight criminals. Four of them had died during the war. Two were missing, one had died during the 50's. The last one remained, the most important one.

"Presumably death by automobile accident."

He would almost have gotten away. He had gotten away for too long. But now he felt the hunter breathing down his neck. No. He should have felt it. But half a century of safety had erased the fear of the past. The old man hated Padoponos because of other, more immediate reasons.

The Greek gently squeezed Rosi´s fingers. She returned the squeeze. They should just drive away. Pick a direction and drive. To return to the village required more willpower than he had ever been required to muster.

Soon it was time.

61

Riement´s library, "Quotes of the Wise Endares", Segments
from Regressions:

*The three of them sat in the shadow of an oak of unknowable
age. It was still wearing a dense leaf cover and grew year
after year, although extremely slowly. The two girls, Devva´s
face marked by tears like soft strokes with a soft brush, were
reclining in the grass. The old man sat on a chair of living
branches. The oak was his and he was of the oak and they
both belonged to each other. He spoke quietly, but when he
spoke, a spell dampened the voices of the birds and insects
and leaves and streams.*

"Mourn, Devva", he said. "Your mourning pacifies. Our
thoughts are images, childish and necessary. Wisdom and
mourning and love do not require many words. We view
them."

"Evil is a black star", he said, "an eternal demon, a dark
fountain which flows at times, but you can never see it. These
too are images. In reality, evil is none of this, but it is there.
We need images to give it a name. We see images of Evil and
images of Good. We do not see the faraway spot where both
of them are one. There is only one entrance, leading to the
realm of Good as well as into the realm of Evil. The demon
guides some of them into the darkness, others into the light.
There is only one demon. Only the people are different."

"There are places which are invisible gateways. Gateways
between many different worlds. Earth, Moon, stars are only
one layer of reality, one standing before us, firm and
unmoving. Only after you have passed through the gate, the
layer you are changing out of turns into a translucent cocoon.
But only for you. For those left behind it continues to exist,

impenetrable.
The gateways radiate and attract. For some, they signify hope, for others, danger. Nobody knows beforehand which world he will step into."
"Evil is alive and strong in such places", the wise man said. "It follows its own cycles. It sinks into the hearts of people. It is like the sun, which does not differentiate between field and rock. On a fertile field it makes the flowers grow. Those hearts which are inclined towards Evil bear fruits of evil. Nobody knows beforehand which hearts will open to Evil, which of them are sterile."

"People are gateways. The gateways are within us. There are places where they are opened up. Common, inconspicuous places."

"Time has direction. It can lose its direction. There are moments when you look into the past or the future, but you cannot tell them apart. Even worse: because you **move** in the past or the future! Time becomes the deepest secret. The rhythm of sun, moon, low and high tide, sowing and reaping, loses its validity. Time is secret inside secret. Everything simple dissolves. What looks smooth from afar turns out to be a labyrinth when up close. You can walk through it. You can walk through everything. It is an endless cosmos of spirit and energy, primal, ever-present power. We are part of it. Every good deed as well as every crime is born from this power and creates new patterns on the map of being and becoming. Indestructible, eternal patterns. However, they are not written into images but into the structure of the whole. As such, every clandestine murder becomes self-mutilation, every good thought contributes to the glory of the enormous unity, which does not condone or negate good and evil because it is good and evil and everything else."

Breathing heavily, he put away the book. Why had it happened? Is there an answer somewhere as to why? Everything questionable, everything unbelievable, everything idle talk! He poured schnapps into a glass of beer, half full, and drank with small sips.

62

A mild springtime evening. The farm buzzed with nervous activity. The crankshaft of the large tractor had broken. A small catastrophe at this time of the year. They had slaughtered four pigs the same day, which needed to be processed. Matte did not move a finger. Without saying a word, he watched his sons dealing with the problems. At least they were diligent workers. But what was it good for when they were not able to use their power? For years he had tried to teach them, in vain. No matter which job he had selected for them, they screwed up everything. They did it without enthusiasm, treated their honorary posts as a burdensome obligation. They did not get it! You don't become the president of an association because you are interested in the association, you become the president because it is a public office. As such it is insignificant, but the signal is important. You show your colors. You show that you are willing to take on responsibility in case you are asked for it. You show that you are doing something for your people. You can call them "my people". And while doing so, you get to handle people. Not his sons. All of the weight that he himself and his property could provide them with would be lost. They would be hard-working farmers for their entire lives, but others would grab the power which they were entitled to. Power is everywhere. Whoever relinquishes it will sooner or later be bothered by those who don't. The young one could make it. He had to take care of him more than before. He had shown potential.

A mild springtime evening. Matte took his cane and strolled along the main street before taking one of the forest trails. He had no idea that at precisely that time the Sheep Inn's keeper was being elected into a council, which automatically made her the village's number one. He had no idea that the past had come alive again. That every step he took signified grave danger.

Matte liked to stroll along the forest trails at this time of the year. Back then in the East, it had been the best time of the year, too. The awakening forest. However, a completely different forest. A lot more deciduous trees, a lot thinner and also much more extensive. It had been a nice time. During springtime he allowed himself to dream about it. To dream of "Friendship".

1943.

The camp lies hidden in the deep forest. The nearest village is an hour´s drive away, the access blocked by guards. Nobody will venture here by accident to stand in front of the ten foot high walls topped off with wire coils which were tightened with more wire. Insulators at the fastenings revealed their function. There are hardly a dozen people in the entire Reich who know about the existence and purpose of the small unit doing its job behind these walls. They are all experts, selected according to their excellent aptitude. Their aptitude is called sadism. Their victims are the stubborn ones from Europe, those who would not even break down in the torture chambers of the Gestapo. There are many among them who don´t have anything more to tell, but they want to be really certain of it. There is no hurry in this camp. Whatever can be learned in a hurry has been learned by the thugs. This camp was entirely dedicated to results. Nobody was quite sure who had given the name "Friendship" to this project. At any rate, it was consistent with the humor of these people. Whenever they let their humor run free they were the worst. Laughing torturers paint a picture of humans which leaves deeper injuries than any other.

Only thirty men were allowed to pass the gate. The outer guards and everybody in charge of external security had to stay outside.

The camp commander is the absolute ruler. He is still very young, a baby face, but already a captain and in charge of "Friendship". In 1942 he has big plans. But back then he is already very careful. The less people know about his special assignment, the better. Back home they have no idea what he is doing here. They think he is at the war front. They don´t even know in which unit he is serving. They are simple people who have enough work running the farm.

You could not say that he foresaw the defeat back then. Cautiousness is only one of his traits. He personally designed the cells for the "clients". They are small, padded holes with an iron grill as the floor. They are padded so nobody can smash his head against the wall. Suicide is a blessing. Blessings are not offered. The cells have an area of one square yard. Ten feet over the floor is a second iron grill. This is the exit. There are 128 of these holes. A single-pitch roof protects them against the rain. That´s all the protection they need. Whoever sits at the bottom hears the screams from block B, day and night. That too is on purpose. To listen to the screams of the tortured without end is torture by itself. They call block B the "health resort". Whoever is brought to the health resort will never return to his cell. They treat him until he has said everything or until they are certain that he has nothing more to say. Whatever is left of him is brought to the "disposal". The "disposal" is a truck doing one trip per day. His destination is an open coal pit. They throw the remains of the clients into the pits. Some of them are still alive. The long fall into the black shaft is not torture anymore, but relief. Once a week they dump a few tons of slag into the pit. People think the commander is overly cautious, but his orders are followed painstakingly. Up the ladder, people are extremely happy with him. He has quite a few liberties. He is also very innovative, continuously developing new techniques and trying them out himself. He does not spill much blood. His victims are weak enough, they are not supposed to die too soon. He takes his time. He knows that a specific pain can become an absolutely unbearable pain as hours go by. He notes the change in their screaming. He enjoys to experiment. He particularly enjoys experimenting with women. He is also a master at psychological torture. He makes his victims watch the torture of others. He makes them torture. He does things that an average SS or Gestapo thug would not have imagined in a hundred years. Yes, one could say that he knows what he is doing.

Sometimes, someone in the group cannot handle it. Only hardcore sadists get here, but even sadists sometimes reach their limits. Some idealists come here, too. Idealism and sadism can embrace each other from time to time. Sometimes there is a mistake in the selection process. Whoever can´t handle it finds himself in a special unit overnight. There he has permanent volunteer status. The commander would prefer to take the disposal into his own hands. But even he does not enjoy that much liberty.

"Friendship" is dissolved in 1944. The commander himself executes the remaining inmates and makes sure that the area is thoroughly torched and demolished. The only remaining traces are those of one of many unimportant camps. Other names will remain in the world´s memory.

Captain Körner has no illusions about the outcome of the war. He had been clever enough to cultivate contacts on all levels and he is always well-informed. And he is not stupid. His only chance is to erase every clue as thoroughly as possible. Behind the back of his men he manages to have them transferred to the heavily-fought eastern front. He himself goes to Munich to occupy a lowly position. That is entirely okay. It´s the wrong time for being ambitious in the Third Reich. Munich is the perfect base for his private Operation Return. He prepares it well and with much diligence. When the last days approach and the advance of the Allies is final, he acts. He takes a car and drives to a forested area outside of the city. Previously, he had picked up an acquaintance. While the car, corpse and uniform still glimmer in the forest, the civilian is already on his way south. There won´t be much of an investigation. It should be enough for a note proclaiming his death. They will uncover a lot, the winners, he is certain of that. So death just before the end of the war is bound to save you some trouble. Cautiousness is one of his traits.

He travels on foot, passing critical points at nighttime. He takes long detours if they minimize even just a small risk. Weeks later he reaches the family farm, exhausted but without being bothered. To the new lords of the land he presents his carefully concocted story of a simple soldier. After only a few weeks he enjoys having the best contacts yet again. With determination he works on his second career and the death of his father is not entirely unwelcome. Once the rebuilding process is underway, he is already one of the powerful people behind the scenes.

63

A mild springtime evening. Awakening forest. You can be a coward or not. Among the courageous ones, there are those who are too stupid to be cowards, a solid majority, and only a few who are too smart to be cowards. Matte was too smart. But when he had walked far enough and turned around and saw the stranger only three yards behind him, he was startled indeed.

The stranger stood there as if put there by an invisible hand. He was not particularly tall. His head was his most impressive feature. Matte still had good nerves. If the stranger wanted something from him, it had to do with Kare. He would not have anything to do with it, right from the start. He murmured a greeting and tried to walk past the man. But he was blocking his path. The forty years of accumulated importance overcame Matte. He hissed like an angry cat.

"Who the hell are you? What do you want from me?"

"Friendship", the stranger said.

The old man froze. This was impossible. After fifty years! No survivors, no traces, no proof. Everything blown up. It was impossible.

"What do you mean?"

"Friendship, captain Körner. A nice word. 1942 to 1944."

"I was on the Russian front back then. I don´t know what you are talking about."

"About the clients, captain. About the health resort and the disposal."

Somehow it had gotten out, despite all the precautions. But it could be no more than a suspicion, nothing conclusive. Had the pastor …? He knew how much Weilrich hated him, but he would have put his hand into into the fire that he would not break the seal of confession. Could it be that he was wrong this time? People had always been material for him, the ultimate material. He judged them with the same certainty as a master carpenter judged a piece of wood. He knew about people like nobody else. There was only one difference with a carpenter: the craftsman loved his material. Matte was incapable of loving people. He also did not love a dog, no flower, no painting, no song. The love of his life was having power over others. There needed not be many of them, but over those, he wanted to have power. The power over the inmates of the camp was among his favorite memories, because it had been limitless. Is there a more absolute power than the power to limitless cruelty?

There couldn't be any proof. If one of the comrades had survived, he would indict himself. Nobody was that stupid. And against the testimony of the cleric stood his own word. Weilrich would never make it through a trial. He would have to abandon his office and would be considered a renegade pastor who even betrays his seal of confession. Perfect prey for any lawyer. Deny everything and fire up the feelings for an old soldier who, like hundreds of thousands, had fulfilled his duty, nothing else. Now persecuted for it by some dubious people. There would have to be a Jew among them, one of these irreconcilable ones, who are like a red flag to a bull for those people who don't want to hear about the old stories anymore. Part of the press would be on his side and the rest would be leftish liberal rabble. In a catholic country, Jews and leftist liberals are still worse than the suspicion of torture and murder. And it had been that long ago … Old Matte had digested the initial shock and felt sure of himself.

"Either you are crazy", he said roughly, "or you are confusing me with someone else. I will go home now. And remember this: if you don't keep your fantasies to yourself, you will get into a lot of trouble."

"There will be no trouble", the stranger said.

"And you will not be going home, either."

The old man snorted and lifted his walking stick. "Nobody has ever stopped me from walking!"

He felt the hand on his upper arm, powerful and hard as steel. The stick slipped from his hand. At first, boiling anger welled up, but then, for the first time in a long time, he became afraid. He thought of Kare´s wrists.

"There will be no trial, either", the stranger said, as if he had read Matte´s thought from a moment ago. "The judgment has been delivered."

"You are crazy", the old man gasped. "That´s not the way it is done. Back then, maybe, but not today. I can only be judged after a fair trial. If you harm me, you are liable. You will be prosecuted for …"

He did not want to pronounce the word to not provide any momentum to the unthinkable.

The stranger did not pay attention. He looked around with a searching gaze and made his choice. A massive fir next to the trail. Without a word, he took his victim along. Dusk had advanced considerably. If the pressure of the steel fingers were to increase, Matte´s bones would break. Pride and arrogance, the elixir of his life, fell off like wilted leaves. What remained was a crying, trembling old man.

"I didn´t do anything", he whined. "I swear, I haven´t done anything!"

The Greek´s expression was somber, his eyes without luster. The collector of an old debt. Merciless, almost absent.

"By my honor!" Matte sobbed.

A short laugh and he felt being lifted up, pressed against the trunk. Something pointy hit his lower body and in that same moment his perception was reduced to a horrific pain burning in his intestines. He wanted to scream but there was no air left. The pain was so immense that he had barely enough air to breathe.

"Friendship", the voice below him said. Then silence. Nothing was distracting him now from the glowing devils burrowing and raging in his body.

64

Matte´s fight with death caused the Monday evening hours to swing, increased the eternal rhythm of horror which keeps the endless circle of cruelty at any hour and at many places of the world going. It did this almost exactly one turn of the Earth after Robby´s sad end.

During dawn of that same Monday Hannes Müller had awoken, bathed in a broth of sweat and blood. The weak bandages had been torn off the chest, the crusts had been shaved. Apathetically, he treated himself, even put in a few stitches with needle and thread. In those lonely years he had learned to deal with it, stitching on buttons. Fabric or skin, there was no difference. Indifferent, he sank back again.

In earlier times his nightmares had followed a script. Perhaps not a logical script, but nevertheless some sort of sequence of events which made sense. This had become rare. The structures were dissolving. Now, when sleep overcame him it was usually a plunge into shivering, screaming flesh, into unadulterated slaughter. Pure horror. Mountains of cut-off limbs, bleeding fragments, heads split open. His own limbs were part of it, his own blood, his torn skin, his muscles and tendons, his own head. All this had lost its meaning. The thing that remained now was a pure concentration of cruelty and murder and horror. Eyes stared at him and dissolved, faces fell apart into shapeless lumps, a mouth with a diseased set of teeth buried itself into his stomach, scraps of decomposed skin around his lips …

He crawled out of these dreams half dead. He was like a machine just before its collapse. Everything was rattling, small wheels lost their verticalness and bent under stress and started grinding, loose parts hit each other with a clacking sound, filigree pistons were grinding up, flywheels lost their axis. At any moment this machine could fall apart. But, miraculously, it affirmed itself time and time again. The dying machine turned into a human again. He was functioning in shorter and shorter intervals, between them he sat there and followed his thought, the sticky threads of madness. Seen from the outside, he was under control. He nodded to people who greeted him. He twisted his lips, like he had done before, when he smiled. But he rarely went out. For how long had he not been at the office? What office? What did he have to do with the office? He fell asleep again, doze off between dreams and waking states and the many dark worlds his defenseless mind was at the mercy of.

65

Bernd was strolling along the narrow band of asphalt which,
at two points, connected the old settlement shaped like a
horseshoe with the main street. He would have liked to gather
a bouquet of daisies, perhaps to give it to Rosi, in secret. But
every time he took a stem he felt the fear and the pain of the
plant and was incapable of harming it. He would not do it
even for Rosi. He was angry about himself. It was Monday
morning, ten thirty. Müller´s car stood at the entrance, so he
was home. Lately he was home a lot. Perhaps he had taken
vacation. Bernd walked past the unlocked gate of the garden.
He hesitated in front of the main door. Usually he went to
people to work for them, to bring them or to pick up
something. He didn´t come just for a visit or to talk. He
pressed the button and waited, shifting from one leg to the
other. It took a long time. Anybody else would have given up,
but time for him was very relative. With interest he looked at
the lawn and the large pile of leaves, still wet. He walked
around the car with the same mix of caution and curiosity as
in his days as a boy. Machines, small and large ones, were
among the deepest mysteries of the world for him. He had a
keen sense for everything alive, the artificial life of engines
confused him. He was always looking for their aura of
feelings and ideals that animals and plants revealed to him,
and he did not find them. Nevertheless, people talked to their
machines, insulted them when they acted up, praised them,
took care of them and often loved them more than father and
mother. Bernd was sad that he was the only one who was
excluded from this community. Sometimes when he felt
unobserved he would talk to a parked car or to one of the large
tractors, but he never got an answer. He bent over Müller´s car
and murmured: "How are you? You can talk to me, it´s me,
Bernd."
The car remained silent.
"I like cars", Bernd asserted and decided to commit a white

197

lie. "I often talk to you." But lying was not one of his strong sides. Müller put the car and Bernd out of their embarrassing situation. He stood at the door and said: "It´s you. What´s the matter?"

Bernd did not know why he had come here, then he remembered.

"Ask", he said. "About Sonja."

Müller looked tired. He was still wearing his pajamas, his hair stood on end, he was unshaven and had black shadows under his eyes.

"Sonja?" he asked, doubtful. Bernd felt his confusion and strengthened himself with it.

"Sonja Lassnig. The daughter of the Lassnig farm."

"Oh yes", Müller said, still not convinced. "What about her?"

Bernd spoke with that tone that some people put on when they talked to him.

"Sonja from the Lassnig farm", he said, very slowly and very clearly. "The Sonja who disappeared."

Müller´s face twitched as if he was in pain. Something like toothache, Bernd thought.

"Come in", the other one said, turned around and went into the house. Bernd followed him. The living room offered a curious sight. There were ripped up floorboards, one wall had been completely cleared and the furniture was piled up in one corner. An empty rocking chair stood in front of the empty wall. Müller sat down in it.

"Get yourself an armchair", he said and looked at the wall.

"A nice fellow", Bernd thought. "A good friend."

He looked for a chair. He was hardly impressed with the mess. He was so occupied with his thoughts that he barely noticed it. But he did notice that the armchair was unusually low and wobbly.

"That´s a strange armchair", he laughed. "Its legs are too short."

"Yes. Müller laughed as well. "They grow too fast. I don´t feel like trimming them every other week, so I was generous."

"I didn´t know that, that you have to trim the legs of armchairs", Bernd said, astounded. He felt the sincerity of his friend. He wasn´t kidding him. He was serious. He felt something else keeping itself in the background, something lying in wait.

"What´s with the wall, Hannes?", he asked. "You´re looking at it like this."

"It´s a good wall, a very good wall."

Bernd checked it with a long, pensive look.

"Yes", he agreed. "A good wall."

For a while both of them looked silently at the wall.

It was Bernd who picked up the conversation.

"I saw you in the forest. You took a club. Do you have any news about Sonja? I would like to tell Mrs. Lassnig. She is nice."

It was a speech that he rarely managed to put together. He was filled with warm and pleasant pride. Patiently he waited for an answer.

"You have to be careful", Hannes whispered after a while, "you have to be careful that they don´t betray you as well. When they betray you, 'it' hurts you."

"Yes", Bernd said with seriousness.

"I can´t remember", Müller continued with a normal voice, "that I was in the forest. I have become forgetful. The last time I was fishing." Suddenly he got up. "Come with me."

He went to the anteroom, where a narrow staircase led to the basement. Obediently, Bernd trotted behind him.

"I don´t know if you know my workshop. I am carving a cradle."

Bernd bent over the table. Müller stood behind him with a crowbar in his hand, which he had reshaped into a pointed tool. He raised his arm.

"That is nice", Bernd said and touched the carved wood. "That´s very nice."

Müller stood there, frozen like a statue, his eyes firmly on Bernd´s neck while his lips took on a life of their own. With extreme force, as if against enormous resistance, they retreated from the teeth, bared the jawbone and snapped back together, starting the game anew.

"Very nice", Bernd said.

The pointy crowbar slipped out of Müller´s hand and pierced the floorboard. None of the men took notice.

"I have a bottle of wine", the host said calmly.

"If you want to, we´ll have a glass."

"Wine? Great. Wine is very nice."

They went upstairs again and moved low armchairs to a table whose legs had also grown too quickly. Müller opened a large bottle of white wine and poured two glasses.

"Cheers!"

They put the glasses together and drank. Bernd was very satisfied. Not only had he simply stopped by for a visit in order to talk - meaning, not to work, not to pick up or bring something - he had been shown a cradle and been invited for a drink. Wine, on top of that. And now they sat at the table, relaxed, totally cool, sipped wine and chatted. Actually, they had not exchanged any more words. But Bernd was determined to turn this great visit into a complete success. He said: "It´s nice to visit friends."

Müller took his time before answering. He was still staring at the wall, although his current position was not suitable to do so. He took *too much* time with his answer. He endangered the recently established chat. Well, if you sit together like this you are allowed to repeat yourself.

"It´s nice to visit friends."

Bernd still thought the phrase was first class.

"Why?" Müller asked after another pause.

This question astonished Bernd, but he did great to get out of this one.

"Well", he said. "It´s simply nice."

"Yes", his friend agreed now. "You are right."

They drank another glass. Bernd, with all his contentedness, realized that the success of such a visit, with talking, looking

200

at things and drinking wine, also included a satisfying departure. Hannes did not help him. He sat there, totally in love with his wall. Sometimes he smiled and had a sip. That was it. Bernd thought hard how to do it. Finally he found the appropriate expression.

"It´s nice to visit friends", he sent along, as it shouldn´t appear that he was only leaving because the conversation had died down. Müller nodded. "But", Bernd added with elegance, "you´re not supposed to stay too long."

He drank the glass in one gulp, stood up laughing happily and left the house. Only a hundred yards away his joy was dampened. There he was, enjoying a perfect visit with talking, looking, drinking wine and departure, and then he forgot to say good-bye. He had not even thanked him for the wine. Nevertheless, the positive aspects prevailed. Besides, Hannes had not even noticed it. He had been strange, he thought. Well, why not? All in all it had been a very nice, very successful visit. Hours later he realized that he had not gotten ahead with his mission. He had not found out anything new about Sonja. Nothing nice for the Lassnig farmer.

"I´ll have to go there again", he thought.

But deep inside he had a different opinion. The memory of this excellent visit was way too valuable as to endanger it by repeating it. And Hannes had really been strange.

Pastor Weilrich´s newfound faith was not sweet any longer. It was a hard, bitter, thorny fruit. The more he talked about God´s love, the more threatening it seemed. Love as an iron rod, presented with an iron fist. Twisted and perverse love. For his entire life he had looked for ascension, had often chosen the steepest trails, had gone to the limits of his abilities and beyond them - now he had slipped and fallen head first into a large funnel.

"Fundamentalism. Intolerance. Hell´s neighbor. The Devil´s baton. Spawning ground of the new evil and the new hypocrisy."

Months ago he had written this with anger into his diary. He could not remember the reason for it. He remembered very little. He recycled page after page of his old life and turned it over to the fire. It was a self-mortification. How blind he had been! How arrogant. Deaf towards God´s warnings. He had to learn from it. Page after page he resurrected the fool. Full of doubt, perhaps full of desperation, too. Always comprehending, always smiling, always trying to forgive, always weak. What had he caused with this weakness! HIS will had to be established, with tenacity and ruthlessness, the herd had to be shepherded along the stoniest of paths. There is no easy way. There is only effort and sweat and tears. Everything else is deception and the devil´s trickery. He had learned his lesson. Now he had to guide the community with a gentle but firm hand towards the new direction. Not scare the horses. People want to be lead. He was ready.

There was a letter lying in front of him on the desk. A letter filled with monstrosities. Obscene, pornographic, immoral through and through. She seemed to enjoy picturing the sins they had committed. He almost began to argue with his new God for not saving him from this experience. Soon he would argue with him. Soon he would pretend his will to be HIS will, as they always do as soon as they get into that kind of groove. Most probably he would believe it, at least pretend to do so. All those who sacrifice their humanness to higher interests are pretending.

She wrote:

"I never thought I could write something like this. But you *loved* to sneak between my sinful legs. *You* moaned and groaned and stammered about my soft thighs. Even though you were not referring to the thighs, but the unspeakable between them, right?" Childish. She called him a disgusting hypocrite and liar. She wrote:

"All of this would be more bearable if you had not gone too far in your self-righteousness. If you hadn´t sacrificed me without a doubt in order to regain the mercy of your god. Never mind how I feel about it. On top of that: the worse I feel about myself, the better. After all, when I feel bad it emphasizes me being bad."

His head was dark red when he read the language of the gutter she directed at him. Then he became pale. She wrote:

"You extorted a promise from me. I should not speak about us. I do not feel bound by it. You should know this. Whenever I feel like sharing a particularly nasty experience I will tell it all. With your name and your address. I will only tell the truth, but without limitations."

She would talk! Expose him. This would not be allowed to happen. He had been too clumsy. He folded his hands and closed his eyes for several minutes. When he opened them again his decision was firm. First he had to calm her down, buy time. If she were to make her threat real later on, he would be prepared. Deny everything with a pardoning smile. There were no witnesses. She would fulfill her role rather well. The mature maid slipping from religious fervor to sexual delusion. In such cases the obvious victim is the priest who takes care of the soul. Nothing new, nothing unusual. But first, buy time. He wrote:

"Dear Monika, God bless you! I have read your letter with much comprehension and at the same time, much fear. There is so much desperation in it that I ask myself ..."

Occasionally, a smile went over his face while writing, one that the old Weilrich would not have liked. But the old Weilrich was dead. The new one would know how to defend himself. He closed the letter with the devout wish: May the Lord be with you!

He read it and was satisfied. The first steps had been taken, the game had begun. She would get what she deserved. The Reverend was certain about that.

67

Tuesday morning.

Maria got up earlier than usual. Her parents would be gone for three days. A meeting of former classmates, put off for years and now finally, against all expectations, coming together after all. The mother wore a bold new hat and blushed cheeks. She appeared so youthful that her husband kept looking at her with excitement and suspicion. Sometimes you actually can turn back time. She said, "I am not at all happy about leaving these days."

Maria laughed. "Dad has secured the house like a fortress and I will not let anyone in. Besides, Isabella can spend the night here."

"Strange name for the doctor", the father murmured and received a punishing look.

"You are impossible", the mother said. "Let´s go now."

They hugged their daughter with a much-repeated "Take good care of yourself" and departed.

The doctor´s practice was in full swing. No time for private gestures. But yesterday he had invited her for lunch. He ate at the Sheep´s Inn every day. He regarded the invitation as a way of thanking her for her nighttime assistance. He was actually looking forward to her company. He was worried. In a certain way he felt guilty for the police´s failure. He felt good talking about it. And about that poor dog. He had the same sympathy for the dog as for the other victims of the madman. She could not understand that. For Maria, a dog was a dog. He felt it and it didn´t surprise him. People who grow up in the countryside often have a more detached relationship with animals than city dwellers. Although they know them much better, they mostly regard them from an economical point of view. Whatever can´t be slaughtered and sold causes them to be suspicious. This way, countryside dogs are living alarm systems, or companions for hunting. They are rarely friends.

Around nine, Hannes stopped by. He didn´t want to wait, only a prescription for an ointment. You could get it anyway, but it was cheaper with a prescription.

"How did the fishing go?" she asked.

For many seconds he looked at her in astonishment before he realized what she was talking about.

"Awful. The water isn´t any good anymore. Too much fertilizer and other chemicals."

He said it with a low voice. The farmers don´t like to hear about it too much. She wrote the prescription, went to get the signature and put a seal on it. He thanked her, and while leaving, turned around again.

"Are you going to be at home in the afternoon? I have carved a cradle. I´d like to show you."

Maria laughed at the thought of a cradle.

"Of course", she said. "Just come on over."

Back then he had been a regular guest. Only during the last one or two years that had changed. Her mother was of the same opinion as all the rest of them. This guy needs a woman. She used to look at her from the side while saying so. But she only smiled in a friendly and indeterminate way.

68

Each morning the world is born anew. After the sun has risen about two or three hand´s width over the horizon there is nothing to be noticed anymore. The day world is old and common. But the time between the beginning of dusk until the moment when the young morning sun floods the damp forests and fields and trails with reddish light and blesses and baptizes it, in that time span the world is as new as on the first day. Time becomes an illusion and the mere joy of existence answers all of the questions humans come up with by making them irrelevant.

Martin, often called Tine, did not know how to express this feeling, but he had experienced and conserved it and that was a thousand times better. He was a farm hand. A simple man who worked hard. He had a wife and three children. He was not interested in either cars or the inn or card games. All his pleasure consisted of that time in the morning while he wandered to his workplace. He usually arrived before the other men, who were brought there by minivan. Sleep-deprived, taciturn and ill-tempered, they awaited another work day of an endless series of such days, which all started with the same bad taste in your mouth. Martin, however, started his days with a wide open heart and the unexpressed knowledge about the value of every hour.

The morning he found Matte´s body was like a golden veil which enveloped nature without creases while accompanying the movement of even the smallest insect. The air was a cool body with a scent, not fleeting, but enveloping and pertaining to all of it. Scents mixed and changed with every step. The fir and pine resin provided the basis which wormwood, sage, wild thyme and mint blended with.

Martin saw what was left of Matte long before he recognized it as human. He was walking along a gently ascending, straight section of the path at the end of which he noticed an enormous trunk with a dark hump. While getting closer the

hump turned into a bundle which someone had hung there, presumably on a broken-off branch. Still closer, he saw that there were shoes at the lower end of the bundle. An unwelcome presentiment turned into a solid suspicion. He ran the last steps. Carefully, he touched the man´s old and stiff hand. It felt like cold wax. A black pool had formed at the base of the tree. The hat of the dead had fallen into it. The tuft of the hat stuck in the coagulated blood like a brush in dried lacquer. Martin tried to lift the inclined torso of the man. It was very difficult. He recognized Matte and discovered the knife which had nailed the old man to the tree. It stuck deep in his lower body. On its handle was the twin angular rune which he deciphered as SS but about which he knew very little. Few know about the rays of the black star, and those who have experienced them prefer to either babble or to remain silent. Martin did not think about it. He only thought about the power which must have been behind the blow. Although Matte weighed less than 130 pounds, it was no small feat to lift him up two feet with one hand while hitting him so hard that the tip of the knife embedded itself deep into the tree trunk.
The power of madness. The madman, again!
There was nothing left of the morning´s gold when Martin ran towards the village with long steps and a hammering heart to notify them of the latest murder.

69

Nobody at the farm had given a thought about Matte's absence. It happened rather often that the old man would return home the following day, and pity those who even mentioned it. When notice of his death spread, they fluttered about like scared chicken. The old farmer's wife felt like being inside a sea of cotton. No pain, no grief, no fear. Whatever happened around her did not get through. Everything was dampened, colors, sounds, movements. She walked around, immersed in herself, listened, rarely spoke, and if she did it was apparently senseless gibberish. Nobody cared much, anyway. Thoughts arose in her lethargically and sank away the same way. "Fifty years married to him." "Fifty years the prime cow in the stable." "Not even fifty years. Missed the golden anniversary by a year." Lethargic. Immersed. Not unpleasant.

It could be summed up in one sentence what the others thought:

"What will happen to the farm?"

They were not interested in the why and how of Matte's death, with the exception of the youngest grandchild. He didn't feel sorrow for his grandfather, but he was taken by the image of an old man pinned to a tree. And, after all, it was *his* grandfather who had suffered it. The surly face of the boy was lighting up noticeably. He would have loved to see the old man hanging there, but he had long been removed and was the object of forensic investigation.

The news spread in the village like wildfire. It jumped from neighbor to neighbor, whoever was still inside was called outside. Telephones rang, agitation and sensation spread like bacteria on a festering wound. The village was a festering wound. A swarm of flies with press credentials ascended briefly and settled down again. The women murders and the incident with the dog had caused much tension, now a new quality had been added to it. Matte had been an *important* person. One from their nest, whose connections reached far beyond the nest, even the region. One of those who never had anything happen to them. And now it had happened! It´s just like it is with racing pilots. If some second or third rate pilot crashes to bits, the horror of the audience is quickly calmed down by the fact that these people really know what they are getting themselves into. The worse they are, the higher the risk. Only the accident of a *real* star causes *real* consternation. Death is not meant for real stars. They die in small light aircrafts and motorboats, but not in their very own cockpits. So is the case with the victims of crazy murderers. They have to be nobodies, people without a special status, simple folks - and not the president, not the head of state, not the secretary, not the number one in the village. And still, now it had happened! The creepiness was joined by sensationalism. It was so much easier, as Matte´s passing away had not caused any personal commotion or pain, not anywhere. Pain presupposes a minimum of love, and nobody had loved him, by God, not even a dog or a cat or a horse.

The innkeeper was annoyed and felt deprived of her triumph. "You could have lived just this one more day", she thought. "At least there was the note from the election council and Rosi can stay for as long as she wants to."

Pastor Weilrich, while not in danger anymore to dry up by turning into gneiss and granite, thought: "It is God´s will. He has punished the sinner. His mills grind slowly." He didn´t think about that afternoon stroll with the Greek anymore. He prepared for consoling conversations with the bereaved family, a large funeral, and a considerable donation.

An old fellow traveler thought: "So now it was your time before mine. But I don´t want to end up like you. But you also lived that way."

Dr. Terrazzo thought: "Two women, a dog, a man. This is pure hatred. If there is anything pure to this, it is the hatred of the person carrying it. And he carries it on the inside."

The news of Matte´s death had turned his waiting room into a busy debating club where everybody wanted to ventilate his opinion and memories and explanations at the same time. The edifying conversations about intestinal problems, ingrown toenails, colics, varicose veins and rheumatic articulations fizzled out and slowly came back to life after a few minutes. Maria enjoyed the sensation as much as everyone else. In some way the series of murders made all of them more important. The village had been mentioned in foreign newspapers by now, in countries where the name of the district town and even the state capital had only caused ignorant head shaking. The madman made something out of them. They were sitting at the pulse of things, knew the victims, most likely knew the murderer, even they themselves were in danger. Many of them therefore felt privileged and superior. They had something the neighbors didn´t have. And on top of it, it was dangerous. The victims of floods and hail storms also show - after an opportune time of detachment - a similar pride. Their flood had been the highest since ancient times, their hail had been as large as tennis balls. Together with a nod, laden with meaning and a mild contempt for those who had not been lucky enough to experience catastrophes of this magnitude. You can show off anything. From spitting further to peeing farther to hosting the craziest murderer. Showing off is the basis of sports. Showing off is meant to combat fear.

The doctor was shaken. Reluctantly, he had handed over the list to the colonel, and now it had happened again. What else did they have to go through? He expected the criminologists to pay him another visit and asked Maria to postpone house visits. There was only one case of importance which he wanted to check out before lunch.

"Do you feel like coming along?" he asked. "Today there´s roast pig on the menu. Not too healthy but very good."

Maria felt like it.

At the Sheep´s Inn, Matte´s murder was topic number one. Rosi seemed dejected, the innkeeper morose. Terrazzo thought about his list and said, "Too bad that Müller left right away. I would have liked to talk to him."

Maria didn´t understand and dismissed it.

"He will take care of the cuts he got while fishing. If it is urgent, I will tell him. He lives right next to us."

"Urgent? No, not that urgent ... or perhaps yes. Just tell him it´s because of the medicine. Do you know him quite well?"

Why did he ask? Was he jealous?

"I used to. Nowadays he prefers to do carvings", Maria said. "He wants to visit me today to show me his new project."

"Aha, he carves?" Terrazzo asked absentmindedly.

"All kinds of things. This time it´s a cradle. Kind of strange, a solitary man carving cradles, don´t you think?"

"Solitary men are, occasionally, able to do what they want", the doctor said. Maria didn´t think it was very charming. A police car drove by and he almost jumped up to ask for the colonel. However, it was common knowledge where he was around noon.

Was he interested in her or was he not? The way he acted today she might as well have been a bothersome chance acquaintance. He was worried about the madman, so what? What did this have to do with their relationship? She became quiet just like him, and when they parted after the meal she had the feeling he had hardly noticed her company. Angrily, she went home.

The shutters on the first floor were closed, the door was locked twice. When she entered the semi-darkness of the house an unpleasant tingling sensation displaced her anger. The sensationalism had vanished, what remained was the memory of three, actually four people who had become the victims of a brutal murderer in short succession. Suddenly she wished her parents would not have left. She was about to take a trip to the city when she remembered Hannes. He had wanted to stop by. With a sigh she went upstairs. Her room was bright and friendly, but the tingling sensation remained. So she flinched when the doorbell rang. She went downstairs and opened the door.

"Hello, Maria", said a familiar voice.

"Twenty, as usual?"

It was the egg lady. Maria accompanied her to the car and took her ration for the week. They chatted for a while over the fence. When she returned the front door stood ajar. She could not remember *not* having closed it. Immediately the tingling sensation returned. She took the eggs to the kitchen and left the door wide open, just in case. Then she looked into each room. Of course there was nobody inside. She was angry about herself.

"Hi, Maria", a voice said behind her. "The door is open so I just came inside."

She turned around.

"Oh, it´s you", she said, relieved. "Let´s go into the kitchen."

70

A pair of buzzards was flying high in circles in the cloudless sky. Only two dots, sometimes almost merged into one, then again clearly separated. Far below lay the green land. Flat areas where the seed ripened and mice hoarded, hilly, mountainous areas with forests and rocky outcroppings and old larches with extensive branches where the buzzard´s nests found support. Like old scars and fresh wounds the trails cut through the land, undergrowth grew in deforested areas if it wasn´t treated with chemicals, the young forest´s thicket hid the nests of small and fearful beings - food, in the buzzard´s language.

A depression between two peaks contained a small lake, shaped like a mangled oval. A chrysoprase of restrained shimmering green, fed by a brook which meandered with abrupt contortions through a marsh. One side of the lake was formed by a rock escarpment, on its other side was a small settlement, half a dozen small houses alongside a country road which turned into a trail behind the last shed. A vacation and weekend settlement, houses with thick window shutters in front of the windows. Large locks on the doors and dried leaves on small terraces. Next to the trail sat a girl on a rock and squinted into the sun. She had long, blond hair and wore a shrill-colored tracksuit.

Sonja felt as if waking up from a long sleep. She knew the settlement, one of the houses belonged to one of her aunts. At this time of the year only one or the other owner could be found here on Saturdays and Sundays. And not very often. She had no idea how she had gotten to this remote place. It was a trek of about four hours from the village. The last thing she remembered was a forest jog with foggy, rainy weather. Had she slipped? Hit her head? The phrase made her smile. She brushed her hand across her hair. Was there the remainder of a bump on her head? The weather was nice, the small lawns around the cabins were green. She couldn´t account for several days. They must have noticed her missing and searched for her. Not at the mountain settlement. If she had stumbled up here, perhaps with a concussion, then she had found the perfect hideaway.

Then Devva's gentle face in the silver mirror appeared in her memory. Devva! An extremely vivid dream. She had awoken from deep sleep.

Devva, shouting something at her while parting.

"Don't forget me", she called. "It is a dream, but don't forget me!" And she saw the Other World fade away, saw the White Land disappear in reddish fog until she felt the new Sun in her face and opened her eyes, blinking.

That was how it had been. This is how the dream had started. She had opened her eyes. She was lying on a bed of moss in the shadow of an oak. Only a few steps away, there was a spring burbling into a small pond whose one half was roofed by a tent composed of two enormous stone slabs.

A young woman put a cloth into the pond. She was wearing a long, white cape and had long, blond hair like Sonja. She stood up and smiled when she noticed Sonja looking at her.

"I just wanted to moisten your temples. You awoke quicker than I thought."

She sat next to the girl.

"My name is Devva. What's yours?"

Sonja replied, confused. "What happened? I have never seen this place."

"Don't be afraid", Devva said. "You are my guest. You can trust me."

Sonja was not afraid, only astonished. She thought Devva was quite beautiful. Her skin was speckless and light, her eyes brown. She did not wear shoes, which was strange at this time of the year, but it was not cold and the ground was dry although it had rained a lot during the past days. She wore narrow, golden bracelets on her wrists and ankles and a broad one on her neck. When she looked into Sonja's eyes her gaze was a little like she was staring into the distance. There are people who are always partly somewhere else. Not because they are impolite, but because a part of them is at home at some other place, no matter where they are.

"This is the White Land", Devva said and made a sweeping gesture. "The Other World. Did you ever hear about it?"

Sonja shook her head.

"Am I dead?" she asked carefully. But the image of a ghost or an angel or whatever she might be, wearing a pink tracksuit elicited a smile from her lips.

Devva smiled as well.

"Do you feel dead?"

"No idea. I´ve never been dead before."

"You are as fine as a fish in the water. Come, I want to show you my home."

Devva jumped up, took Sonja´s hand and pulled her up.

"Would you like to drink?"

"Yes", Sonja said. "I had been running."

Devva pulled a silver cup from her cloak, filled it at the well and stepped in front of Sonja.

"Drink", she said solemnly. "Drink from the Water of the Other World."

Sonja drank with much thirst. The water was cool and clear and almost without taste, yet it contained a hint of any taste imaginable within it.

"Come now", Devva said. "There is so much to see."

71

An extremely vivid dream. Sonja now remembered so clearly
that she could not tell the difference between real experiences.
What had she experienced and what not? She had to get home,
calm down the family. How long had she been absent? Absent
in both senses. She did not feel hungry. The aunt's house.
Most likely she had been cooking at the aunt's house. She
knew where the spare key was hidden. Almost everybody here
hid a spare key. Too often the keys in particular were
forgotten. This meant breaking into your own home or return,
taking the very steep road, which was in really bad shape. She
must have eaten at her aunt's house. There were supplies for
many months. The aunt was one of these people who felt
secure only when all of the shelves were bursting.
Notwithstanding the fact that she came here only for a few
days at a time. After all, you never knew …
But she had not the slightest memory of it. However, the
memory of the dream was pulsating, alive, *real*. It would have
been easy to unlock the aunt's house again and look for signs
of her presence, but something inside her resisted. Who knew
if she would indeed find signs. She was a very orderly person
by nature. When she got out of her bed she had done it a
moment later, when she used dishes she rinsed them
immediately. Most likely there were no signs. Certainly not.
She did not want to know. Sonja stood up and left the
settlement with the strange feeling that she would never return
to this place. In passing she glanced at her aunt's house. It
looked like all the others. Uninhabited, withdrawn into itself.
She had managed to keep her presence a secret. Perhaps she
wanted to hide? People do the strangest things after a head
injury.
The dream: forest. Wonderful forest. Loose, light, airy, leafy,
wavy forest. Enchanted and magical forest. The Other World
was the world of the forest and clearings, the world of the
flowers and brooks and rocks covered with moss. The world

of the circling buzzards, that were looking at many worlds from up high. Nobody can tell what they see. Nobody can speak for everyone. Not for humans and definitely not for buzzards.

Venerable old trees. Trees with strange names. Birch trees called Airos or Fleinsta, maple trees named Ekkel and Maruta, alder trees bowing to the sound of Kandire and Banene. Trees that held these names with honor long before the first human stepped into the Other World. Devva told stories from forgotten times. Stories of trees and trees, stories of trees and animals, stories of trees and people. Then she talks about people. "There are seven ways to see, to hear, to smell, to taste. Every human knows only one of them. It is the only one he can imagine, the others frighten him. This is where suspicion and fear come from. Trees speak one single language."

They wander along shadowy and sunlit paths winding through forests, pastures and hills, they accompany brooks for a while, crossing them on large rocks, they circumvent rock formations, they cross steep stairs with a few select steps. The wind is mild and pleasant, the light has a glassy clarity in contrast to the dreamy landscape. Roes and deer back up a little when they come along, but then they stay to observe the young women. The air is filled with the songs of countless birds and the humming of fat bumblebees. The forest smells of woods and resin and blooms. Just to take a breath is a joy. Devva's talk burbles like a brook, Sonja does not say much. She is taken by a deep sensation of contentedness with this world. Her initial curiosity is gone.

"This region has to be far away from home", she says at one time and receives the reply, "Further away than you can imagine. At the same time as close as each one is to itself." Devva often says things which are rather mysterious to Sonja. She hardly thinks about it. As little as she does about her own situation. Only once she asks: "Why am I here?" The answer: "You were in grave danger."

But things lose their importance in a dream, insignificant things become important and the other way around.

Can there be a dream that is so absolutely sharp, firm and real? Can there be Another World? Sonja was walking quickly and nimbly. She watched the vegetation and tried to estimate how much time she had spent at the mountain settlement or inside her dream. Two weeks, one month? But it could be many years. One spring in many years. She observed her mirror image in a pond. Not many years. Only weeks. Her parents would be terribly worried. She had thought of them. Not in the settlement. The settlement was as if erased. In the dream.

"My mother must be worried."

Devva thought about it. "Write a message", she decided.

"I will deliver it."

"I don´t have anything to write with."

Devva cut a piece of her white coat.

"Take this. Here is charcoal."

She hands Sonja the fabric and a piece of charcoal, which she picks up from the ground. It is difficult to write something readable with these materials but she succeeds nevertheless. Devva takes the note and says: "You just rest. I will be back soon."

She walked through the underbrush next to the trail and after a few moments disappeared from Sonja´s view.

Sonja remembered every word they had exchanged, every step she had taken. This really only happens in a dream. No waking memory is ever this attentive and strong. The closer she got to the village, the slower she walked. Without being able to say why she decided not to reveal her dream. She would tell about life in the settlement, the loss of her identity. She knew the clearing next to the path. Now she recognized everything and sat down on a tree stump. The upper third of the clearing had a few hazelnut shrubs and wild roses, which had escaped the chainsaws, a fortress covered with leaves, almost impenetrable because of the long thorned tendrils.

There, Rüdiger and herself had built their summer nest with a well-camouflaged entrance, some leaves and much open sky above them. When they heard a helicopter they did not move. Rüdiger said that you could see any movement from a helicopter. She thought of Rüdiger and felt great. Whatever had happened to her, it had changed her. She remembered the silver birch.

A clearing inside the loose forest. In the center of the clearing, the highest birch she has ever seen. Even from the smallest of its hanging branches blinks a dewdrop in all rainbow colors. The tree blinks like a giant jewel, only much more impressive because of the solemn dignity expressed by its age and size. Devva felt happy about the sensations which were mirrored on her friend´s face.

"The silver tear birch", she explained. "The wonders of the Other World. Every tear contains its own story from beginning to end which is again the beginning. Every story is a world onto itself. When the wind brushes off the drops, new ones form, even clearer ones. They convert light into all the colors you wish."

Forest, even more forest. She is never hungry, water is sufficient.

"You have to learn not to desire anything. You should not see your life as a series of successes and failures. Life is not a stage race which starts anew every day. Only when you are free of ambition you start to live. Then you will develop numerous activities. Out of joy about what you are doing, not to achieve anything. That is the first step."

"That´s strange", Sonja said. "This is not like me."

"You are right", Devva laughed. "But you will think about it often."

The only bad vibe in the dream. Sonja pushed it away, she had prepared everything. Only a quarter of an hour, ten minutes. Again, the Other World faded. Even Devva faded.

Sonja´s calm could no longer resist the onslaught of the memories. She was sixteen. When her parents´ house appeared at the edge of the forest she started to run.

72

The immediate family, maid and farmhand sat around the large table. They had sent out the children. Matte´s place remained empty. His wife had lit a candle and placed the crucifix next to it. She wore all black, same as the daughter-in-law, the men wore black armbands. They had come together without a real reason, had followed an urge they could not name. Wife and children had been paid the mandatory amount by the old man. It was derived from the unity value, a fraction of the real value. Prior lifetime gifts, such as those to his daughters, had been discounted. It was a shock which was sitting deep in their bones. But he had also bequeathed others. Clubs, friends, the pastor - and the members of his household.

"He must have laughed his head off", said the older daughter-in-law, the corpulent one with the wide hips. "Giving me his old riding breeches."

"I am getting his wool socks", the maid said. Whenever Matte had gone into her chamber at night he had always complained about her cold feet. She didn´t say that. She didn´t have to.

"A burned-out pipe", the farmhand grumbled. "If it were possible, he would have left me his saliva." A glimmer of satisfaction crossed his face. "But I am still alive, he is not."

"I am getting the hunting gear", said the elder son. "But all the good rifles are going to his friends. What is left is the cleaning equipment and two rusty traps."

"You are lucky", said his brother with a hint of black humor. "To him I was only worth a watch without glass and without hands. This must mean that I am only good to be thrown away."

The younger daughter-in-law said with a low voice: "For me he came up with an old muzzle. But I won´t take it. I asked the notary. You don´t have to take any of it."

Until now all of them had spoken with a strange, factual calmness. But the old farmer´s wife sobbed when it was her turn.

"We were married for almost fifty years. I am not talking about the fifty years. But now he knew that I can hardly walk from pain and he leaves me his mountain boots. That´s what he thought of me all the time."

The son sitting next to her tried to put his arm around her shoulder but she pushed him away. She forcefully hit the burning candle and it fell to the floor. She flipped over the crucifix. They all sat there as if struck by lightning, waiting for the unavoidable tempest of the old man.

The fat daughter-in-law was the first to move. She stood up and brought two bottles of champagne from the freezer, handed out glasses, opened a bottle and raised her glass.

"He can´t bother me anymore with his riding breeches. The champagne is on me. This much I have put aside. Cheers."

They hesitated, the maid taking the longest, - champagne for the maid! - then they drank in rare unity. It was like people exhaling after having held their breath for years.

Meanwhile, small Johann, old Matte´s grandson, was busy torturing ants. He caught a few of them and put them into a flat glass cover whose rim he had lubricated with oil. The ants did not like the oil. They were running in circles in their round prison. Johann knelt next to them, magnifying glass in his hand. It was not easy to track the animals with the small, hot dot which the glass turned the sun into. Johann was skillful. Whenever an ant felt the heat on its body, it panicked and walked faster. Ruthlessly, he pointed the concentrated rays on it until the insect bent over and froze while a thin wisp of smoke rose up. Every time this happened, a weak smile crossed Johann´s face. He liked the small red ones the most. They could really get wild and were hard to hit. The large forest ants died harder. This was enjoyable, too. He tried to burn them as slowly as possible. He could burn thin black holes into their lower bodies while they dragged themselves along with wildly swinging feelers snapping desperately, trying to find safety or at least an end of the torture, but it was futile.

His father and his uncle, his mother and his aunt, his brother and the cousins were treating him differently since his grandfather had named him the main beneficiary. He had written the testament a few days before his death. Three identical copies. Two of them he had given to friends. He simply had not trusted anyone. Johann's father was to lead things until he was of age. Eleven more years, then *he* would be the boss of the farm. Johann knew exactly what this meant. Already he was making small, clever, evil plans for the future. But for now all his attention was taken up by the game with ants and frogs, with mice and other animals. The idea of playing the same game with humans was only an embryo of a thought deep inside of him. Nobody knew about it. Nobody could foresee whether this embryo would develop. There is always a series of coincidences, situations and opportunities which determine such developments. Few realize that there are moments in every life where we escape the abyss by a hair's breadth. Those who are conscious of it shudder at the thought of it decades later. Often it is only a word you say or you don't say, a move you make or you don't make. Only with hindsight do you realize how fragile the choice had been, how close to catastrophe. But Matte's grandson felt nothing of this while he tortured small animals to death with his magnifying glass. He only felt an obscure satisfaction because of the power in his hands. If someone had asked him about it, he would only have shrugged morosely. Without embarrassment, without a guilty conscience. He just did it, why talk about it?

Rüdiger was floating on cloud nine.

"You really lived for three weeks like Robinson without knowing who you are?"

Sonja nodded.

"And the message? Your mother showed it to me."

"I cannot remember", said the girl. "I must have delivered it myself."

Incredulous, Rüdiger shook his head.

"It´s incredible, but surely it must have happened like this. Suddenly there is a simple explanation for all of it." He laughed. "Almost a pity."

Sonja laughed with him.

Padoponos was also fascinated by Sonja´s return. Every night he had rediscovered parts of his vision in his dreams. There was a structure. Recognizable but not comprehensible. Sonja´s return fit into it. Fear, hatred, hope, trust, love. A structure within a larger one, inside an even larger one. But not a Russian doll. Reversible. Each one in each other. The small inside the large, the large inside the small. The image of a world which resists all attempts to explain it.

He was always several people at once. Entire generations were piling up inside of him. He was his father and his mother, which he had hardly known, he was aunts and uncles, cousins, neighbors and colleagues, living and dead. They all messed around, they all wanted to take charge. Only "it" kept an overview and saved him from drowning in this flood of personalities. "It" extinguished them, one by one, mercilessly. Finally he was alone once again. "It" was not his enemy after all, but a faithful ally. How blind he had been to fear what was his only ally. "It" explained to him that he had to fight to survive. He had to extinguish his enemies just like "it" extinguished them. Even the faces and voices from the walls and ceilings had turned against him. But this time he would not retreat, this time he would fight. He took a knife and started to stab at them. Fifteen minutes, half an hour. The wallpaper was hanging down in tatters, small and large pieces of plaster covered the floor. It was hard work and he broke into a sweat. And it didn´t work. Instead of the old and weak faces new ones appeared, more coarse, more pronounced, hostile. He realized that he would not get anywhere. He had to hit the face behind the faces, the snake behind the snake, the eye behind the eyes. Like a lost shadow, he sneaked around his demolished apartment, knife in hand, always ready to attack. Then came the hunger. When had he eaten for the last time? In the evening? Yesterday? The day before? He took some bread out of the drawer and saw that it was completely moldy. They had sold him moldy bread! They were capable of doing even that. He opened the fridge and sniffed at the sausage. It was bad. Everything was bad and moldy and in the process of decomposing. They persecuted him even in his sleep. In his own house, in his bed, and now in his kitchen. He was terribly affected when he realized that they even negated him a piece of bread, which he needed in order not to starve to death. Tears welled from his eyes, the eyes turned into wounds, into continuing bleeding, eternal bleedings which continued even after there was not one drop of fluid left in him.

For hours he sat on the floor, desolate. Then his gaze slowly started to change. Four o´clock. He had a date, the last date. He would get the snake behind the snakes. He shot up and went into the basement. There was the cradle. The sharpened crowbar was still sticking in the floor. He pulled it out and sharpened it for the very last time. He put the crowbar into the cradle and put it under his arm. The snake behind the snake was expecting him.

75

The doctor had actually hardly noticed Maria. Now he was reproaching himself for it. Yes, he was interested in her. Since he had arrived at the village he had not had a stable relationship. He had not looked for it. Now …
But his thoughts did not remain with her. They circled endlessly around the six names on the list. What would the police do to these people after the latest murder? At least five of them were innocent. Wouldn´t they all be fair game? He had turned them in. Not that he thought the colonel was inept, but his trust in his discretion and caution was negligible. On top of that, these policemen were on a hunt for a killer while being chased by the press. There would be many instances where they would disregard precautions which they would otherwise adhere to. And they also had little experience. Even the most experienced ones among them. Murders are rare in this country. And the majority of those few ones ends with the perpetrator turning himself in. He should not have disclosed the names.
Terrazzo returned to the surgery and waited for the colonel´s call. But it did not come. He had gotten what he had wanted from him. Without much enthusiasm, he browsed some trade magazines, read one or the other article without being quite there. The minutes passed slowly and he chided himself for having postponed the house calls. He looked at the mail. This was something he usually reserved for the evening. He noted a letter from a major newspaper. There had been a few reporters trying to interview him. They thought along similar lines as the colonel. Of course he had been very low-key with the press. He was curious whether they would try to get to him in some other way. Perhaps with his own column. "Through the eyes of a doctor" or something like that. Well-paid, of course. As long as there is enough suspense in the story. He grimaced and ripped open the envelope. It contained a second envelope and an accompanying letter. He first read the cover letter.

"Dear Dr. Terrazzo!

The enclosed letter was sent to our complaints department of which I am in charge of. I am not sure whether this is only a strange joke or whether there is something more to it. If the author is, as he insists, really your patient, I thought you should know about his concerns. You can certainly help him much better than we can."

Below it was an illegible signature and a blurred seal.

The doctor opened the second envelope and took out a handwritten sheet. The script was quite noticeable. Small letters, words and lines, cramped next to each other alternated with generous passages where one single long word took the entire width of the paper. There were many underlined sections and words in capitals. If the letter had been written by a first grader, it would have been nice to frame it. Apparently, it came from an adult. Terrazzo began to read.

"Dear Chief Editor of the Daily Mail!

As a regular reader of your publications I am sorry to note that there are continuously more errors getting into your newspaper, which affect its lecture, and they are given to cause great confusion. I would like to mention right away that we are a small village with only a few readers and perhaps therefore not that interesting to you, however, I would mention that even a large edition consists of many small buyers who have a right to be well-informed for their money. There is a country doctor living among us who has a large group of patients to attend to and whom you could get into great trouble with each wrong date (births!). However, it would be so simple if you were only willing to get a TV set. A small portable one would suffice, even a black and white set.

This expense should be no big deal for you, more so if you want to improve the quality and stop annoying many of your regular clients. You should get such a TV set, even if there is competition among the media. Even if there is competition, one should acknowledge whenever someone is better at something and learn from him. You will certainly only profit from this. Unfortunately, I do not know at what time the Daily Mail is being printed, but even if it is outside of the Early News, there is no difference, really. A written note addressed to the gentleman in charge of the date will suffice. The date of the Early News is always correct!!

I would not have bothered to contact you, if this would have happened only once. Everybody makes mistakes, and although I once went to work on a Sunday because of it, I am not angry about it. But now it has happened repeatedly that I pick up a newspaper which states a different day and date than today's. That would be Saturday. And nevertheless, it says Thursday on your front page. However, this happened when I went to see Dr. Terrazzo, who is a fine doctor. You understand how embarrassing it would be if I simply relied on your Thursday. But a reader should be able to trust his newspaper. Therefore I am happy to give you this little bit of advice because it is really no big deal and until now there has never been an error. I would be very happy to contribute to your further success.

Sincerely,

Hannes Müller

P.S.: I don't want any compensation for my tip, or a thank you. It is really just a trifling thing which doesn't cost me much except for paper, envelope and stamp, and we will all benefit from it. I don't want to be published, either!"

Terrazzo read the strange letter a second time. If he understood correctly, Müller was picking up some old newspaper and complained that the date was not corresponding to the current day. This indicated severe disorientation. Too bad he had not read the letter in the morning. His patient would not have gotten around a serious conversation. He remembered the prescription for a lotion. Maria had made a remark about it while having lunch. Something about angling. So Müller was fishing. The only water for fishing in the area was the river. They had found Robby at the river. He had to find out at what time Müller had gone fishing. Maria had mentioned something else. He cursed his absent-mindedness. Something about carving. Müller was angling and carving. That was nothing special. Again he thought about Robby, his severed legs and the brutal sign they formed. It could have been an M. M as in Müller, M as in murder …

Suddenly he heard her voice. "A cradle. He wants to show it to me today."

A shiver went down his spine. M as in Maria!

76

Hannes was carrying the cradle under his arm and placed it on the kitchen countertop. Maria thought about opening the shutters, but she limited herself to switching on the light. He would not stay around that long and if she were to close them again in half an hour she would feel ridiculous. She would close the shutters. That much was certain.

"Do you like it?" he asked.

It was a very short cradle. Way too short. All of its surfaces were covered with carvings. She stepped closer. At first she could not recognize a theme, the patterns were so wildly intertwined. Then she saw the snakes. Snakes with human heads, heads with fangs, distorted, deformed faces, limbs without context, everything confused, confusing and crude. The tingling on her back turned into goose bumps.

"Nice", she said hesitatingly and turned around. He stood between her and the door. He held his hands behind his back. He smiled.

"Do you want to have something to drink?"

He didn´t hear what she said.

"So, you like it?"

"Yes", she said. Still uncertain, but nevertheless fairly certain as to her feelings. All her instincts were sounding alarms. He seemed very pleased.

"That is good", he remarked. "We will have children. I like children."

"What do you mean?" Maria asked. She noticed the upwelling panic in her voice and tried to suppress it.

"I don´t know for sure", he said. Without any doubt, he really didn´t know for sure. He was not faking it, he was completely honest. He was honest in a way that she had never experienced before. Even the most honest of people still keep a certain distance to others and to themselves, observe themselves; they have intermediate stories and nuances, safety zones and counterbalances. Hannes had none of that. His inner world was lying as it was, naked, in front of her. Uncovered and exposed and frightening like a living organ. A pulsating heart, a brain without its skullcap. She looked at him and saw the violet shimmer around his eyes. Colored glass ...

He saw her. He saw her in detail. She wasn't small. How wrong he had been about that. He saw the swaying body, the snake's head on Maria's body, Maria's head and the snake body. If there was any more proof necessary - but he had been absolutely certain - then this sight of her was it. Again, he had been absolutely certain. There is a knowing beyond proof. He had to kill the snake to get to Maria. "It" began to drum quietly. "It" sat inside of him and drummed quietly. "It" was drumming a rhythm which was so old that nobody could tell how old it was. Older than their cities in any case, older than their churches, older than the old mines, the excavations, the caves where burnt bones and skulls of bears could be found. She moved, over here, over there. She was dancing. She was listening to the rhythm. He danced with her. The pointy crowbar's handle was in his hand. He drew figures, sidestepped, he let the pointy iron whirr through the air. She showed her teeth, she laughed, she liked it. Since when do snakes have that many teeth?

She took two, three steps to the side, as did he. He was still between her and the door. The battle had not started yet but war had been declared. Now he showed her what he had kept hidden behind his back. A narrow crowbar. Not a regular crowbar. A crowbar with a tip which was coarsely sharpened. Maria's consciousness was like a shaft. She thought about dozens of things. "It is him. Why didn't I open the shutters? There are so many policemen out there. I have to get to the door. I will scream. Why is nobody coming? I have to defend myself. Talk to him. But say what? He is crazy!"

And at the center of the cyclone the certainty: "He wants to kill me!"

He had not gotten closer yet. Maria screamed. With a jump she managed to get the kitchen table between herself and him.

She pushed the table forward. He was still smiling. He started to draw circles into the air with his crowbar, punching. Now he came closer, as if he had all the time in the world. Perhaps he had. The shutters closed, the kitchen towards the back - she screamed regardless. He came closer. She used the table as a cover. She was young and nimble. The fear did not paralyze her, it made Maria fast and bold. They held the table between them, like children playing tag. Right, left, feinting, ahead, back. He was completely mad, but he did not open the way to the door at any moment. She hoped he would jump onto the table. She would have toppled it or crept under it. But he didn´t jump, he made no decisive attack, he was waiting for something. And suddenly she saw her opportunity. They were at the same distance from the door but there was an armchair in his way. Maria screamed again, jumped, once again, a third time - then she was hit by the arm chair. Now she knew what he had been waiting for. He had been smarter than her. She fell, and the next moment he was on top of her. She had never seen such violet eyes.

He pressed the snake to the floor with his weight and tried to push the spike between her eyes. They were strange eyes. Human eyes, snake eyes. They changed all the time. The snake had long hair. Her hands were holding his wrist and pushed upwards with despair. The slim reptile body was writhing under him. Like a woman. It had been a long time. He got an erection, which doubled his disgust. Again the girl´s face changed into the blunt, scaly snout, the head flattened and the split tongue shot out of the mouth without lips. The hair remained. He felt the strength of her arms wane. Inexorably, the spike sank lower. He also felt the confusing thighs and increased his effort.

77

There were not many opportunities in the village to take the wrong turn. But in his agitation, Terrazzo wound up in the longer loop of the horseshoe. He pressed past a tractor and stopped in front of Maria´s house. The shutters on the first floor were closed, so was the door. He heard a rumble and hesitated no more. The door was only closed, not locked. Again he heard something and ran past the hallway towards the bright square of the door. He saw Maria and simply ran against the man who was lying on top of her, wrestling her. The man, the armchair and Terrazzo flew through half the kitchen, the spike whirred through the air and cut the linoleum floor when it landed. The small rip in the linoleum left a lasting impression on Maria. It was this ridiculously harmless image of the damaged floor which she would connect with the horror of these days for the rest of her life. It took a split second. She was alive. She stood up. She thought "He loves me." The doctor was kneeling on top of Hannes, choking him although his opponent did not defend himself. Maria watched, then she shook the doctor until he let go. Terrazzo stood up, perplexed, and picked up the spike.

"Did anything happen to you?" he asked.

"No", Maria said. "You?"

He shook his head. They both arranged their clothes. Müller remained lying on the floor and looked at them, mute and harmless like a dog that does not understand why someone is angry at it. Before there was another word spoken, they heard the sirens.

When the colonel entered the kitchen with grim men and grim pistols, Müller was still lying on the floor. Terrazzo sat next to Maria on the kitchen bench. His arm was around her shoulders.

Two policemen lifted Müller from the floor and put handcuffs on him.

"He is sick", Terrazzo said.

"Let him go", ordered the colonel. To Müller: "Sit down."
The prisoner obeyed. He didn´t show either surprise or fear.
He looked at everyone present with a friendly and polite
expression, as if he had gotten himself into a crowd of people
to whom he did not belong, but he would not acknowledge
that under any circumstance.

"Are you going to confess?" asked the colonel.

"Yes", Müller said graciously. "I would love to."

"Get the stenographer", the colonel ordered.

During the following minutes Terrazzo described briefly what
had brought him here just in time.

Meanwhile, the stenographer was taking notes.

"We found out, too", the colonel said. "But you were faster.
Fortunately." He smiled at Maria, who smiled back. "Your list
did help us and it confused us, doctor. At first we thought
Müller had an alibi for the murder of Martha Riement. He was
actually seen in the morning at the office for road construction
and took part in a meeting around eleven. His colleagues
thought he was in his office during the time in between.
Plenty of time for an excursion."

"Yes", Müller agreed, noncommittally.

"His father had been a policeman - hence the rubber coat. You
wore it when you killed Grete Strutz, correct?"

"I don´t really remember. Most likely you are right."

"The dagger which was used to kill Matthias Körner could
also be from your father."

"I don´t know anything about it. But I am actually quite
forgetful lately."

The colonel looked at Terrazzo with a curious expression, the
doctor shrugged. He was not a specialist for mental disorders.
At any rate it would be difficult to get a conclusive testimony.
But that was not his problem. He still held Maria in his arm.

"We found out that you went to the river on Sunday. After
you had some trouble with your car and left it behind."

"That´s right", Maria commented. "I was there. It was out of
fuel."

"Yes. You were very lucky. After you had gotten away, he killed the first living thing he encountered."

"Robby", Terrazzo said.

The colonel nodded and addressed Müller again.

"A pattern started to emerge. Yesterday an officer went to pay you a visit. You weren´t home or didn´t answer the door. He didn´t have orders to enter by force. But next to the shed was a hatchet. We are particularly interested in such hatchets. There was no weapon found in the area where the dog was."

"Poor Robby", Müller said. The regret in his voice was genuine.

"When we received the report from the lab we did not hesitate. Too late for the old Körner, unfortunately."

Unexpectedly, Terrazzo intervened. He put his questions in a friendly and firm voice.

"Where did you hide the body of Sonja Lassnig?"

The colonel put on an expression of surprise and wanted to interject, but he did not say anything when the doctor winked at him. Müller didn´t notice. Calmly, he answered: "I don´t know."

"Where did you kill her? How?"

"I don´t know." He hesitated. "I was in the forest. I was told I was in the forest. With a club."

"Who told you that?"

"I don´t know."

"Perhaps an inner voice?"

"Perhaps. There were so many faces, many voices."

"Did the voices order you to kill?"

"I had to defend myself. Every person has the right to defend himself."

"Defend against whom?"

"Treason", Müller whispered. "Punishment and treason."

"Sonja Lassnig, Grete Strutz, Martha Riement, Matthias Körner - they all committed treason against you?"

"I don´t know. Yes. I think. I don´t know for sure. The pain …"

"Did you beat the girl to death?"

"I don´t know. I was in the forest, yes."

"You beat her to death?"

"I think. I can´t remember."

"Where did you hide the body?"

"I don´t know."

Maria had started to shake. The colonel addressed Terrazzo.
"I understand where you are going. Is it possible that he really
does not remember?"

"I am afraid so. Perhaps a psychiatrist could find out more."

Müller saw the officer, the doctor, Maria. He would have
liked to know what was going on here. He felt weary and
tired. Had he defeated the snake? He would have liked to talk
about the snake but they were asking so many questions. He
would have liked to go home to sleep. He wouldn´t really be
bothered by the bound hands. He looked at Maria and said:
"I better go now. Didn´t know you had visitors."

A police officer burst out laughing.

"It´s terrible", Maria whispered. Why was she whispering?
Was he the only one who was supposed to hear it? He smiled.
He wanted to reply something, whispering too. At that
moment "it" let go of him completely. The people standing
around him did not notice anything. Only Terrazzo saw the
change in his eyes. He thought about slowly fading headlights,
a retreat beyond the last line. Terra incognita. Area without
return. Nobody should ever know that "it" had had a
connection with him. Müller´s mind slipped through
increasingly narrow sluices which all opened in only one
direction. All movement became irreversible before all
movement stopped. He found himself in complete
contentment and complete paralysis. He opened a new pair of
eyes and looked over an endless, flat, snowy surface which
faded into a uniformly white sky. But he was not looking at a
real landscape, he was looking deeply into a foreign land. Too
foreign for humans.

The sounds which still reached him were as mysterious as a

cosmic thunderstorm. Slowly they faded away. From now on everything was as quiet as it was supposed to be.

"He will talk, eventually", one of the officers said with confidence.

"I don´t think so", Terrazzo contradicted him in a low voice. "Could be I am wrong, but perhaps we just witnessed a dying which doesn´t end with death. Death will follow later on."

The officers looked at him without comprehending.

"You mean he is totally gone?" asked the colonel. "Well, we will see."

He gestured to his people. They took Müller between them and led him away. The weapon and cradle had already been removed. Only the tear in the linoleum remained. The colonel shook the doctor´s hand and said with a wink:

"Doctor, you are a hero. You saved a life. Allow yourself to be venerated."

He said goodbye to Maria and followed his subordinates. He walked with more of a spring in his step than he usually did. After all, he had captured a crazy killer. Why not allow yourself to be venerated a little as well?

Maria shook herself.

"It was terrible, but it all happened so quickly. A few seconds later ..."

"Yes", Terrazzo said.

There they stood, looking at each other, undecided.

"Would you like to have a drink?" she asked. "I have some apricot liqueur up in my room. Homemade.

"I´d love to", he said. He despised liqueurs.

"It´s more comfortable upstairs, too."

She had blushed and felt for his hand. Hand in hand they went to the front door to lock it and then up the stairs. She poured two glasses and took off her glasses. Perhaps the frame was too severe after all. His clear contours turned into a soft outline, but when he kissed her she closed her eyes anyway. Shaky hands loosened two clasps and the dress slid from her shoulders like a tired wave which doesn´t want to remain at the shore.

Later they were lying next to each other closely, felt the warmth of their bodies and the smoothness of their skin. He was in a strange mood. Excited, happy, bitter, sarcastic. A cocktail of sentiments, not entirely wholesome.

"You don't know anything about me", he said. Then he stayed silent for minutes and suddenly laughed.

"I am a hero. A provincial hero. It looks like I will be sticking to this place more and more. Like a fly on flypaper."

"What are you saying?" Maria asked.

"I am talking about getting stuck. Getting settled. Here."

"Here's your practice", she said. "You came because you chose to."

"Yes, my practice. Not entirely my choice. Not entirely."

She propped herself up and looked at him. His eyes were closed and the corners of his mouth were raised with irony. But he wasn't making a joke. He was being serious.

"Explain that to me", she asked.

"Why not? There isn't much to explain. I had good chances to have an academic career. You know: assistant, medical specialist, lecturer, eventually, professor. A bourgeois life, a conceited career with a few minor perks. Perks like social prestige, investigative activities and of course a solid private practice to scoop up the cream. To skim off the cream you need a convenient position. It doesn't work if the jug of milk is on the third floor and you are sitting in the basement. The jug is always up there."

"And what …?"

"Patience, darling. So, I was in a fortunate position, well-trained and all that, you know. My professor liked me. He thought highly of my capabilities. I was going strong in that race until I stepped on the banana peel. The stupid thing was that I had thrown it onto the track myself. Plunk, I wasn't ahead anymore, but lying on my nose."

"What's that supposed to mean", Maria asked, annoyed. "Can't you tell it in a normal way?"

"This way it´s easier for me. The banana peel was something very stupid which happened due to my credulity. It could have landed me in court. The professor was disappointed, but still on my side. He covered up the unfortunate affair and put me on probation. Temporary exile, gain experience. A medical practice in the countryside."

"Does it mean you want to leave?"

Maria´s private plans were being shifted around.

"That was the idea, but meanwhile there has been a change."

"Which one?" she asked, breathless.

"The professor´s second heart attack", he replied dryly. "As of now he is a private person. There is a provisionary successor at the institute, who doesn´t like me. I don´t like him either, by the way. At any rate, he has other plans than to help me with my comeback. The race is definitely over."

"You are staying?"

"For now, yes."

"Wonderful", she moaned and tried to affirm his decision.

Later they were lying next to each other again.

"What kind of banana peel was it?"

"Hm? What kind of stupid thing I did?"

"Yes."

"You really want to know?"

Maria nodded vehemently. Yes, she wanted to. It could always help to know these things. Perhaps it would be helpful at some time. She had some very specific plans. They went as far as a second home in Tuscany. Terrazzo played an important role in these visions. She would firmly keep him there. By all means permissible. There are certain situations where *all* means are permissible. Perhaps he could have read it from her face, but it was dark and he had closed his eyes again. He had been guileless on top of it. After all, she owed her life to him. The fool.

"Drugs. A nurse was taking the poisons I was experimenting with and for which I was responsible. She sold them in her circle of friends. One of her clients almost died, which got the whole ball rolling."

"It wasn´t your fault."

"Well, firstly, it was my job to make sure they were locked away safely, and secondly, she was my girlfriend, too. Bad people like these combinations. They are very productive, you know? If the professor had not believed me … nevertheless, I have to pay for my mistake."

It still was the great love. But later, Maria suspected, he might well prove to be correct. But it would have been wrong to accuse her of bad intentions from the start. She really loved him. The other thing, well, it was simply there. Put away inside the last drawer. The emergency drawer.

"The main thing is that you stay here", she said and snuggled up closely. "And that this nightmare is over."

Terrazzo too could see several good points with respect to the latest developments. A remark by the colonel was making his way through his mind while he was half asleep. Something about patterns. Was it really all over?

The next day he made a long phone call, asked for and received information. Later he drove to town and consulted with the detectives for a long time.

78

When Riement entered the room where they had sat together so often he sensed the change without being able to classify it. Perhaps it was because of the schnapps. He was drinking schnapps every day now. Clear fruit spirit, half a bottle, sometimes more. He sat in his usual armchair and watched the usual ritual of his friend removing the cork. There it was again, the hollow gurgling in the neck of the bottle, which could only be heard while pouring the first glass. As always, a small sprinkle landed on the polished table, as always, he wiped it away with his hand while the other was still looking for his handkerchief. It was obvious that none of them quite knew how to start. Riement cleared his throat.

"Of course we can talk about it", he said. "The thing with Martha was certainly a heavy blow, but as you know, we had drifted apart a long time ago. What could it be, causing such an inconspicuous person as Müller to suddenly commit such deeds?"

"We don´t know the real reason", Terrazzo said, lost in thought. "Whatever we explain remains inside the narrow boundaries of our thinking. Things beyond that can only be grasped with auxiliary mental constructions. We describe symptoms and work on causes and connections which can somehow be brought to coincide with our perceptions. We can´t and don´t want to do more. It would also be too dangerous. Nobody knows whether there is a return once we leave the familiar path. The strangeness in our mind is powerful and unpredictable. All of our instincts warn us about it."

From the street there was the sound of car doors being slammed shut. Saturday night. Time for visits, eating, drinking.

"Do you think that this strangeness has something to do with the mystery around Sonja?"

Terrazzo raised his hands helplessly.

"I don´t think she has lost her memory. But she is also not the kind of girl who would disappear like this for three weeks. Whatever happened to her, it has not done her any harm. Perhaps", he added after a slight pause, "she wants to protect somebody. Herself or a third person or even us. I spoke with her briefly. It is as if she had been cleansed by her experience. Despite her youth, one has the impression of talking to a rare and special person. I think the evil gossip is bunk. They can´t get to her. She smiles about it. Perhaps she found a faith in those three weeks which makes her invulnerable. This is how I imagine the first Christians, or some of the yogis and shamans."

"Doesn´t sound like you at all", the teacher teased him.

"I can´t dispute that. This past month has changed all of us. All of us."

Terrazzo poured his glass to the top. The light of the lamp reflected in the dark wine and made it sparkle, seemingly hypnotizing both of them. When he continued to speak it sounded as if from very far away.

"Müller didn´t kill your wife."

Riement was flabbergasted.

"He himself admitted to it."

"He also admitted to having murdered Sonja. The murder that never happened. He would have admitted to anything. You only had to ask him."

"That doesn´t prove that he did *not* kill Martha."

"It only proves that his confession is worthless. I became suspicious because of something else. You remember that your wife was knocked down before the perpetrator inflicted these deadly wounds?"

"So she couldn´t call for help. That´s pretty obvious."

"Exactly. For you, for me, but not for Müller. Whenever he killed, he was literally beside himself. I have seen the Strutz woman. Whether his victim was screaming or not, he didn´t care at all. He never thought about the consequences of his acts. Most likely he didn´t "think" at all. Remember the hatchet with the blood on it. He had simply left it next to the pile of firewood. I don´t want to say that he consciously wanted to reveal himself. His subconscious however might have worked in that direction."

"Most likely Martha tried to escape and that is why he knocked her down."

"That´s possible. But there is still the pattern."

"A pattern?"

"Your hypothesis. You remember? You put it something like this: 'It is not about a shoe or a piece of jewelry or deep footprints. The clue can be something trite, obvious. Something everybody will easily understand once he knows the context. Every occurrence leaves behind clues. They don´t have to be mysterious or well-hidden. They only have to be recognized. A person is embedded in his environment, physically and psychologically. If he is pulled out of it from one moment to the next, there are ripples left behind. They can provide clues …'

I have found a clue. The pattern of the incisions. Once the blood was washed away it could be recognized. Poor Strutz was literally torn apart. The cuts on your wife were placed almost accurately on top of and next to each other. Stabbed, pulled out the knife nice and straight, didn´t rip it out, stabbed again, pulled out, and so on. Almost like lines and paragraphs. This perpetrator was not beside himself. One stab would have been enough. But he was aware of the fact that this did not fit with the image of how Strutz had been killed. However, he was too restrained. Perhaps because he was timid, more likely not to get more blood on himself than necessary."

"If this is correct", the teacher exclaimed, "then who killed her?"

"You", Terrazzo said.

Riement laughed out loud.

"That´s incredible. How did something this crazy occur to you?"

"The situation was too tempting for you. You had hated

Martha for a long time because she was like a living reproach. You had longed for the day she would finally leave you. But she didn't do it. Perhaps she would have never done it because you were her sustenance. That meant more to her than her freedom. You couldn't throw her out. That would have been too expensive for you. You don't make that much money. Also, you are a thrifty man. The madman killer in the village was like a gift for you. With such a guy you don't look around much for motives. And if he kills two people, he might as well kill three. You only have to act quickly before he is apprehended."

"I don't believe it", Riement said, partly angry, partly stunned. "Only because of an imaginary pattern you accuse me of having murdered my own wife?"

"I once observed you making entries in a catalog. You did it the same way. First row, first column, first line, second row and so forth."

"How are you supposed to fill out a catalog otherwise?" the teacher asked, more amused than worried.

"I have looked at one. The number of the fields on a page corresponds exactly with the number of stabs. The power of habit."

Riement stood up.

"This is plain bunk, nothing else. Who would sentence me because of such a wild story, or even charge me?"

"Nobody. I knew that. It can't even be used as evidence. But it was enough for the idea. Once the idea was there, the details followed. Straight from my memory. Things you retain without interpreting them. Ultimately, I was pretty convinced. Once there is a suspicion, the police can find out a lot of things. I believe they have pretty much dismantled your rock-solid alibi."

Two free periods on that morning. Two hours where he had been swallowed by the earth. They would trace the yellow Opel or some idiot who had seen him driving towards the old gravel pit. Then they would find the bag with his prints and her blood.

"You sent the police after me?"

"Of course. What was I supposed to do? Forget the whole story? You killed your wife, Franz. That´s not like smuggling cigarettes or passing the speed limit."

The teacher looked around with a wild gaze. A cornered animal, a cornered person - the differences disappear. At any rate, they are not as pronounced as we would like to believe. Terrazzo felt that these were the most dangerous moments of his life. Nobody could tell what might happen the next moment. Not him, not the other one. Everything seemed to be within the realm of possibilities.

"They are standing outside the door", he said.

That was decisive. Riement tightened, said, "They won´t be able to prove anything. Nothing. There is nothing to prove. I am not worried. But you have disappointed me enormously. Friend!"

These were the first sentences of his defense, directed at those listening out there. At the same time it was the first step to capitulation. As soon as the police know what to look for they will find something. You can´t commit a murder in broad daylight without leaving behind some memories inside of someone. Innocent observations. But then, one joins the other and suddenly your clever plan lies out in the open. The only thing you can do is deny, invent someone, raise as much doubt as possible. Perhaps it would turn out okay. With a very good lawyer … but it wasn´t probable.

"I was your friend", the doctor said with a low voice. "I have been wrong about you. I am through", he added, louder.

The gaunt colonel entered, two of his men took the teacher between them and led him out of the room. The colonel nodded to Terrazzo and followed them. It all happened without a word being said. The door fell into its lock. The engines of two cars started.

"Inglorious end of a detective career", the doctor said to his glass. "Nailing a friend who has become a murderer to the wall."

He drank up, refilled and drank up again.

Perhaps he should drive to the city with Maria. Have a nice meal, talk about the future, have a few cognacs. Hopefully she had a driver´s license. Hopefully she was up for it. Hopefully he could deal with what he had found out about himself and others this month. He took the phone and dialed her number. Whether as a doctor or a private citizen or as an abandoned speck of dust inside an unknowable cosmos - it was not an evening to be by yourself.

Epilog

Hard to say what Rosi thought about herself. She did not think about herself, really. Her self-image had something primeval, close to earth. This is certainly not a merit and usually not an advantage. In Rosi´s case it was. She had a natural, firm, straight character, which could probably never be bent. Her parents did not have it, her grandparents did not have it, and the long succession of ancestors had not given any indications about it. These people had been people like your left-door and right-door neighbor, people like him and her, you and I. A sort of conglomeration. Much inside, baked hard, pure and impure. Not a gem. Rosi was a gem.

She was not particularly intelligent, she had no special talents. She was not rich either, and she would never be rich. But she was beautiful. Her beauty was the outer side of her character. Beautiful because she was strong and unbreakable. Not for front pages. At first sight. At the second ... who knows? But model scouts don´t go into villages which are only on the map because some people are very meticulous about it.

Rosi sat on a stool and cried. Jason had left the room. It was three in the morning. He had been lying on the bed for hours and talked. She had let him talk. She was not surprised. He informed her, unreservedly and freely. About himself, about the organization, about his motives, including the murder of Matte and its necessity. He didn´t say "killed" or "executed". He said "murdered".

Finally, he asked the question of all questions. Rosi said no. She considered and said no. There was more at stake than she had ever dreamed of *and she loved him*. But she said no. Instinctively, she had detested and despised Matte, and now she despised him more than ever. But she said no. This is something you do not need to understand, you can only accept it. She simply had more character than the rest of the village, including Adelheid and Terrazzo and Robby the rover, that did not count anymore now. Perhaps too much character. But who could determine that?

She went into her chamber and waited for the coming day. Meanwhile, Padoponos was walking aimlessly through the night. He walked along moonlit trails and through sections of forest which were so dark that he was lost like a blind man without his stick and without help. He left the empty house where the thug had attacked him behind; eventually he passed the spot where the dog had to die because a girl had been very lucky. But in front of everything he could see or could have seen was the image of Rosi. With every step he took, her "No" hammered inside his temples. He almost went mad from sadness. In those hours he was actually a little mad because he knew that she loved him. Because she said no, regardless. Because she did not judge him but reject him, although it broke her heart. If she had only judged him, she could have forgiven him! But that was too easy for her. A cheap solution with the image of generosity. She didn´t like cheap solutions. Especially not about the most powerful thing she had ever experienced. So he was no match for her. Nobody was a match for her. He was a little crazy because of his sorrow while walking through the night, followed by his own shadow, which was pressed against the earth by a soulless moon.

Then at dawn he saw the mountain and stopped. Dark, old and heavy it stood there against the sky´s leaden mass. Nothing special about it, except for its size and the aura of eternity. It was this mountain which had taken the girl and released her weeks later. The mountain of his vision. The mountain where, on its southern slope, old Matte had been born and where he had died by his hand. In the shadow of which he had grown up to be the monster that would later fulfill himself by torturing people. The mountain which seemed to dominate this small speck of land with its gloomy power from ancient times. Was it a coincidence that, after Matte, a second and even a third villager had fallen into the grip of madness and murder?

Padoponos was now really a bit crazy. He hurried back to the village, packed his suitcase, left a considerable amount of money on the table and started his car. He drove towards the mountain. Bad roads, second gear, first gear, second gear, many curves. He was driving up the mountain in the morning light and felt as if he did not have to drive, as if an invisible power was drawing him towards it. Without thinking, he turned into country roads, again and again, until he had to stop. The road ended in front of a dirt hill which a Caterpillar machine had left there. Behind it were trees, tall firs and pines. He had no idea where he was, but he was still a little crazy. He stepped out of the car and continued on foot. To the top, straight through the forest. Soon he was scratched all over and soaked with sweat. He found a trail, rather, a steep furrow. Perhaps it had been used to extract wood. He followed the furrow without knowing what he wanted. Rather, he knew, but what he was up to was impossible. He wanted to find the clearing of his vision. A clearing on a plateau with oak trees, which had disappeared long ago, and there would be no clearing either. He was the young boy climbing higher and higher to see Africa. He didn´t know what he was expecting to see here. At any rate, something which was even farther away. Something only a few get to see. Something well-known which he had inside of him without ever having met it. Only here would he meet with it. He was gasping because of his effort. Suddenly he realized that he was also hurrying towards great danger. The weight of his life, the burden of his conscience, the dead men of his vengeance - all this required a counterweight, required the faith in the ideal of justice. And it was this faith which seemed to abandon him while climbing higher and higher up the mountain.

There he stood on the plateau and there was a clearing. The ground was rocky. Only a few low shrubs, flowers and moss could thrive here. The many centuries had not changed anything. Padoponos stood there, wet and steaming, eyes half-closed, swerving slightly. Images swept over him. Images of his own life and that of many foreign lives. Human lives,

animal lives, plant lives, mountain lives. He held his hands stretched out in front of him and let himself be pulled by the images, crossing the plateau towards the edge of a cliff. There he opened his eyes and looked into the abyss. Slowly he lifted his foot for the last step.
"No!"
As if a heavy bubble had burst, all the weight fell from his shoulders. Jason whirled around and barely managed to hold onto the edge. One minute later he sat on the plateau and looked over the valley. Those white peaks over there, lifted by the morning sun - was that his Africa? The end of the chase? He sat for a while, got himself together, registered every detail, then he began his way back. When he reached the edge of the forest he turned around and saw a blond girl sitting on a rock. But it was a mirage, a faraway cloud, a cloud of white and gold.

While on his way down, Padoponos decided to take a long vacation. Vacation in his village on the island. Six months, perhaps a year. Then, a new assignment would await him, a new duty. There are too many of them who get away. But not all of them.

He reached the car. It had gotten bright, just before noon, when he finally found the right trail. He even found the shortcut to the main road. A shortcut which allowed him to avoid the village. Padoponos did not look towards the village, and for a long time he did not look into the rear view mirror. Village and mountain - he never wanted to see either of them again, ever.

Rosi stood in her chamber and looked into the patio. Bernd was leaning against the stable wall on the other side. Tall, strong, awkward. The trouser legs of his old suit were too short, so were the sleeves. He had the face of a young dog. Good-natured, curious, easily distraught. Now he was facing the sun with closed eyes and thought. She could read it on his forehead. Thinking was more work for him than piling up

wood. And he piled well. His piles stood firmly and solidly.
She thought about Jason. About his gentleness, his experience,
about how he spoke to her. Never had a man slept with her
like this, never had anyone spoken to her like this. She would
never have dared to hope that he would ask her. A waitress at
some village inn, uneducated. Then he had asked her and she
had said no. He had killed old Matte. He didn´t deny it. He
had not come for any other reason. He had killed other people
as well, and none of them had deserved any better. He
explained it to her and she thought it was fair. But she said no.
He was even more affected because he knew how difficult this
answer was for her. He was shaken to the core because she
owned the most honest of hearts. She had tested him and
discarded him although everything in her was longing for him.
Without a word he had left the room and the house, without a
word he had returned later and driven away.
Rosi looked out the window.
Jason´s car was speeding along a country road, then took the
main road and disappeared from view. Much too late she
raised her hand, only briefly, and put it down again.
Bernd was leaning against the stable wall and warmed his
large body in the sun. The sun was a friend. He had thought
much lately. Nevertheless, many things were confusing.
Hannes had killed these people, so they had told him. He is
much crazier than you are, yet nobody had noticed, they had
said. At least you are not pretending, they said, nobody has to
be afraid of you. Nobody has to be afraid of me, I am not
crazy. Sometimes people got on his nerves. He didn´t know
that these moments were his most normal moments.
Old Matte was gone, dead. That was good. Old Matte had
insulted Rosi because he could read his thoughts. He had
uncovered the hidden thought and shown it to Bernd, to insult
Rosi. For this, someone had pinned him to a tree. That was
very good. Bernd would not have been able to do that, he
could not harm a living being. But he was very happy that
someone else could do it.

How had he found out that Matte had insulted Rosi? This was one of the mysteries he thought about.

There was Rosi. She was coming towards him. She wore a short skirt which showed her knees. Again he felt the wound which old Matte had inflicted on him. It was choking his throat and made him want to flee. But Rosi extended her hand to him.

"Come", she said. She took his hand and walked with him across the patio to the back entrance of the Sheep's Inn, up two floors, to her chamber. She sat on the bed and the skirt slipped up even more. All this time she didn't let go of his hand.

"You are a lovely fellow, Bernd", she said. "You are my friend. I am your girl."

She leaned over to him, who had turned bright red from joy, and gave him a gentle kiss on the lips.

"My girl?" he stammered. "Really, like, my girl?"

She nodded and smiled like only a few women can. It was the smile of pure, unlimited magnanimity. Men are never able to be this altruistic. Men always reserve a small place for themselves. There they remain and find joy in their gesture or their humility, depending on their cravings. The small place is the limitation that distinguishes them from those very few women.

Only Bernd was worth this smile, nobody else, not for light years around. Because only Bernd was capable of responding to her limitless magnanimity with limitless adoration.

She sat on the bed and smiled and had tears in her eyes. With an expression of heavenly rapture, Bernd was kneeling in front of her, caressing her knees. So softly and cautiously that she barely felt the touch. Tears ran down her cheeks and dripped onto her skirt. She suppressed the upwelling sob. Under no circumstance did she want to expel him from his paradise.